PLAYING WITH FIRE

Patricia listened with dismay and near despair to her husband's words.

"The Viscount Reading may never visit us again," said Mr. Biddles. "You have discouraged him with your coldness, though you know he can give me entry to the *ton*. The next time we meet him, you will smile and charm him and be so agreeable to his wishes that he will seek you out every chance he gets."

"But Alvin," Patricia exclaimed. "You cannot possibly mean . . . that you want me to make love to the Viscount."

"Who said anything about lovemaking?" Biddles muttered, his eyes avoiding her horrified gaze. "There are ways for a woman to lead a man on without being unfaithful, ways to make him think her surrender is only a matter of time, and so encourage him to continue his pursuit."

Thus the game of deception was begun, though Patricia could not say whom she would deceive—the Viscount . . . her husband . . . or herself. . . .

THE ENCHANTING STRANGER

SIGNET REGENCY ROMANCE

COMING IN JUNE 1989

Emily Hendrickson
Lady Sara's Scheme

Sheila Walsh
The Notorious Nabob

Gayle Buck
Willowswood Match

The
Enchanting
Stranger

by
Barbara Hazard

A SIGNET BOOK

NEW AMERICAN LIBRARY

A DIVISION OF PENGUIN BOOKS USA INC.

Copyright © 1984 by B. W. Hazard Ltd.

SIGNET TRADEMARK REG. U.S. PAT. OFF. AND FOREIGN COUNTRIES
REGISTERED TRADEMARK—MARCA REGISTRADA
HECHO EN DRESDEN, TN, U.S.A.

SIGNET, SIGNET CLASSIC, MENTOR, ONYX, PLUME, MERIDIAN
and NAL BOOKS are published by New American Library, a division of
Penguin Books USA Inc., 1633 Broadway, New York, New York 10019

First Printing, October, 1984

2   3   4   5   6   7   8   9   10

PRINTED IN THE UNITED STATES OF AMERICA

There is a lady sweet and kind
    Was never face so pleased my mind;
I did but see her passing by,
    And yet I love her 'til I die.

            Thomas Ford, 1580–1648

PART ONE

Bath, England
1813

1

The early-morning mist that rose from the River Avon had burned away long ago by the time Guy Leighton, Viscount Reading, left his aunt's house on Great Pulteney Street and strolled along to the bridge that spanned it, for it was past eleven and promising to be a fair, warm day. The viscount had risen much later than was his usual custom, for the evening before had been spent with friends newly arrived from London, but even so, his head ached still and he cursed himself for his carelessness in allowing James to crack another bottle of wine at two in the morning.

As he crossed the bridge, he nodded to a middle-aged gentleman walking toward him, and lifted his high-crowned beaver to his companion, a young lady of about sixteen who blushed rosy at this attention and then lowered her eyes in confusion. The viscount's lips twisted in a cynical smile as he settled his hat again at a jaunty angle on his dark-brown hair. The smile did not reach his cold, hooded gray eyes.

I would wager anything, he thought, that if I turned my head right now, I would find her peeking back at me. He did not consider himself conceited as he did so, for he could not help knowing that his tall, rugged physique and handsome face generally had this effect on members of the opposite sex, and even before the death of his father ten years ago, when he was twenty-one, he had used the boon to full advantage every chance he got. His father had been a handsome man and his mother the reigning toast of her day, and the few times he had ever bothered to think of it, he had been glad they had bequeathed their looks to their only son.

He decided not to bother to check on the girl, although she had been a tempting little armful with big blue eyes and blond ringlets, worthy of any man's second glance, for his head was aching abominably and there was a throbbing behind his right eye that was most unpleasant. If he did not feel better in a short time, he knew he would have to send his regrets to Lady Mills, begging off from her party this afternoon, but he hoped the walk in the fresh air would help, at least enough so his aunt's watchful eye would not notice his indisposition, for then she would press him to drink some of the mineral water for which Bath was famous. He was glad she found it so helpful to her condition; for himself, he abhorred it.

As he reached the more populous part of town near the abbey and the Pump Room, he found High Street crowded, and he was often forced to step aside to allow others to pass, or to avoid a muffin seller and the old flower woman who crouched in her usual place calling, "Vi'lets! Sweet vi'lets! Who'll buy my vi'lets?"

Besides those walking like himself, there were sedan chairs everywhere for the infirm and the elderly, for Bath streets were very steep, the town at its inception being set in an amphitheater of rolling hills. Drays and carriages of the gentry as well competed for the available space, and as he reached the corner of West Gate Street and prepared to cross, he discovered all traffic had come to a halt. A fat elderly beau, red with frustration, was calling from the seat of his dusty gig, while ahead of him a lady leaned from the window of her coach to find out the reason for the delay. Neither person interested him, and his eye moved on, passing over an open landau containing two women, to the cause of the standstill itself: a farmer's cart blocking the intersection.

And then he caught his breath, and his eyes swung back to the landau. From her sober dress, the plump, middle-aged woman was obviously a servant and was quickly dismissed, but seated on the side nearest to him was a lady he judged to be in her early twenties. As he watched, she leaned toward her maid and made some remark, and then she smiled.

Lord Reading stood very still, his eyes narrowed, and he could have sworn at that moment that all the noise of the busy street faded away. She was so beautiful, with her pale, creamy complexion and delicate profile, the chestnut hair that curled beneath her chip bonnet shining in the sunlight. He willed her to face him, and as if she sensed his command, she turned her head to inspect the shop windows behind him.

He stood very still, not daring to move as he devoured the sweet expression on her face, her large, luminous eyes, and the gentle curve of her lips, and then the tangle in the street was resolved and the vehicles began to move again. He had a sudden, insane urge to rush into the street and detain her, and it was only with the greatest difficulty that he restrained himself. Her landau moved away, but still he stood there at the curb, oblivious to the jostling of those behind him.

He was just about to sprint after her when he saw her carriage pull over to the curbside a short distance away, and thanks to his superior height, he was able to see her quite clearly as she stepped down on her groom's arm. Smiling her thanks, she entered the shop before her.

As she disappeared, Lord Reading was released from the spell, and he pushed his way through the crowds until he reached the shop she had entered. Without a moment's hesitation, he went up the shallow steps and opened the door.

She was standing at the counter directly before him, so close he could have touched her with only two steps, and when the bell over the door announced his arrival, she turned her head. As she stared at him, he saw her widening eyes were a deep violet-blue, and his heart began to pound as he drank in the lovely oval of her face, her graceful neck, and the swelling of her breasts above a slender waist, discreetly covered by a simple gown of sprigged muslin. He removed his hat as he moved forward, and then he became aware of several other women in the shop as one of them dropped the filmy garment she was holding to the counter and exclaimed out loud. As she did so, some reason came back to his overheated brain, and he saw he had entered a boutique selling lingerie and was now the cynosure of every feminine eye. One corner of his mouth quirked in amusement.

"Your pardon, ladies, I mistook the address," he said in his deep, careless voice as he bowed and backed to the door, never taking his eyes from the lady he had followed, and knowing even then that he had been waiting all his life for this moment without even being aware he was waiting. When she turned away, he forced himself to leave, and once outside again, he drew a deep breath to steady himself while he pondered this extraordinary event.

Guy Leighton had had the customary calf love when he was seventeen, and since that time a number of affairs with willing married ladies of the *ton*, and actresses and demi-mondes as well. He was happy to take these ladies under his protection and make love to them, but he was not at all distressed when the time came that they drifted apart. He had certainly never been in love or expected to be; but whatever emotion was raging within him, it had dealt him a telling blow to the heart that left him helplessly committed to a stranger. That he would never feel this way again was as certain to him as his knowing that the sun would set and the moon rise for all the nights that were to come.

He knew he had to meet her and talk to her, but he did not know how he was to accomplish it. It would be unheard of for him to accost her without a proper introduction, but perhaps there was something he could do, some tribute that he could give her that would make her remember him, make her want to meet him. The vision of her deep violet-blue eyes came to his mind, and he strode back down the street to where the old violet seller crouched over her basket.

She cackled her delight and called him "your Worship" when he bought all her flowers, but he hardly heard her. Returning to the shop, he waited until the lady's groom was looking the other way before he heaped the nosegays on her seat. Then he crossed the busy street and took up a position in a doorway opposite, determined to wait until she should finish her shopping and reappear.

He saw one woman leave the shop, the lady who had exclaimed at his intrusion, and when he saw the disdainful look she gave him when she saw him waiting so obviously across the street, he bowed to her with a flourish of his hat and a sneering smile, and she sniffed and hurried away. He turned his back on the street then, to look into the windows of the shop where he was loitering, glad it contained nothing more exotic than tobacco and snuff, and glad as well that its owner kept the bay window polished so he could be sure to spot her in its reflection when she came out.

As he peered into the window, he wondered at his actions. He had a reputation for cool urbanity, for always being polished and controlled and giving nothing of himself away, and yet here he was, behaving in as silly a manner as any moonling. He wanted to lay his coat under her feet like Sir Walter Raleigh, so she would not feel the bruising of the cobblestones; he wanted to take her in his arms gently and hold her against his heart to shelter her; he wanted to take her hand and lead her far away where they could be alone together forever; he wanted . . .

Lord Reading stiffened as the door opposite opened to disclose her. Her groom hurried to assist her into the carriage, and as she spotted the violets on the seat and gathered them into her arms, he could see her questioning the servant. From the groom's puzzled look, Lord Reading knew she could have no idea where they came from, and he saw her glance around, that glorious face perplexed. Taking a deep breath, he turned to face her. She had buried her face in the flowers, and then a large coach lumbering by hid her from view. When it had passed, her carriage was already in motion. Again he willed her to notice him; again her eyes met his, and he removed his hat and gave her his most elegant bow. By the time he straightened up, all he could see of her was the back of the little chip bonnet that just showed over the folded hood of the open carriage, and he felt as if his heart left his breast to follow her before he was disgusted at himself for this flight of fancy.

He stood there until the landau disappeared around a corner, and then in a sober, thoughtful mood, he retraced his steps toward the Pump Room, where his aunt was waiting for him. The lady was gone and he did not even know her name, but he was not disturbed, for Bath was not that large a town and surely they must meet again. He would accompany his aunt every morning to the Pump Room and keep watch there; he would attend every function in the Upper and Lower Rooms, no matter how boring they might be to an active, sophisticated Corinthian; he would haunt the libraries, for they were Bath's most popular lounges; and he would search the streets until he found her again. He had been thinking of returning to London, or taking a look at Brighton in a few days, for Bath was too stodgy and dull a place to hold him for long. If his favorite aunt had not taken up residence in Bath for her health, he would never have visited it at all, but now he knew he must remain, for he was tied here with bonds as strong as iron manacles.

He found his aunt with her companion, sitting to one side of the Pump Room, listening to the music of a string trio in the balcony at the end of the large room with its elegant columns and oval windows set high on gold walls. He wondered, observant as she had always been, that she did not appear to notice anything different about him, but she only smiled and patted the little gilt chair beside her.

Lady Sylvia Randolph, his mother's eldest sister, was a slim, gray-haired lady of some sixty years. Her intelligence and good sense were well known, but it was her unfailing kindness to her nephew, left motherless at the age of ten, that endeared her to Lord Reading.

"Guy, my dear," she greeted him, her gray eyes, so like his own, twinkling. "This is a surprise, for I was sure you would not make an appearance at all after the raking you did last evening. Gregson let slip the hour you came home, you must not accuse me of prying!"

He smiled a little and took the seat beside her as she added, "And how are Lord Williams and your cousin James? If they have come on purpose to remove you from Bath, I shall let them know my displeasure, for you have been with me such a little time."

Her nephew picked up one thin veined hand and kissed it. "They would not succeed, Aunt, for nothing could take me away now."

Lady Sylvia raised a pair of elegant eyebrows, but before she could ask for enlightenment, old General Cowles tottered up, and after an exchange of greetings, Lord Reading was dispatched to fetch his aunt's old friend a glass of the famous water.

He was absentminded for the remainder of their stay, which she was quick to note, not missing the way his eyes went so keenly to every new person who entered the room, and the faint look of disappointment when he did not find whom he was seeking. He walked beside her sedan chair on the return trip to Great Pulteney Street, for her companion, Miss Kincaid, had errands to do, and he chatted easily to her, although once again she noticed his searching eyes scanning pedestrians and carriages alike. Lady Sylvia wondered whom Guy had met last evening. Surely he had said it was only to be a convivial gathering of old friends, some cards and conversation, and from what she could see of the lines of dissipation on his face, far too much wine. And yet, in her opinion, he acted as if he had fallen under the spell of some entrancing female. She smiled to herself. Respectable Bath was thin of the muslin set, and girls from good families were kept close to home, for there was nowhere near the freedom here that they were permitted in London . . . so, who could it be?

Glancing at the handsome profile beside her chair, she hoped the lady was intriguing enough to keep him in residence for a long time. She did not dare to expect that this time he had met a girl who would make a suitable bride, for her nephew seemed determined to remain a bachelor. Sometimes she had had to bite her tongue when she saw him going his careless way, seemingly intent only on transitory pleasures. She had always been very careful not to condemn his way of life. His mother, the late viscountess, had been her favorite sister, and she wanted nothing but the best for her only child, but any direct action from her would only estrange him. Someday, she told herself as the sedan chair was lowered so she could step down before her tall, honey-colored stone house, someday Guy will fall in love, but until he does, there is nothing that I or anybody else can do to hurry the matter along. But, oh, how I will welcome the day! Surely he will be happier then, less bored and restless, always searching for some new experience or daring challenge to fill his days.

She allowed him to help her up the steps, leaning heavily on his arm. Lady Sylvia had contracted a joint disease some years ago, and it became progressively worse, a fact she kept from her family and her friends. Only her companion, Wilma Kincaid, realized how much she suffered and she was bound to secrecy. Lady Sylvia knew that although the hot baths alleviated the pain and stiffness, they would not cure her, and she was not sure of the efficacy of the waters, even though she forced herself to drink the prescribed three glasses a day, but Bath appealed to her, for her illness had forced her to retire from the world. The climate was temperate, the pace slow, and there were all manner of amusements suitable for an ailing lady. As long as members of the family came to visit several times a year, she was content to remain here with her friends, her books, and her hobby of translating French literature.

At the luncheon table, Guy set himself to amuse her and soon had her laughing helplessly at some of the stories of the *ton* that he had heard last evening. Even Gregson, his aunt's elderly butler, was hard put to keep his composure when Guy related the story of Sir Gerald Stone's disastrous elopement to Gretna Green with the widowed Lady Mary Edison, who, after two days of traveling in a constant downpour, insisted he take her back home at once. She did not care if her reputation was in shreds; she would sooner marry a monkey than a man who had no more sense than to journey in such distasteful weather, a sentiment she made known to all her acquaintance as soon as she reached London again.

"But how bad of Lady Mary," Lady Sylvia said, wiping her eyes. "Surely she could not hold Sir Gerald responsible for the rain!"

The viscount agreed it seemed most unfair, and then he signaled the butler to leave them. As the double doors closed behind the old retainer, he reached over and took his aunt's hand. "May I have a moment of your time, *chère tante*?" he asked.

Lady Sylvia settled back into her chair. "As many as you like, my dear. I suspect something of great importance has happened to you, am I right?"

"So, you sense it, after all," Guy replied, not seeming to hear the teasing note in her voice. "Yes, the most amazing, marvelous, wonderful, unexpected—"

His aunt chuckled. "Aha! I know that dangerous, glinting look of yours. It can only be *une femme*! But you were not enamored when you left the house yesterday, I believe, so it must have happened last evening."

The viscount waved an impatient hand. "Not last evening, Aunt. That was only a bachelor affair, as I told you. No, it was this morning on the way to the Pump Room that I saw her. The most glorious chestnut hair, the most melting deep-violet eyes, the sweetest expression I have ever seen, her figure so slim yet shapely—why, she reminded me of an angel."

His aunt ran over her acquaintance for red-haired, blue-eyed misses who might fit this lyrical description, but no one came to mind. "But have you not decided on very short acquaintance, Guy?" she asked. "Do consider Sir Gerald's experience with Lady Mary and how quickly her sentiments changed when the sun disappeared."

"She is nothing at all like that," her nephew said, his eyes glowing so with his fervor that Lady Sylvia felt a twinge of alarm. "I know she is the truest, most honest person in the world. I cannot imagine her impatient or rude or out of temper, Aunt. I do not pretend to know anything about love, but surely this emotion I feel now must be it. I have made up my mind . . . I will marry her.''

His aunt swallowed her quick retort that his knowledge of love was nonexistent and that what he was feeling now was only lust and infatuation. Instead she asked, ''But where did you meet her? And what is her name? Do I know her?''

She thought he looked rueful as he said, ''You may know her—in fact, I pray you do, for it is certain I do not. And now I must search all of Bath until I find her again.''

By this time, Lady Sylvia was definitely alarmed. Guy was no green young man to have his fancy taken in a moment by a sweet smile or an inviting look. ''You . . . you were not introduced?'' she asked faintly.

For the next several minutes, the viscount related his story, and his aunt sat quietly and did not interrupt. Indeed, she could think of nothing to say. This was so unlike him that she was stunned. To think of all those Seasons of avoiding matrimony and laughing at the traps set for him, all those long years he had gone his own way and reveled in his freedom, erased in a moment, if he were to be believed, by a pair of violet eyes and a sweet smile. She herself did not believe in love at first sight, and she could only feel that her nephew was standing on a precipice about to leap into a dark endless void of trouble. He had certainly not even considered that the young woman might be completely unsuitable, and although Lady Sylvia was not a proud woman who insisted on pomp and ceremony, she knew only too well that, as Viscount Reading, her nephew must marry one of his own kind. For all he knew this girl might be a tradesman's daughter, or much, much worse! She shuddered as he concluded, ''But you will help me, won't you, Aunt? I must find her.''

Lady Sylvia assured him of her assistance, her face white and strained, and Guy came out of his reverie and said, ''I am so selfish. You are tired, for I know you always rest at this hour. Come, let me take you to your room, Aunt. I do not despair, you know,'' he added as he lifted her to her feet and handed her her cane. ''No, Bath is a small place and there are not that many of the gentry here that I will not find her eventually.''

As he helped her up the stairs, he said jokingly, ''You may be wishing me at the devil if I do not, before too long, for I intend to remain with you until that happy day.''

Lady Sylvia told him that his attendance was always a
delight to her, and wished him luck in his search, already
deciding to ask a few of the busier Bath matrons to tea as
soon as she could arrange it. Living secluded as she did,
uninterested in large parties and balls, she did not hear much
of the town gossip, but surely Miss Warrenstoke and Lady
Helmsley, being such accomplished quizzes, could help her.
As Guy left her at her door with a kiss, she had the happy
thought that perhaps the young lady had just been passing
through town, or making a short visit, and might never be
seen again. She hoped it was not wicked of her to pray that
this might be the case, for she could not throw off the terrible
sense of foreboding she had about this sudden enchantment of
her hitherto sensible and sophisticated nephew had been cast
under. Somehow she knew in her heart that this mysterious
lady would bring him nothing but trouble, and she wished
him out of the adventure as soon as possible.

The lady they had been discussing was even then leaving
Bath. When she had seen the violets heaped on the seat of the
landau, she had paused in astonishment before she gathered
them into her arms to inhale their sweet, woodsy scent. But
then, looking around, she saw the handsome stranger giving
her an elegant bow from across the street, and she realized he
had bought them for her. She felt a little tingle of delight at
the tribute in spite of herself, and like Lady Sylvia, a sense of
foreboding as well. She was glad when her coachman drove
away. Her maid was darting suspicious glances her way, and
she knew it was only a matter of time before she began to
question her mistress openly.

The lady wished she might keep even one of her posies as
a remembrance, but she did not dare, for then the maid would
be sure she was involved in some intrigue and mention it at
home. And so, when the landau reached the poorer section of
Bath, she signaled the coachman to pull up.

"Here, Betty," she said, her voice cool, "give these
nosegays to the children playing over there. I have no idea
how they came to be put in my carriage; surely there was
some mistake! Since we have no way of returning them to the
rightful owner, at least we can make sure some good will
come of the error, for the children can sell them again."

As the maid climbed down and took the violets, the lady

kept her face calm and indifferent. In her mind, however, she was remembering the handsome gentleman who had honored her. She could not help feeling attracted to him, for he had been so good-looking and aristocratic. She had known at once, from the light in his gray eyes and the intentness of his posture, that he was interested in her. She told herself she was not sorry there was no chance that they would ever meet. After all, she had seen many a handsome beau who stared at her fervently before this; she knew what was in his mind. Her little smile was rueful. The path of her life was already determined; there could be no change in her circumstances, not now. No matter how tall and handsome and distinguished he was, she knew he was not for her. To meet him would only be futile and distressing.

As the maid took her seat again, the lady waved to the delighted children who were calling out their thanks and bobbing curtsies for this unexpected boon. As the horses moved away at a smart trot, she put the disturbing stranger from her mind. Turning toward her maid, she began to chat of the purchases she had made that morning, the glorious weather, and the crowded Bath streets. It had been an amusing interlude, but that was all it had been, and now it was over.

Unaware that the lady had left Bath, Guy Leighton changed into riding clothes. He was restless and so anxious to begin his search that he knew he could not remain indoors, reading the papers and idly passing the time until he was due to meet Lady Mills and her party at three for a canter along the Avon. No, he decided, stamping into his polished boots in a way that caused Chums, his valet, to raise his brows in horror, I will ride about the town and perhaps have the good fortune to spot her carriage once again. He knew women spent a good deal of time on their shopping, and it was by no means impossible that she still had errands to do.

He ran down the stairs whistling, and smiled at his aunt's butler, who held the door open for him. Gregson bowed, wondering what the man was up to now, for his demeanor was so different from this morning's when he had gone out with a frown, his gray eyes cold and bored, and his mouth twisted in a sneer. Perhaps he had had a drink of the mineral waters and it had put him in better spirits, the old butler

thought as he closed the door. I should live to see the day!
No, with a rake like Lord Guy, it had to be a woman.

The viscount rode through Bath for an hour, going up as
far as the Royal Crescent, then back to the Circus and down
Gay Street to the center of town again. Always his keen eyes
searched the cross streets and sidewalks, but he did not find
the carriage he sought or its charming passenger. He had
never realized how many young ladies resided in Bath, nor
how many of them favored chip bonnets and sprigged muslin,
for several times he urged his horse to a faster trot to come up
with some lady so attired only to be disappointed. He was
smiled on by blondes and brunettes alike, but of chestnut
curls there was nary a glimpse, and not even the most melting,
seductive glance from a lady with strawberry-blond hair had
the power to deter him from his search. At last, hearing the
abbey clock strike the quarter hour, he turned toward the river
and his rendezvous with Lady Mills and her party.

His cousin, James Debenham, was before him, mounted on
a hired hack and looking disgusted, as if he had never crossed
such a slug in his life. Mr. Debenham was a cynical forty. He
had never married, and when questioned about it, he admitted
he had never found a woman whose company, out of bed, he
could bear for more than twenty minutes at a time. "Assure
you, my dear sir," he had concluded to his awed questioner,
"but find me one who can hold my attention for twenty-one
minutes and I will seriously consider it."

He had a tall, thin figure and bright-blue eyes that missed
very little under their sleepy lids. He wore his black hair
longer than was fashionable, and his clothes were chosen
more for comfort than for high style. With his beak of a nose,
he could not be considered a handsome man, but he was
much sought after for his drawling conversation and outrageous *bons mots*.

Now he saluted his cousin with his riding crop. "Thank
heavens you have come, Guy," he drawled. "So tiresome to
be first! I had almost decided to go away and return in an
hour. Ladies, you know, are so unpunctual. I fear they
cultivate the trait hoping it will make them more interesting."

The viscount cast one last glance around the busy street
corner and then gave his attention to his cousin. He wondered
what James would say if he told him what had happened, but
before he had time to consider doing so, the other members

of the party arrived, and after greetings were exchanged, the horses were set in motion. Until they left the crowded streets, conversation was general and spirited, but as soon as the road to Bradford-on-Avon was reached, the eight riders separated into pairs and began to canter.

The viscount found himself beside his hostess. Clorinda Mills was a plump, pretty woman in her late twenties who was well known for her flirtations and love affairs, none of which seemed to bother her husband in the slightest. He was often heard to remark on the happiness of his marriage, happiness that seemed to depend on his turning a deaf ear and a blind eye to even the most outrageous of his wife's activities. Guy Leighton knew Lord Mills was in London, and he could see from her smoldering gaze that the lady intended to make good use of his absence.

The pretty little village was soon reached, and after a cursory inspection of the church and the cottages, the riding party dismounted to enjoy the refreshments provided by the landlord of the Bradford Arms, served on the banks of the Avon.

Guy made himself keep his mind on present company. He was glad now that he had not blurted out his sensational news to his cousin, for he knew he could not have stood it if James made it general knowledge. He could almost hear their jeering laughter and lewd jests, for he himself had often mocked others' affairs that way.

He remembered he had even considered making Clorinda Mills his mistress while they were both in Bath, as a way to pass the time. Now he wondered why he had ever thought her attractive, or Miss Bates and her sister Anne at all out of the common, and as for Janice Reed, she was loud and vulgar. They all seemed coarse and overblown to him, joking and flirting so openly with the gentlemen. He could not imagine his lady of the violet eyes in this group, for he could not picture her being at all comfortable in an atmosphere of such loose intimacy and barely veiled sexual comments. He sipped his ale and watched the others, almost as if he were a spectator at a play.

"You're quiet today, my boy," his cousin remarked softly from behind his shoulder. "Can it be that that final bottle of wine last evening has soured your spirits?"

The viscount turned and smiled. "Perhaps. It was devilish

late when I reached home, I know that. But where is Charlie today? I was sure he was promised to Lady Mills too.''

His cousin shrugged. "Indeed, but on the way to the rendezvous he spotted a satin waistcoat in a shop window that took his eye, and nothing would do but for him to relay his apologies to Lady Mills so he might purchase it at once. Lord, was there ever such a fop!''

Guy grinned. Charlie's weakness for fashionable attire was well known, and his wardrobe acknowledged to be the most extensive in England, surpassing even the Prince Regent's.

"I feel I should warn you, Guy, as an older member of the family, y'know,'' Mr. Debenham purred next, "that unless I am very much mistaken, Lady Mills has decided that you are to be her next, mm, how shall I put it? 'Victim' sounds so crude, 'lover' so specific, and 'flirt' not nearly close enough to the mark. Look there where she is even now bending such a burning gaze your way.''

Guy glanced at the lady and she blew him a kiss. "I hope not,'' he said, turning away. "I should be desolated to have to disappoint her, for I find she is not at all to my taste. But stay! Perhaps it is you she is smiling at, cuz?''

Mr. Debenham's blue eyes gleamed for a moment before the sleepy lids came down to hide them. "Surely not. I see I must admit that I am before you by several years, for Clorinda and I have already enjoyed a liaison, and she has not reached the unenviable state of having to repeat a lover. My, my! I wonder what she will do when the shocking day arrives that she finds she has run out of eligible gentlemen to seduce? Will she descend to the ranks of commoners or throw herself into the Thames in despair? At the rate she is working her way through the House of Lords, it cannot be far distant. Come, Guy, a wager on the date!''

The viscount returned a joking answer and wandered away to join the group around Lady Mills, who was beckoning to him in a way he could not disregard. She insisted he sit down close beside her, and he had never been so impatient for a party to end. When at last they all strolled back to the inn where they had left the horses, he could not restrain a stifled sigh of relief.

As they rode back to Bath, he made his plans for the evening. There was a concert of sacred music in the Lower Rooms this evening, and although he hoped that such entertainment was not high on the lady's list of enjoyable pastimes, he would look in on it to make sure. Early tomorrow he would search the libraries before he joined his aunt in the Pump Room, and then in the afternoon he would explore both Sydney Gardens and the Parade Gardens, where so many Bath residents promenaded beneath the soaring sixteenth-century walls of the abbey, admiring the colorful flower beds set above the gently flowing river.

At his side, Lady Mills pouted, tossing her black curls while her dark eyes smoldered with anger, for not even the most blatant hints of her availability were answered by the viscount, and when he gave her a bow from the saddle in parting, she had the feeling he was looking right through her and did not see her at all.

2

The concert of sacred music was not graced by the lady with the violet-blue eyes, nor was she to be found the following morning in Meyler & Sons near the Pump Room, nor in Duffield's on Milsom Street, or any of the other libraries for which Bath was famous. Neither was she among the crowds of strollers in the parks or gardens that afternoon, although the spring day was warm and sunny, with only a little breeze to stir the air.

When the viscount returned to Great Pulteney Street late in the day, his expression of annoyed disappointment was noted by his aunt with relief. She was seated in the drawing room with her companion when he came in, and she offered to order a fresh pot of tea for him.

"No, *tante*, do not trouble yourself," Guy replied, his gray eyes remote and serious. "I shall have a glass of your excellent sherry instead, before I have to go and get ready to dine with Lord and Lady de Riche. I wish you might have been persuaded to accompany me."

Lady Sylvia shook her head, and before Wilma could inform the viscount that his aunt had spent a wretched day in almost constant pain, she said, "I am happy to remain by my own fireside this evening, my dear, but do say everything that is proper to Lady de Riche for me."

The viscount swallowed some sherry and then wandered over to the long windows at the front of the house, as if even now he could not give up the hope that the lady he sought might be walking by on the flags below. Behind him, he heard his aunt ask Miss Kincaid, her dithery but loving companion, to leave them for a little while.

"You had no luck, Guy?" Lady Sylvia asked softly as that lady shut the drawing-room doors behind her.

He turned from brooding down into the street and came

24

back to her chair. "None at all. It is disappointing, but I do not despair, for it can only be a matter of days before I find her. I shall consider this interval a test of my devotion, like any knight sent on a quest before he can win fair lady." He paused, and then he shook his head at his folly, his expression cynical again. "Bah! I sound like an idiot, don't I, Aunt? No, no, do not shake your head at me. I have thought too many times myself, when one of my friends fell in love, how ridiculous he became with all those sighs and impassioned vows, his constant references to the lady's qualities and beauty, and his complete uninterest in either his former pursuits or his long-suffering friends, all of which conspired to make him a dead bore. I shall try very hard not to condemn you to such a fate, but even so, I make no promises. The thought of her burns too brightly."

His aunt laughed at him. "You may bore me as much as you wish, my dear," she assured him cordially. "What are aunts for, after all?"

The viscount pulled a chair closer to hers and perched on its edge. She watched his eyes grow intent and serious. For a moment there was silence in the drawing room, and then he asked softly, "Is it always like this, Aunt Sylvia?"

At her look of incomprehension, he added, "What I mean is, is love always so painful, so all-consuming? Does everyone feel the way I do when they are caught in its spell?"

Lady Sylvia considered carefully before she answered. "It can be all-consuming, of course, for when you first fall in love it is difficult to think of any other subject. As for the pain of love, that only comes when the one who is loved does not return it. There is no worse pain in all the world than that, my dear. I hope you never know it. But, I might add, there is no feeling to compare with the exultation of knowing that your love, so freely given, is returned with equal fervor."

The viscount ran a hand through his gleaming dark hair. "I cannot imagine that fate will be so unkind to me, Aunt, as to deny me that. Surely we have only to meet for her to share my sentiments."

"But, Guy, what if she does not?" Lady Sylvia could not help asking.

Her nephew rose and began to pace the room, and she watched him with anxiety. At length he came back to her, his eyes blazing and his jaw outthrust, and said with great force,

"Then I shall set myself to make her do so. She *will* love me!"

His aunt did not like to point out that his determination might not be enough, for no one, not even her handsome, rakish nephew, could command another's affection, and so she changed the subject. "Have you thought, dear Guy, that your own feelings might change on further acquaintance?" she asked, and at his incredulous look, she hurried on, "For example, suppose she has a loud, coarse voice or is afflicted with a common accent or stutter? She may have a silly laugh or some other mannerism that will offend you. Then too, there is the question of her character. I beg you not to place too much reliance on this love at first sight until you meet and speak with her, for I would not have you hurt."

Throughout this speech, the viscount had appeared cynically amused that his aunt could attribute such revolting qualities to his lady, and now he took her hand and kissed it. "Thank you for your concern, *chère tante*, but it is not necessary. I know she is an angel; no one who looks as she does could be anything else."

He glanced at the gilded Cartel clock on the wall and rose. "It grows late and I must leave you now."

After he had given her a kiss, he put his hands gently on her shoulders. "Go to bed early, Aunt, for you are looking pulled this evening," he ordered, his deep voice full of concern.

"I shall cease worrying about you at once, Guy," Lady Sylvia retorted. "If you can still notice my looks, you are not as completely consumed by this love as you imagine, and I am in no danger of being bored to death. Run along now and send Wilma to me, if you would be so kind."

Her nephew laughed and left the room, but when he was gone, her gay smile became a frown, and when Miss Kincaid came in, she asked at once if she should fetch a powder for the pain.

"No, thank you, my dear. I have no time for that. Let us retire to the library, for I wish you to pen some invitations for me to a small tea party in two days' time. It is most important that they be delivered first thing in the morning, but I know I can rely on you, my friend."

*   *   *

It took only a glance for the viscount to discover that the lady he sought was not among the de Riches' twenty dinner guests that evening, and immediately any enjoyment he might have had in the party disappeared. Lady Mills did her best to engage him in dalliance, her abundant charms generously displayed in a low-cut gown of crimson silk, and the look in her black eyes suggestive, but the viscount continued immune. From his part of the drawing room after dinner, Mr. Debenham watched and smiled to himself before he strolled over to rescue his cousin from the lady's clutches.

As the two of them left together some time later, the viscount refused an invitation to join Mr. Debenham for a nightcap in his rooms at York House, where he was putting up.

"Charlie will be so disappointed, cuz," Mr. Debenham urged, "especially since you refused his invitation to drive out this afternoon. He is most anxious to have your opinion of his new waistcoat."

The viscount waved an impatient hand. "Tell Charlie I shall call on him at York House tomorrow morning late. There is something I must do before that."

"What?" James asked baldly.

Guy turned quickly to see his cousin smiling gently, one eyebrow raised in interrogation.

"The reason that I am so bold as to ask, dear cuz, is because it has been devilish hard to get your attention, even for someone as luscious as Clorinda Mills. Why, just this evening you ignored the veritable banquet of feminine delights that she spread before your eyes, and even if you do not want her, it is most unlike you not to take full advantage of such a display. If I did not know that you, like I, are immune to permanence, I would wager anything you like that you have fallen in love." He laughed softly and continued, "But since I am sure that is not the case, what can it be?"

The two strolled along in silence while the viscount struggled to find some explanation for his behavior. At length he said, "I cannot tell you, James. Believe me, I regret any rudeness and inattention, but I cannot explain my reason—not yet."

His cousin shrugged. "As you wish. You will forgive me for saying so, Guy, but I will be delighted when this, mm, dilemma of yours is solved. You are not the most enlivening of companions at the moment.''

Thus put on his mettle, the viscount thrust that perfect face to the back of his mind and set himself to amuse his cousin until the steps of York House were reached. A time was set for the morning's meeting and they parted amiably, before the viscount continued on his way, free to return his thoughts to the lady he was in such desperate need of finding. Surely it could not be much longer before he learned her name and could take her hands in his at last.

But in the days that followed, it appeared that she had disappeared from the face of the earth. No matter how diligently the viscount searched, she eluded him. Lady Sylvia, who had gained nothing from her tea party but a headache, was delighted. It appeared that Guy's lady of the violet eyes had indeed just been passing through town, for neither Miss Warrenstoke nor Lady Helmsley could recall any young miss of that description either residing in or visiting Bath, and she was able to sigh with relief as day after day passed and her nephew's downcast face each evening told its own tale. She was sure that such a violent passion that had sprung up so suddenly would just as suddenly disappear, although in one way it was regrettable that it must be so, for then Guy would revert to his former, dissolute habits, the late hours and drinking bouts, the gambling and wenching that made up his days. She longed for another pretty face to catch his eye, even going to great pains to point out a neat figure and slim ankle, or a pair of pansy-brown eyes in the Pump Room.

But the viscount was not to be turned aside. One afternoon, two weeks after his first encounter with the lady, he ordered his horse saddled, and in complete frustration decided to go for a lonely gallop in the countryside. He did not think he could bear to haunt the Bath streets for even one more hour, and he wished to be solitary so he might ponder what on earth he was to do next. It never occurred to him to give up the search and admit defeat, for as the days passed, the memory of her remained as fresh and vivid as at first meeting.

He had heard Lord Williams mention an expedition to Chippenham, and not wanting to come up with any of his acquaintance, he rode out in the opposite direction. He took the road west out of town leading toward Prior Park, the great Palladian mansion that Ralph Allen had commissioned John

Wood, the architectural genius who had had so much to do with Bath's beauty, to build for him of native stone. Passing this landmark without a glance, the viscount headed toward the Mendip Hills, in his dark thoughts ignoring the play of light and shadow on the face of the quarries from which so much of the warm-colored stone that was used in the local building had come, as well as the beauty of the perfect spring day. Although he rode for a long time, he could not think of a single thing that he had not already tried in his search, and in some despair and no wiser than before, he turned again for home as the sun began its descent.

He had come through the little village of Midsomer Norton and was just urging his horse to a canter again, when he saw in the distance ahead of him, a lady in a dark-brown habit, mounted on a chestnut mare. There was something about her that quickened his breathing and sent his riding crop slashing down his horse's side.

As he drew nearer, he saw the chestnut curls beneath her riding hat, and he prayed hard that he was not to be disappointed again. Perhaps disturbed by the pounding hooves behind her, the lady turned her horse into a shady lane, not much wider than a path through the woods, and with hardly a check, he followed her. When she heard the pursuing horse still behind her, she turned her head in some alarm before she urged her mare to a faster pace, her face pale and frightened.

The viscount drew in his breath, for it was his violet-eyed lady indeed.

"I have found you at last!" he exclaimed. "Wait for me!"

But the lady only bent farther over her horse's mane as she continued to try to escape. Guy could not know that his exultant words and the wild look of triumph on his dark, handsome face made her think him mad. But the chestnut mare was no match for the viscount's gelding, in spite of the narrow, winding path, and a few moments later, deep in the woods, he drew abreast of her and reached out to grasp the bridle of her horse and pull it to a halt. They were both panting from their exertion, and it was a moment before he could say, "Do not be afraid, I beg you. It is just that I have searched for you for such a long time, I could not let you escape me again."

The lady's wide eyes made her look like a startled fawn. "You," she whispered, "the man in the shop that day."

His eyes devoured her face, worshiping each perfect feature that was surely even more beautiful than he remembered, and for several moments they remained perfectly still as they gazed at each other—he with obvious hunger, and she atremble still with fear.

At last he said more quietly, "Your pardon. My name is Guy Leighton, Viscount Reading," and then, unable to help himself, he transferred his reins and her bridle to one hand and reached out with the other, almost as if even now he had to convince himself that she was real. As that hand came down to grasp her shoulder, she started and, twisting away with one fluid motion, slid from her sidesaddle, picked up the train of her habit, and ran into the woods.

"Wait! I mean you no harm, my dear," he called, trying to watch the way she had gone as he dismounted and quickly tied both the horses to a nearby branch. He hurried after her, but she had run as fast as the wind and disappeared. He searched for a while, but he realized she must know these woods well if they were near her home, and he had little chance of finding her. He stood still and listened, hoping to hear her moving. There was no sound in the woods but the cheerful chirping of a bird far above him, and somewhere in the distance the chattering of an angry squirrel.

As he made his way back to the horses, he told himself that he must not despair, for at least now he knew where he could find her again, and then, as he mounted his gelding, he realized he could do even better than that: he hit her mare on the hindquarters with his crop. Obediently, the chestnut moved away, and he followed it closely until they came out of the woods and it jumped a fence and cantered across the fields to a distant stable.

Turning his horse back toward the road, he continued on his way, approaching the front gates of what he could see was a large estate, for across the fields and gardens there was a stone manor house of some four stories and numerous outbuildings. As he reached the gate house, he pulled up the gelding. A small boy was playing by the doorstep, and at the viscount's command, he came to the wrought-iron fence to stare at him.

"Who lives here, boy?" Guy asked, smiling down at his towhead and round blue eyes.

"The Biddles, m'lord," the boy answered, and the viscount threw him some pennies to thank him for the information. He rode back to Bath lost in his dreams. Tomorrow he would return, and somehow he would make the acquaintance of Mr. Biddles—or M'lord Biddles, as the case might be—and then he would ask for permission to address his daughter. It was going to be all right, after all. He had startled her today, but when he had a chance to explain, he was sure she would understand and come to love him as deeply as he now believed he loved her.

But the next morning he woke to discover that the spell of fine weather had broken, and he could not control a growl of disappointment when he saw the large raindrops cascading down his windows. He would not be able to ride out today, after all, and he resigned himself to further delay.

He spent a long time with his aunt, telling her everything that had happened, and Lady Sylvia stored the name "Biddles" away to ask the Bath quizzes about. Somehow it did not seem at all suitable a title for an alliance with a viscount, and her foreboding increased, but still she exclaimed over the way fate had relented at last and led him to the lady he sought.

That evening there was a cotillion ball in the Upper Rooms such as was held every Thursday during the Season and which he had promised to attend with his cousin and Lord Williams. Although he had no desire to go now and have to chat and dance with others, he knew he could not, in politeness, refuse the engagement. In any case, he told himself, it will make the evening pass more quickly, and surely it will not rain again tomorrow.

He dressed in his evening clothes, assisted by his valet, and went on his way looking every inch the accomplished, handsome aristocrat that he was. The tight-fitting black coat of superfine fit his broad shoulders and narrow waist to perfection, his knit knee breeches and white silk stockings clung to his muscular legs in the approved style, and in his white cravat, a diamond twinkled. He wore his massive signet ring on his right hand, and his dark-brown hair gleamed as he climbed into the waiting sedan chair to be carried to York House, where he was expected for dinner with his cousin and Lord Williams before the ball.

York House was known for the excellence of its table, and he made a good meal, but not even Charlie's innocuous chatter or James' sly comments could keep his mind entirely from the lady he had found at last. The rain had almost stopped, for the sky to the east had lightened during the afternoon, and in his mind, over and over again, ran the thought, Tomorrow, surely I will see her again tomorrow!

Lord Williams did not appear to notice his abstraction, for he was more concerned with his dinner and the new way he had invented of tying his cravat, which he explained in great detail to his friends while disposing of a plump duck, several slices of red sirloin, and some early asparagus. Lord Williams was only of moderate height, and inclined to corpulence. He had round blue eyes as guileless as a baby's, and blond hair that was carefully brushed to conceal his impending baldness. Now, his fat cheeks wobbled as he laughed at one of Mr. Debenham's sallies, for although he was not needle-witted, he was known for his good nature.

As the waiters took away the first course and its removes, he poured more wine for them all as he remarked that Bath might be devilish flat, but the quality of the food at York House almost persuaded him to remain for an indefinite period of time.

"Surely not," Mr. Debenham murmured, and at his inquiring look, he added, "If you were to stay, you would soon be forced to purchase an entirely new wardrobe, Charlie, for nothing will fit you if you continue to eat as you do."

"I say, James, that is too bad of you," Lord Williams protested, his blue eyes indignant. "Why, 'tis nothing but a slight repast. A man must keep up his strength, y'know."

Guy and his cousin stared at his plate—now heaped with filet of sole in a wine sauce, a large slice of game pie, some new peas and duchess potatoes—and saw him eyeing the tarts and jellies on the sideboard as well, and they burst into laughter. Charlie ignored them as he tucked into his meal.

Mr. King, the master of ceremonies in the Upper Rooms, was delighted to welcome three such eligible gentlemen to the ball, even though they arrived well past the appointed hour, having lingered over their dinner. After they had paid sixpence each for tea, they were free to join the other guests. Mr. Debenham wandered away when he saw an acquaintance across the room, and Charlie excused himself to make his bow to Lady Harris, an old friend of his mother's. The viscount stood slightly apart, leaning against the wall, his arms folded as he surveyed the crowd. And then, a couple standing directly in front of him moved away and he saw her again. His gray eyes grew keen, and he straightened up in surprise, all boredom gone in an instant.

She was standing talking with a small group of people, and for a moment he remained perfectly still as he stared at her. Vaguely he was aware that the others laughed, and the middle-aged gentleman beside her smiled fondly, even though all his attention was directed only to her.

This evening she was wearing a gown of pale-blue silk, trimmed with rosettes of matching ribbons, and on her head and at her throat she wore some of the most magnificent diamonds he had ever seen. They glittered in the candlelight as she moved her head, the chestnut curls dressed high to show off her slender neck. Briefly he wondered why she wore so many, for surely the tiara, to say nothing of the elaborate necklace, pendant, and bracelets, were much too opulent for a simple Bath ball, but as he continued to drink her in, all such thoughts left his mind. How very beautiful she was in the blue gown that showed off her graceful figure and slim waist, how perfect.

He tore his eyes away from her at last and went back to Mr. King. He did not notice that the M.C. looked disconcerted when he made his request to be introduced.

"Of course, m'lord, if you are sure you would care for it," he said after a moment's pause. "But perhaps you do not know? I mean, are you aware—"

Guy was impatient. "Never mind all that," he interrupted, his face intent and harsh, "I wish to meet the lady—now!"

Mr. King shrugged and escorted him to where she now stood alone with the older man. "I beg your pardon, m'lady, sir," he began, his voice stiff. "May I introduce m'lord Guy Leighton, Viscount Reading? Mr. Alvin Biddles and his wife, Lady Patricia Biddles, m'lord."

The viscount bowed, which gave him an opportunity to hide the bleakness in his gray eyes and the sudden pounding ache of disappointment and shock in his heart. Lady Patricia Biddles? She was married? He felt so ill it was all he could do to keep his features composed and unconcerned.

"M'lord! An honor, sir, a distinct honor!" the middle-aged man was exclaiming, bowing as low as he would to royalty.

Guy stared at her and saw a slight tinge of color wash over her face.

"M'lord," she murmured, and curtsied.

Guy watched Mr. Biddles put his hand under his wife's arm, and gritted his teeth. To think that the only woman he would ever love was the wife of another, and such an unworthy consort for her, too! He was in his late fifties, short, heavyset, and almost bald, and his pleasant smile did not mask the shrewdness in his brown eyes, now beaming with delight at the viscount's attention. Anyone seeing them together would be sure she must be his daughter, although there was not the slightest similarity. She looked the complete aristocrat, and he resembled nothing so much as a retired merchant.

"The honor is mine, sir," Guy said in strangled accents.

Mr. Biddles positively glowed as he rocked back and forth on his heels and caressed his wife's arm.

Guy clenched his fists to keep himself from tearing that hand away before he throttled him for daring to touch her, to own her, when by all rights she should belong to him. He was not aware of Mr. King's murmured excuse as he left them, nor of the way Mr. Debenham was watching from across the room, his blue eyes intent under his half-closed lids.

"I must apologize to Lady Patricia," Guy said when the stiffness in his throat allowed him to speak. "I am afraid I startled her yesterday while I was out riding near Midsomer Norton."

The lady waved away his words. "It was nothing, m'lord. I did not quite understand—that is, your style of riding made me think you were pursuing me."

Her husband laughed with great good humor. "My love, how could you be such a silly widgeon? As if anyone of the viscount's stature could be a highwayman or some other villain! But why did you not bring the viscount up to the hall? I should have been glad to welcome you, m'lord."

Guy tore his eyes from her face and tried to look pleasant as Mr. Biddles added, "Come out anytime! I daresay you might like to see the estate, for it is extensive and I have made many costly new improvements. I can offer you an excellent dinner as well, eh, my dear?"

Around them, the other guests were moving to the sides of

the room as the musicians took their seats again to begin another set. Guy noted that Lady Patricia did not reply to her husband's prompting and add her invitation to his.

"I should be delighted, sir, my thanks," he said, and then he asked, "May I beg a dance, m'lady? That is, if you would be so kind as to allow it, sir?"

"Of course, of course, my pleasure," Mr. Biddles replied, bowing even more deeply before he gave up her hand to Guy. "Not much in the caper merchant line m'self, but delighted to see my lovely Patsy dancing with such as you, m'lord. Run along, m'dear, and enjoy yourself."

With another bow he left them, to take up a position against the wall where he could watch them, beaming all the while.

Guy could sense her reluctance, but she allowed him to lead her into the set that was forming, and he remarked softly, "How eager he is to accommodate me. If you were mine, I would never allow another man anywhere near you."

His voice was harsh and strained, but Lady Patricia colored up, but she made no reply. As Guy put his arm around her and looked down into her beautiful face, now so close to his own, he could not help saying, in accents as bitter as if they were torn from his throat, "How could you marry him when you must have sensed that I was in the world, waiting to find you?"

"M'lord, please," she whispered, her violet eyes begging him to control himself. "I do not understand you or your words, but you must be aware how improper it is to speak to me thus."

She moved away from him then in the figure, but when she came back and took his hand again, he said, "There can be nothing improper between us, my dear, for I fell in love with you the first moment I saw you that morning in West Gate Street, and I have been searching for you ever since. And now, when I find you at last, you belong to another man. And such a man!"

His laughter was harsh, but when he felt her stiffen in his arms, he looked down into those pools of violet-blue and wished he might drown in them in reality, for if he could not have her, he felt he might just as well be dead.

"How cruel fate is," he said, in a quieter, sadder voice.

"If you continue to speak to me this way, m'lord, I will be

forced to leave you alone in the middle of the dance," she said, her head high and her manner formal. He admired her look of haughty indignation as she added with scorn, "No one falls in love that way, you exaggerate."

He shook his head. "How I wish that were so, for then in a little while I would be able to forget you. No, what I said is true, to my deep regret, but we will speak of it no more now, m'lady, since you request my silence."

She nodded in thanks before he added, "When we meet again in a more private setting, I shall try to explain my feelings to you. I beg you to listen! You owe that much, m'lady, to one whose whole life now can only be a wasteland of loneliness and despair."

"I think it would be best if we do not meet again, sir," she said firmly.

Guy's arms tightened around her slender waist and her eyes flashed fire. "But your husband has invited me to his estate and in courtesy I must come there and visit," he pointed out. "Would you have Mr. Biddles slighted?"

"Is this some sport for you, m'lord?" she asked, furious now. "Do you think me fair game because I married Mr. Biddles, and make mock of me?"

Guy looked startled. "Make mock of you? Never! I love you."

"This constant reference to your love has no power to move me, sir, for I do not believe you. I am well acquainted with your sort—oh, yes, very well." For a moment she paused, a bitter look coming over her lovely features, and then she went on, "Rakes and libertines are not unknown to me, nor the way they make a farce of the word 'love,' since they are incapable of understanding it, never having known its power."

She stopped then, her color heightened, and he could see her struggle to regain her composure. "Your pardon, m'lord," she said more quietly. "I should not have called you that."

"No, you should not have," he agreed, and her eyes flew to his face. "You know nothing about me, not yet. Perhaps at one time I could have been considered a rake, although certainly no one has ever dared to call me one to my face before, but I assure you, from the moment I first looked into your sweet face, I knew I would love you until I die."

The music ended, and she stepped back out of his arms to curtsy, her eyes as bleak and unhappy as his own.

As he bowed, Guy murmured, "Believe me when I say I wish I had never seen you, for then I would have been spared the pain of knowing I can never claim you for my wife. Even so, I know I cannot stay away from you."

As he offered her his arm to lead her back to her husband, she lowered her eyes and bit her lip. "I am sorry, m'lord. I wish you had not seen me either, or conceived this ill-judged passion for me. I beg you to remember that I am a married woman, and dealings between us can only disappoint you. I remain faithful to my vows and my husband."

They reached Mr. Biddles' side before the viscount could reply. He bowed and, after expressing his thanks, excused himself. Mr. Biddles reminded him with cheerful insistence that they would be looking for him at the hall in the near future even as he made good his escape.

As he walked over to join his cousin, he wished he might leave the ball at once, but then he realized that there was something more here than he was aware of as yet, and so he must remain. Besides, if he tore off after one dance, it could only cause comment, and he did not want to do anything that might distress Lady Patricia. He forced himself to smile at James as Charlie walked up to them.

"And who was that prime piece of perfection, Guy, if I may be so bold as to inquire?" Mr. Debenham asked. "I do not think I have ever seen such beauty even in town."

Lord Williams raised his quizzing glass to inspect the lady, for if Guy had found a new paramour, he must also join the ranks of her admirers.

Across the room, the lady turned her head aside at his blatant inspection, but her husband bowed and smiled, and then bent his head to whisper to the lady. Guy did not look their way as he replied in what he hoped was his normal, bored tone of voice, "Yes, she is beautiful, is she not? The Lady Patricia Biddles. The man beside her is her husband."

James shuddered. "That cit? How . . . how very singular! He certainly has the look of a man named Biddles, but she does not. Hmm. There is something in the back of my mind, now what can it be? Biddles, Biddles? The name has meaning to me, but I cannot recall why."

"Too bad she is taken, Guy," Lord Williams sympathized,

"but I do not think you will want to have anything to do with someone so common. I wonder who she was before her marriage?"

"And I wonder what made her accept an offer from such an older, unattractive suitor," James pondered, and then he sneered. "He must have the wealth of the Indies."

"I have no idea. The lady did not confide her reasons to me in the space of one dance, nor was I so gauche as to ask," Guy said, his voice taut with anger, and his cousin and Charlie exchanged startled glances. The viscount did not see, for he was looking about the room.

Spotting Lady Mills sitting with Miss Reed and some others, he excused himself and strolled over to her side, to Clorinda's delight. She was further encouraged when he asked her to dance, and she rose with a look of triumph for her conquest. What they talked about, or even what dance they performed, the viscount could not have told you, but he remained by the lady's side for the rest of the evening.

Although he did not show it by even a flicker of an eyebrow, he was aware that the Biddles did not join any of the groups in the rooms, and were left very much to themselves, and he noticed they left the ball well before eleven, when the festivities concluded.

3

In the luxurious carriage that carried them home, Mr. Biddles raved about the success of the evening, and perhaps it was just as well he found so much to say, for his wife was strangely quiet.

"There now, Patsy, my love, you see I was right, after all, and tonight is only the beginning," he enthused, leaning back against the velvet squabs and smiling broadly. "For where Viscount Reading leads, others are sure to follow! Oh, yes, it is all coming true at last, even as I knew it would when I married you. I do not begrudge one farthing that I spent to get you, either, for just see how our marriage has answered. Alvin J. Biddles, late of the London docks, hobnobbing with the gentry and making conversation with a lord."

He pinched her averted cheek and added, "Not that I am such a nodcock that I think it was me he honored. Oh, no, for I cut my eyeteeth years ago!" He chortled then, his huge stomach shaking with his mirth. "The look on his face, Patsy, when he came up to us and discovered you were a married woman I shall never forget. But he will not retreat now, not after his dance with you. No, we can expect him at Biddles Hall within the week."

He paused and looked to his wife in happy triumph, and she murmured, "I am sorry if it displeases you, Alvin, but I hope he does not come. I cannot see any good in this situation at all."

"You are all about in your head, m'dearie! No good? When you know what an alliance with a viscount will do for our consequence? Before you know it, we will be welcomed everywhere in all the finest homes, and I shall have the pleasure of seeing you take your place beside me in the *ton,* attending all the grandest parties and showing off the jewels and gowns I have bought you, the envy of even a duchess."

He patted her hand and added, "And it is not impossible that I might be able to buy a title even now, with well-born friends behind me, although that part of it has always riled me. Why should I have to purchase what others get for nothing from their birth? Is not plain Mr. Alvin Biddles good enough? Ha! When they come and beg me to lend 'em money, they're mighty humble, I can tell you, those grand lords and ladies! But while my money is good enough for 'em, they make it plain that I am not. Well, they shall see—oh, yes, now they shall see."

He began to run his hand up and down her arm, and he said more softly, in a wheedling tone, "I am very pleased with you, my dearie, and very proud of you too. You were beautiful tonight, and no one was your equal. The diamond set becomes you, but did you notice the paltry stuff the other ladies wore? I am sure they envied you."

After five years of marriage, Lady Patricia knew what the caress and soft words meant, and steeled herself, although not a muscle moved in her soft cheek. When he was pleased, Mr. Biddles came to her bed, and soon he would buy her yet another large, vulgar piece of jewelry or some new toy he thought she might like, a carriage or a monkey or a little black page boy, none of which she wanted in the slightest.

She tried to put the viscount from her mind and concentrate on what her husband was saying again, but it was difficult to do so when his extraordinary words kept echoing in her head and his handsome face refused to leave her mind. She knew it was her duty to be attentive to her husband. Indeed, in the five years since their marriage when she was just nineteen, she had schooled herself to be a pleasant, agreeable companion to him, never denying him anything he wished, from her bed to his ostentatious way of life that she could not help deploring, and forcing herself to accept his gifts as if she were perfectly content with her lot.

And I know he does not suspect how unhappy I am, she thought as the carriage turned into the drive. He may be a cruel, unethical businessman, but he is kind to me and he has never blamed me for my failure to make him socially acceptable. I knew what I was doing when the bargain was made; there can be no regrets now. If the viscount dares to come to the hall, I will find a way to tell him that he must leave me alone, and discourage him so he will take his fancies elsewhere. And somehow Mr. Biddles must be convinced as well that her title and background would never gain him acceptance from the *ton*, for they snubbed her now, too.

She had begun her married life in a magnificent town house in St. James's Place, but after two years of being cut by the neighbors and never once gaining admittance to anything but public entertainments and balls, her husband had seen that a direct assault would not answer and had bought the estate near Bath. He told her society was more easygoing in the country, but up to tonight their only acquaintance had been other elderly cits and their wives, whom Lady Patricia had nothing in common with and could not like, and whom her husband tended to snub in turn. Her visits to her family had almost ceased, for one and all they had made it clear that their invitations did not include Mr. Biddles, and she could not, in good conscience, force him to endure that slight. She often wondered why a position in society was so important to him when he had everything else he wanted, but she had never dared to ask.

As the groom helped her to alight, she smiled a little at men's follies. Here was her husband, thinking that with one introduction he was on the edge of social success, and the viscount considering her so naïve that he expected her to believe everything he told her. So, he had fallen in love with her in a moment, had he? It was truly ridiculous. He was just toying with her, trying to set up an affair. How easy he must have thought it would be to do so with a young woman married to a vulgar old man when he himself was so handsome and compelling and sophisticated, so much a part of the world she had once enjoyed and now had left behind her forever. Perhaps he thinks I will welcome his attentions because he is part of that world, she thought as she greeted the butler and took Mr. Biddles' arm as he urged her up the stairs. He cannot know how much I despise society for the way it has treated me, how shallow and hateful and conceited I think it.

She remembered how her friends had dropped her one by one as soon as they learned of her engagement, and most especially Lady Maryanne Whitton, her closest friend, who, without a word of explanation, was suddenly not at home when she called and who never answered her notes and letters. It was the moment that they met in the Burlington

Arcade one morning and Maryanne turned her back on her
eager greeting that had shown Patricia how she was now
regarded. It had caused her intense pain that, of all people
Maryanne could treat her so, but it was from that moment on
that she had begun to school herself to accept her inevitable
exile. She had ceased making calls and stopped sending the
notes of invitation that were now always refused.

The two years in London might just as well have been
spent on a desert island. She had been lonely and miserable,
but she was determined not to beg. The more outrageous the
cut, the more arrogantly she held her head, but if it had not
been for Mr. Biddles' insisting they drive in the park, attend
the theater and such public balls as were open to them, as
well as making use of the box he had provided for her at the
opera, she would have lived as a recluse. Instead, richly
gowned and hung with jewels, she had to take her place by
his side, ignoring the whispers and the sneers.

There had been other men like the viscount who considered
her easy game and tried their luck with her, but they had been
repulsed one and all, unbeknownst to her eager, beaming
husband. One speaking glance of scorn from those flashing
violet eyes had caused even the most determined rake to
retreat, feeling a vague sense of shame that he had so mis-
judged the lady. That the viscount's approach was novel did
not obscure his real purpose. She knew that because she was
married to Mr. Biddles, he thought her common, too.

At her door, her husband leaned over and kissed her, his
fat lips demanding, and then he whispered, "I shall come to
you soon, puss! Do not linger with your maid tonight."

She nodded and smiled, hiding her relief that she could
escape him for even that brief period of time as she went into
her room and closed the door and began to brace herself so he
would not know from the expression on her face or the
response of her body how much his touch repulsed her.

The viscount did not come in the days immediately following the ball, but there was another caller. Patricia had been
coming down from her room one afternoon when she heard a
strange voice raised in anger, and she paused halfway down
the stairs to listen. Suddenly the door of the library was flung
open and a young man who could not be much more than
twenty backed out into the hall, waving a clenched fist and

shouting, "You are a devil, Biddles! Somehow I'll make you pay for this, you old scoundrel, you mark my words!"

From inside the library came her husband's contented chuckle. "What's more to the point, Mr. Granford, my fine young sprig, is that *you'll* pay, and pay, and pay! I am not such a niddicock that I lend money without hope of return, and if my interest rates don't please you, why, then, go somewhere else to seek a further loan. But be warned that I expect a prompt return on the money you already owe me, else I'll have to apply to your brother. No, perhaps your father would be better. I hear he's not well? Too bad, too bad. It would most likely carry him off entirely if he were to find out how badly dipped you are."

Mr. Granford started back into the library, his face murderous, and Patricia's hands went out to grip the banister hard. The slight rustle of her dress brought his head whipping around to regard her as her husband rang for the butler.

For a moment they stared at each other. Mr. Granford was only of medium height and slim. His blond hair was disarranged, and in his white face his blue eyes were wild with his angry feelings, but the look of fear in her own eyes made him pause, and in a moment he was in the grasp of two husky footmen, directed by Ames, the butler.

As the servants forced him to leave, he called over his shoulder, "Devil! Satan! Oh, that such slime as you should live!"

When the door had been closed behind him, Patricia waited for a moment before she continued down the stairs, avoiding the butler's eye. As she entered the library, she was surprised to see her husband pouring himself a glass of wine, a wide, contented smile on his face, quite as if nothing out of the ordinary had occurred.

Patricia was shocked, but then she remembered the time in London when they had been at dinner, and an older man, a Mr. Alderstoke, had forced his way past the butler to demand that Mr. Biddles admit that he had in his possession an important paper that belonged to the intruder. He had stood there and begged to have it returned, telling them both of his wife's illness and the expense of special care for her, and then he had demanded that Mr. Biddles return his canceled loan that in his jubilation to be free of the moneylender at last, he had forgotten to take with him.

Patricia had stared at her husband in disbelief. His self-satisfied smirk had made it clear that he was dunning the man for a loan already discharged, even as he announced that the paper had disappeared and there was no other record of payment at hand.

"But you know I repaid you every penny, and the interest too," Mr. Alderstoke had cried, leaning on the table in his distress. "Surely even you would not be so dishonest, so unethical as to—"

Mr. Biddles had thrown his napkin down and risen, beckoning to his butler to remove the man. "How dare you come here, sir?" he had asked in an indignant voice. "I do not conduct business in my home. I am the husband of the Lady Patricia Westerly that was; this is a gentleman's house!"

Mr. Alderstoke had laughed, a jeering, derisive laugh even as his shoulders had slumped in defeat. Before the butler could reach him, he had turned and bowed deeply to a horrified Patricia.

"My deepest apologies for disturbing you, m'lady, but notwithstanding your presence, there is no gentleman here. Good evening."

Mr. Biddles' face had grown very red, and Patricia remembered how he had sputtered and threatened and yelled as the man was led away. When she tried to speak to him of the incident, he controlled himself and brushed her questions aside with a careless wave of his hand.

"Now, puss, you are not to concern yourself with business matters. Just be glad that such as he buys your gowns and jewels."

"But, Alvin, he was so sure the debt had been paid in full. You must remember! Surely you would not continue to press him just because he forgot to take the paper."

Mr. Biddles had smiled broadly at her shocked tones as he reached for his fork again and proceeded to go on with his meal. "Of course I would," he had said thickly through the large mouthful of beef he was chewing. "If the man is such a fool that he forgot a valuable paper, he deserves to be dunned. Stupid idiot! You'd never catch Alvin J. Biddles being so careless where money was concerned, but these gentry with their notions of 'honor' and their 'gentlemen's codes'—bah! There is no such thing in business dealings, Patsy, as I learned when only a young boy. To succeed you must be ruthless and as hard as nails. At least Mr. Alderstoke has learned that valuable lesson, although there's no denying he will pay dearly for it. Oh, yes, very dearly indeed!''

And then he had laughed and urged her to try the partridge before he ordered the butler to pour them both more wine, and when she still tried to dissuade him from continuing such a cruel, dishonest course, she had been told in firm tones that it was none of her affair and to cut line.

Some few weeks later at the breakfast table, she had looked up in inquiry when Mr. Biddles gave a startled oath and threw down the newspaper he was reading. Muttering about fools and cowards, he had left the room without any explanation, and she had picked up the paper he had dropped. Amid the advertisements for Water of the Nile lotion and potions for gout, white swellings, and catarrh, she saw a small story about a certain Mr. Alderstoke of ————, who had been found dead in his library by his butler, a smoking pistol beside him and a bullet through his brain. The authorities saw no reason to investigate such an obvious suicide, especially in the light of the note he had left behind him.

It had been a long time before Patricia was able to regard her husband with anything but horror and revulsion. To think that he had been responsible for driving a man to such a desperate, final action, and his only regret had been that Mr. Alderstoke had escaped his grasp by killing himself. Patricia tried to forget what a monster she was married to and since that time had never asked him about his business again. Now, however, she could not help remonstrating with him.

"But surely if Mr. Granford's father is so ill, you would not do such an infamous thing, Alvin," she said heatedly, her violet eyes distressed. "I cannot believe it, for the poor man is not responsible for his son's debts."

"Aye, perhaps not by law he ain't, now Granford is no longer a minor, but he'd pay, if only to keep the young cub out of jail," Mr. Biddles said, rubbing his hands together in glee, and then he came and gave her a hearty kiss and hugged her all the while he told her she was a silly goosecap to worry about his business affairs. She remembered that any bold stroke that ended in triumph made her husband eager for her and more than usually amorous, and she forced herself not to shudder and push him away in her disgust.

When nine days had passed after the cotillion ball and the

viscount did not come, Patricia relaxed, although Mr. Biddles
became increasingly more short-tempered and moody in his
disappointment. And then on the tenth day, the viscount
trotted his gelding up the long drive to Biddles Hall.

Guy had had a miserable time of it since the ball. Leaving
his cousin and his friend at the doors of the Assembly Rooms,
and refusing Lady Mills' invitation to escort her sedan chair,
he had walked toward his aunt's house alone. When he
reached the Avon, he crossed the bridge with its shuttered
shops on either side, and then he descended a flight of stone
steps to the embankment of the river. He knew he would not
be able to sleep, and the murmuring sound of the water as he
leaned against the railing and stared down into the blackness
was comforting.

He ran both hands through his dark hair and cursed fate
aloud. How could the powers that be do this to him? To think
that he had finally found the one woman that he wanted to
spend the rest of his life with, and then he had been denied
her. And she had not believed him when he told her of his
love. No, she had refused to listen to him; she had called him
a rake and a libertine and as much as accused him of playing
with her feelings for sport.

The viscount began to walk again in his agitation, although
he knew it was dangerous, alone there in the dark. If he
slipped, who would hear him call out at this hour, and even if
they did, how could they find him? For one mad moment, he
considered dropping into the river to be swept downstream
and drowned, thus solving all his problems at once, and then
he scoffed at himself, the cynical sneer back on his face. That
was not the way a Leighton behaved, taking the easy way out
of his difficulties.

It was very late when he let himself into his aunt's house
and wearily climbed the stairs to his room, to lie awake till
dawn, tossing and turning and wondering what he was to do.
Always in his mind's eye was her beautiful face, those gentle
lips and glowing eyes to taunt him with what he could never
have.

He slept at last, only to find that even in his dreams he was
not free of her spell, and it was almost noon before he
summoned Chums to help him dress. The valet, knowing
how late to the minute his master had come in, remained

silent as he did so, for he did not think, from his cautious peeks at his master's face, that m'lord had overindulged or even spent the night in someone else's bed. No, there was such a look of raw unhappiness there that Chums could only feel a pang of sympathy for his obvious pain.

The viscount, clad in his riding dress and fortified by several cups of coffee, met his aunt as she returned from the baths and the Pump Room, where she had spent the morning.

One look at his face was enough to make her exclaim, one hand to her heart, "Guy, my dear, what is it? What is wrong?"

He tried to smile as he bent and kissed her cheek. "Do not ask me now, *chère tante*, if you love me. I am going out and I do not know when I will return."

"But, Guy, what about your luncheon?" she asked, upset at the stark misery she read in his eyes.

"I shall not be in, and do not expect me for dinner either, if you please. I shall tell you about it, *tante*, I promise, but not now."

Lady Sylvia nodded, shaking her head at Miss Kincaid, who had come in in time to hear her nephew's last words and who was anxious to ask if there was not some medicine she could fetch to relieve whatever illness he was suffering from. Before she could voice her offer, the viscount left the house.

"My dear Lady Sylvia," her companion exclaimed as she helped the lady with her cape, "whatever is wrong with m'lord? Should he go out alone in that condition?"

"I don't know, Wilma, truly I don't," the lady replied, shaking her head. "Come with me into the library and we will have a glass of sherry, for I have seldom felt the need of one more."

As her companion poured her a glass, she added, "I think I will ask my nephew James to visit me this afternoon. Yes, I will write the note at once."

Mr. Debenham was not too surprised when the boots at York House brought up her urgent note. In the light of the flambeaux he had seen the agony on his cousin's face when they had left the Assembly Rooms, and he was able at last to relax the strong control he had kept over his features until then. And then, of course, he had said good night so abruptly, and turned and left them without a courteous word of thanks for his excellent dinner, or some appointment made for the

morrow, that even Charlie had been amazed and commented
on it.

As James made his leisurely way to Lady Sylvia's house,
he was sure it was all the result of the viscount's meeting
with Lady Patricia Biddles. He had watched him carefully
although unobtrusively throughout the remainder of the ball,
and nothing untoward had happened to overset him. Biddles
. . . Biddles . . . now why in the devil did that name tease
him so? Was it four years ago or five that he had heard it?
And in what connection?

Suddenly he stopped dead still on the street, upsetting the
flow of pedestrians, and his eyes narrowed. Of course! The
wealthy shipowner and moneylender, Mr. Alvin Biddles, had
married the Lady Patricia Westerly then, and it had been a
thirty-day wonder at the time. How could he have forgotten
it? It was bad enough that she was only nineteen and he a
man in his fifties, but she was, more important, the daughter
of a marquess and he a very common commoner, not even
admired for his business acumen. There had been too many
shady deals, too many unkept promises, too many important
papers gone astray, to inspire anything but hatred for the
man. He remembered Lord Hadley's remarking when he
learned that Biddles aspired to society's ranks, that although
he might have to borrow money from the old slug, he'd be
damned if he'd sit down to dinner with him.

It was obvious that Lady Patricia had been sold to the
highest bidder, Mr. Debenham thought with scorn as he
began to walk on again. He was busy remembering all he
knew of the affair, and by the time the butler admitted him in
Great Pulteney Street, he had it down pat.

Lady Sylvia did not waste time on the amenities, for, as he
had suspected, she wanted his advice on Guy's mysterious
behavior, and she began to question him as soon as Gregson
left the room.

James leaned against the mantel while he told her about the
ball.

"I knew that woman would bring him nothing but trouble,"
she exclaimed. "I felt it in my bones! But who is she? Is she
as beautiful as Guy would have me believe?"

"Oh, a pearl without price, Aunt," James told her. "She
was the Lady Patricia Westerly before her marriage some five
years ago to Mr. Biddles."

At his aunt's frown, he explained, "Mr. Biddles is a very wealthy older man—a cit, of course, and one universally detested for his shady idea of business ethics—you take my point? He made his fortune in shipping and moneylending, and everyone was astounded that the Season's leading incomparable would stoop to such a union."

"Everyone who did not know her father, the Marquess of Westerly," Lady Sylvia retorted. "I have known of Lord Westerly these thirty years. He is a gambler and a spendthrift, and as dissolute as a man as the *ton* has ever known. Of course, it was all his doing that his daughter married such a person."

"I am sure you are right, Aunt. As I remember it, Lord Westerly was on the brink of bankruptcy, his estates mortgaged and his pockets to let. And then there were those two sons of his, each wilder than the next. The younger was languishing in Newgate for failure to pay his debts, and the heir escaped the same fate only by fleeing the country and was in exile abroad. It was left to the Lady Patricia to tow them all out of the River Tick by selling herself to Mr. Biddles." He paused and whistled softly. "It must have cost the man a fortune to set those three on their feet again. But I would be willing to wager anything you like that the marriage was not the lady's idea. No, her father must have engineered the whole thing and forced her to go through with it. What a pity her mother died while she was still so young! She might have been able to prevent her daughter being made the sacrificial lamb led to the slaughter. I pity her sincerely."

"I hope Satan has a special place in hell for such as Lord Westerly," Lady Sylvia muttered. "But sad though the story is and no matter how sorry I am for the girl, I am more concerned about Guy." She paused for a moment and stared at Mr. Debenham, as if considering whether to tell him anymore.

James raised an eyebrow, and she pointed to a chair across from her. "Sit down, if you please, James. What I am about to tell you is in confidence and must never be revealed. Do you understand? No little hints to Lord Williams, no sly digs at Guy—is that clear?"

Mr. Debenham lowered his sleepy lids over suddenly angry blue eyes. "I think I may still be trusted with a secret, Aunt," he drawled.

"Very well, but remember that I will hold you to your word," she ordered, and then she proceeded to tell him about Guy's falling in love with a stranger in an instant, and what he had been doing ever since, up to his meeting with the lady in the countryside where he had discovered her name.

"So that is why he has been so preoccupied, and so often absent from our revels, and why Clorinda Mills could not entice him into dalliance," James murmured. "Of course it also explains his behavior last evening, for it was at the ball that he found out she was a married woman."

"Yes, that would surely overset him, determined as he was to marry her himself. I thought this only one of his fancies, one that would fade quickly, but when he could not find her for almost two weeks and still persisted in claiming this ridiculous love, I must admit I felt some pangs of disquiet. He did not come home last night until dawn, and when he left the house this morning, he looked so unwell I knew I must ask your advice."

Mr. Debenham smiled. "No, we cannot have him throwing himself into the Avon, now can we, ma'am? Bad *ton*, to say nothing of how it would distress the family."

Lady Sylvia did not look amused, little knowing that her nephew had thought of doing just that. "Do you think he will recover from this passion, James?" she asked, her brow wrinkled with her concern.

"Either that or he will make her his mistress, and that would solve the problem, too. Since she is married, there is no other course open to him. You will forgive me for speaking so plainly, Aunt," he added.

Lady Sylvia waved an impatient hand and James continued, "Someone must warn him that the *bourgeois* do not consider these little affairs in the same light that society does. Mr. Biddles might take after him with a horsewhip—or worse!"

"Perhaps Guy can be persuaded to confide in you, James. I would find it impossible to bring the subject up. Why, every feeling must be offended. Besides, I don't want him to become any further entangled with the girl. His mistress, indeed!"

She sounded so proper that James hid a grin. "I shall do my best to make Guy confess to me, Aunt, you may be sure." As he rose to take his leave he added, "And I shall watch over him as far as it is in my power to do so."

Lady Sylvia reached up with both hands to pull his face down so she could kiss him. "You have a good heart, James, or I would never have confided in you. Why you feel you must hide it behind that mask of cynicism you affect, I shall never know."

He laughed and went away, and Lady Sylvia sat down again to ponder their conversation and wonder what she might do that would help.

She had little chance in the week that followed, for Guy was seldom home. She knew he was not seeing Lady Patricia, even though he rode out early and did not return until late, for his expression remained grim, and although he seemed calmer, it was obvious that there was a weight on his mind.

Nine days after the ball, he came to her in the library, where she was working on her accounts, and asked if he might speak to her.

"I have been waiting for you to do so, my dear," she said with a warm smile as she laid aside her quill and folded her hands on the mahogany writing table.

"As you have no doubt guessed, *tante*, all my problems stem from the lady I told you I love," he began, and then he went to pour himself a glass of wine. He looked at her inquiringly, but she shook her head. Taking his seat again, he continued, "I found out the night of the cotillion ball that she is the Lady Patricia Biddles, a married woman. The disappointment when I learned that almost unhinged my mind, and I do apologize for my behavior. You must have thought you had a lovesick, third-rate actor in your house!"

He snorted in derision and she said quickly, "No such thing, Guy. Of course it was a blow to you. But, my dear, what have you decided to do? In a way I am surprised you remain in Bath, for I know you would find it less painful if you left the vicinity."

Guy shook his head, his gray eyes remote. "I cannot leave her, *tante*," he said softly.

Lady Sylvia was alarmed. "But she is married, Guy! There can be nothing but trouble and scandal if you continue to pursue her. And it is not fair to her either, my dear."

He looked at her then, his face darkening. "What do you mean?" he asked in a harsh voice.

"Lady Patricia agreed to marry Mr. Biddles, although

from what I have heard, it was arranged by her family, and she is now his wife, whether or not she is in love with him."

Guy snorted again. "In love with him? Of course she is not! He is fat as a flawn, common to boot, and old and coarse. How could she love such a man?"

"But if that is the case, and I am sure it must be, for you to tease her with your lovemaking can only distress her. Look at yourself! Tall, handsome, titled, dashing, and so young—her husband's complete opposite. Of course she will fall in love with you, but where can it lead? Would she contemplate divorce and its accompanying scandal? Would you both be willing to wait the many years it may be until Mr. Biddles dies? Or do you think to make her your mistress, stealing around behind her husband's back to make love to her? From what you have told me of the lady, she is too fine to contemplate that course with any degree of complacency. Perhaps, Guy," she said more slowly, "it is just that you cannot have her that makes her so intriguing to you. You have never been thwarted in any way in your life. To be denied something you want is a new come-out, is it not?"

Lady Sylvia paused, wondering if she had gone too far, for the look on her nephew's face was black and thunderous. There was a moment of silence in the library, and then he said, "I am not a spoiled brat, ma'am! May I remind you that I loved her before I knew of her marriage? I would not do anything to distress her, on my honor, and I see from your words that my best course would be to stay away from her. But I cannot . . . I *will* not leave Bath without seeing her again. I must tell her what is in my heart, and I must hear from her own lips that there is no hope for me."

"How will you manage that, my dear?" his aunt asked.

"The least of my problems, *tante*. Mr. Biddles himself was most insistent that I visit his estate near Midsomer Norton, and remain for dinner as well."

"The man must be mad!" Lady Sylvia could not help exclaiming. At Guy's look of surprise, she muttered, "To put the two of you together like that, why, it would be like throwing gunpowder into a fire."

A ghost of Guy's old grin crossed his face. "I cannot understand it myself, ma'am, but there it is. He must have some hold over her I do not know of to be so sure of his omnipotence. That, too, I must find out." He rose and put his wineglass back on the tray. "I intend to ride out there tomorrow, so do not look for me till late. And perhaps a small prayer or two might be in order, if you would be so good."

Lady Sylvia promised a most fervent one, and he took his leave to join James and Charlie in a stroll around Bath. He did not know that she was praying he would come out of this with a whole skin and that Lady Patricia would send him about his business with alacrity.

And this she certainly tried hard to do. She was cool and formal when the butler admitted him to the drawing room, her violet-blue eyes indifferent, the hand she gave him in greeting lying unresponsive in his clasp.

Mr. Biddles more than made up for any stiffness of hers, however, for after determining that the viscount had no desire for a mug of ale or a small repast, he insisted on showing him the hall and the surrounding buildings himself. Lady Patricia was ordered to accompany them on their tour, in spite of her expressed wish to remain at her desk writing letters. Guy noticed how her lips thinned and her color rose as her husband boasted almost continuously of his wealth as they proceeded through the hall: how much this oil painting had cost, that statue, those damask draperies. There was nothing in all the large, stuffy, overdecorated rooms that he was allowed to miss, no item too small to be told its value. For one mad moment Guy thought Mr. Biddles would even tell him what his wife had cost him as well, for he paused after showing Guy a full-length portrait of the lady dressed in lavender satin and wearing enough jewels for several coronations, to consider her where she stood slightly apart, her eyes downcast.

After the entire hall had been seen, right down to the modern improvements in the kitchen, which Guy could see flustered the servants, ordered as they had been to prepare a dinner fit for a lord, Mr. Biddles took him outside. In the stables, the horses were led from their stalls one by one to be admired, and the formal garden and maze had to be gone over, inch by inch, as well as every outbuilding from the gazebo and folly to the barns and dairy yard.

Guy tried to appear interested, but his eyes were never far from Lady Patricia, dressed in a smart afternoon gown of rose muslin with a triple strand of pink pearls around her slender neck. She is more beautiful than ever, he thought, even in her embarrassment over her husband's boorish behavior and boasting words. He was wondering desperately how he was to see her alone, when Mr. Biddles solved the problem for him.

"There now, sir, what do you think of Biddles Hall? Fine as any duke's establishment you've seen, I'd wager!"

Guy told a graceful lie and Mr. Biddles clapped him on the shoulder as if they were old friends. "I look forward to seeing you at dinner, sir, but now I must have my rest, and then there are some papers I must see to. But Patsy will be delighted to take you around the grounds, wouldn't you, m'dearie?" he asked, turning ponderously toward his wife.

Guy thought she looked as if she wished she might refuse, but something in her husband's face caused the words to die unspoken on her lips.

"Of course, if you would care for it, m'lord," she said, her voice wooden.

Guy tried to control his elation as he thanked her, and Mr. Biddles rubbed both fat hands together and beamed. "Run along and don your habit, my dear, and I will have your mare saddled for you. And mind now, be sure to wear the purple velvet with the ermine trim, Patsy."

She nodded and moved away toward the hall, her graceful figure in the rose gown watched by both men. The soft spring breeze set her skirts arustle and lifted her shining curls, and Guy wished he might be as intimate with her as that breeze.

"A lovely lass, ain't she, m'lord?" Mr. Biddles asked, his shrewd brown eyes twinkling.

"Very lovely, sir, I agree. You are to be congratulated," Guy replied as calmly as he could.

"Be sure she shows you the home wood and do not let her chouse you out of seeing the Venetian bridge I had built over the stream that feeds the ornamental water. For some reason, my Patsy don't care for it, but I assure you, m'lord, 'tis all the crack! Three thousand pounds it cost me . . ."

He continued to brag of his wealth and his astuteness in shipping and money matters as they walked slowly back to the hall after ordering the horses saddled. Mr. Biddles often paused to catch his breath, especially when they climbed the slight knoll near the hall, and by the time they reached the front door, his red face was streaming with perspiration.

He remained with Guy until his wife came back downstairs,

breathtaking in the velvet habit that matched her eyes, although privately Guy thought it made her look like an actress, it was so overtrimmed with fur and braid, besides being much too heavy for such a warm day. He was sure her husband had bought it for her without her consent.

Mr. Biddles bowed and left them then, and together they went outside to the horses. When Lady Patricia saw the viscount coming to help her into the saddle, she was quick to beckon to the groom, and Guy mounted his gelding without comment. They started down the drive, still without speaking, but after a few moments, Guy said quietly to the cameo profile that was all he could see as she stared straight ahead, "I told you I would see you again, m'lady, even though I am sorry it distresses you."

Her face turned toward him for a moment, and he caught a glimpse of those magnificent eyes flashing her scorn. "I was beginning to think you would not come, sir, and I admired you for your forbearance. I am disappointed now, for obviously you did not choose to believe I meant it the other evening when I asked you to let me alone."

"I could not, not until I told you what was in my heart, m'lady." He paused and glanced back at the hall. "Mr. Biddles insisted I see the Venetian bridge. In what direction does it lie?"

She pointed her crop toward the sheet of blue water on their left, and they turned their horses to ride along the shore. At the end of the lake there was a small stream, hardly bigger than a brook, and arching over it was a miniature copy of the Rialto Bridge. It was so tiny and ridiculous that Guy could not help laughing out loud. Lady Patricia tried to look haughty, but his laughter was so infectious that her lips curled in an answering smile.

"Your husband said you did not care for it, and now I see why," Guy told her, pulling up his horse for a closer look. "Whatever possessed him to build such a . . . such a monstrosity?"

Lady Patricia was forced to halt her mare in turn. "He considers it the final touch to a gentleman's estate," she said. "It is faithful in every detail to the real bridge, and in perfect scale."

Guy was not reluctant to take his eyes from Mr. Biddles' *pièce de résistance*. "Will you dismount and walk awhile,

m'lady?'' he asked. Seeing her hesitation, he added with a
touch of hauteur, ''You will be quite safe. I am, after all, a
gentleman.''

She nodded then, and in a moment he had dismounted and
was holding up his arms to her. As she slipped down against
him, she felt the quiver that ran through his strong frame as
he grasped her waist in his large hands, but he released her
the minute her riding boots touched the ground.

After he had tied their horses to a branch, they began to
walk along the bridle path that followed the stream, both
strangely reticent again, Lady Patricia because she had nothing to say to this handsome lord, and Guy because he was
choosing his words.

At length she stopped beside a rustic bench. ''Well, m'lord?
I believe you have something you wish to say to me? Let it be
now,'' she decreed, and at the warm, glowing look in his
eyes, she lowered her own. ''I shall not grant you another
opportunity,'' she added in warning.

''I thank you for even this boon, m'lady,'' he said formally.
''Won't you be seated?''

He waited until she had arranged her skirts and folded her
hands in her lap, and then he walked a few paces away, his
head bent. She stared at that broad back and narrow waist
until he turned and came back to her to begin telling her what
had happened to him since he first caught a glimpse of her.
All through his brief but passionate recital she kept her eyes
lowered, but when he vowed he would never love another,
she looked up in skepticism and caught her breath. His face
was almost boyish in his fervor, and he had removed his
riding hat so the soft breeze ruffled his hair, and a dark-
brown lock fell over his broad forehead. His glowing gray
eyes blazed into hers as he leaned forward, one booted foot
resting on the seat of the bench as he tried by his words and
his expression to convey the depths of his feeling.

He paused at last, his hands outflung to her, but when she
did not speak, he asked in a quieter tone, ''I know why your
marriage to him was arranged, Lady Patricia, but how could
such as you, so fine and so beautiful, ever agree to it?''

''I cannot tell you that, m'lord,'' she answered past the
lump in her throat, her heart beating strangely.

''Very well, we will leave it. Tell me, instead, why your
husband allows me to see you alone. I should think he would

be fearful I might fall in love with you and you with me, if I do not sound too conceited to say so; and yet at the ball he allowed me to dance with you, asked me to call, and today it was at his instigation that we are alone together. Most strange!''

She hesitated, and then she put up her chin. ''He aspires to the *ton*, sir, and he feels if he can make friends with you, you will pave the way for his acceptance.''

Guy's laugh was derisive, and she flinched. ''The man must be mad! With his reputation he will never be accepted, no, not even your birth and beauty beside him can help him.''

''I know that,'' she said quietly. ''The *ton* has made it very clear in what light they regard Mr. Biddles, and myself too.''

''Surely they have not rejected you, my dear?'' he said as if he could not believe such a thing.

Now it was Lady Patricia's turn to laugh, and he could hear her bitterness. ''Of course they have. Mr. Biddles is hated by so many and with such fervor that I myself do not escape the same censure. I have been snubbed time out of mind these past five years.''

Her violet eyes darkened in angry misery as she remembered the painful slights, and Guy wished he might take her in his arms and comfort her. Instead, he changed the subject. ''But, still, isn't Mr. Biddles afraid I will make love to you? Or can he be so base as to try to trade your lovemaking for my sponsorship of him in society?''

He looked so furious at the thought that she answered without considering her words. ''No, no, he trusts me, and for very good reason. He holds my father's notes still, and he has told me he will call them in and ruin him if ever I leave him or play him false with another.''

''Good God, what a monster to hold that over your head,'' Guy exploded in strong tones of loathing, ''and you his wife!''

Lady Patricia regretted she had spoken so honestly, and made haste to explain, ''Mr. Biddles is a shrewd businessman, m'lord, even though in this case he has nothing to fear. I have no intention of breaking my vows. No, I made a bargain with my husband, and I intend to honor that bargain.''

Guy groaned and ran his hand over his hair in frustration. ''I cannot bear to think of him touching you . . . holding you . . .''

Lady Patricia paled and then she rose from the bench,

smoothing her overfancy habit. "Shall we return to the horses m'lord?" she asked, and there was dignity as well as anger in her voice. "I do not care to hear any more. My life cannot change. My father and my brothers may have forced me into my marriage and society may scorn me, but I will be true to it. I will be no man's mistress, even though men have affairs without number, think nothing of breaking their sacred vows and treat women as if they were playthings set here on earth only for their amusement. Bah! What beasts you all are!"

"But all men are not like that, my dear," Guy protested, and she tossed her head, her eyes blazing with scorn.

"I have not had any other examples to go by, sir," she said as she turned to go.

"Then regard me as one, and know that I will always love you. There can be no other woman for me, not ever."

His quiet words stopped her, and she turned to face him as he continued, "I see I have not made myself clear. You accuse me of trifling with you, of trying to start an affair. Well, I have had my share of them, but I would never offer you such an insult. That is not how I think of you. I intended to make you my wife, the mother of my sons, and my dearest friend. Much as I long to make love to you, I could not bring myself to change the picture of you as Viscountess Reading that I treasure. I am thirty-one, and I think by that age it may be safe to say I know my mind. I honor you for your commitment to your vows, much as it tears my heart, and would not willingly cause you a moment's pain. I do, however, ask you to remember that as long as we are both in this world, no matter how far apart, I will love you. And if you ever need me, know, too, that I will come to you as soon as can. You yourself may refuse to acknowledge my love; you cannot stop me from adoring you."

Lady Patricia's mind was in turmoil. His words had been spoken so solemnly and with such conviction that she knew he told the truth.

He put his hands on her shoulders then, his grasp light and unthreatening, and bent his head so his gray eyes could search her face. "Will you leave me with no word, no sign to warm me through the lonely years ahead, my lady Patricia?" he asked softly.

For several moments they stood there staring into each other's eyes. The afternoon sun filtered through the new green leaves of the beeches above them as the breeze stirred them. In the distance she heard her mare nicker and the cheerful songs of the birds, and she knew she had never been so confused and miserable in all her life.

Which one of them moved first, she was never sure, but suddenly she was in his arms, drawn close to his broad chest. For a moment he held her there and she could hear the thudding of his heart, and then he tipped her chin up, his gray eyes asking permission before he caught his breath and covered her lips with his own. His kiss was gentle at first, as if he were afraid he might frighten her, but as soon as her mouth moved under his, he tightened his grasp, drawing her closer into his arms and caressing her back and her waist with his strong, lean hands. His mouth was warm and firm, demanding a response she was unable to withhold. She had never been kissed by anyone but her husband, and she had always found him revolting, so she was amazed at the way she answered the viscount's caressing lips. A tremor ran through her body, and somewhere deep inside her, a warm tingle of yearning blossomed from a tiny pinpoint to an explosion of delight. Then, to her surprise, she began to cry.

Reluctantly, he raised his head when a salty drop touched their lips. One gentle finger came up to wipe it away as he whispered, "Do not cry, my love. I cannot bear to see you cry."

She shook her head and drew away from him, her violet eyes still sparkling with tears and enormous in the pale oval of her face.

His eyes never left hers, but he made no move to keep her in his arms as he said, "Thank you for that sweet kiss. I will not ask you for another."

Lady Patricia tried to calm her breathing. Through her tears she saw his handsome face taut with self-imposed control. Only one muscle near the corner of his mouth moved a little as he clenched his fists at his sides. He was looking at her with such an expression of longing, and so much love for her in those intent, ardent eyes, that it was all she could do not to run back into his arms.

"Tell me, must I go away?" he pleaded. "I promise there will be no repetition of what just happened, but I would stay near you for a while longer."

"M'lord, I—"

"Guy," he corrected her.

"Very well, Guy. I think it best you go. You have confused me, made me forget the obedience I owe my husband. To see you again would only complicate the problem and cause us both pain. Please, I beg you . . ."

He frowned, but then he nodded, and stepping back to her, he tilted up her chin again as he asked, "Now do you begin to understand how much I love you, my dear?"

Her eyes answered for her, but he waited until she murmured, "Yes."

"And do I dare to hope that you might return that love?"

Again he waited, but when her lips parted to speak, he put his hand over her mouth. "Do not answer! It was unfair of me to ask you, and besides, I could not bear it if this time you said, 'no.'"

4

By the time they finished their ride and returned to the hall, Patricia again had herself under firm control, and for that, she knew she had the viscount to thank. Although he had asked her to write to him care of his aunt in Bath if she should ever need his help, and had given her the direction as they walked back to the horses, once he tossed her into the saddle and mounted his own gelding, all trace of the eager lover had disappeared. It was as if he knew she needed the time to compose herself before they met her husband again, and so he asked her some idle questions about the estate, told her a few stories of London and the current Court gossip, and generally behaved as any casual guest would, perfectly polite but always with formality.

Only once did this mask slip. When they arrived at the hall and he saw the grooms running to take the horses, he said quietly, "I thought to spare you by leaving immediately, but I was afraid that your husband might suspect something, and since he insisted I remain for dinner, we had better go on in as normal a manner as we can manage."

His gray eyes caressed her for a brief second as she smiled her gratitude, and then the hooded lids came down and the moment was gone.

How kind he was, and how wise, she thought, to know that Mr. Biddles would be very angry if he cut his visit short, and probably demand answers of her she did not know how to give.

Guy did not offer to help her dismount, which she was ashamed to realize caused a pang of regret. She would have liked to feel his hands spanning her waist one more time, and she was so angry at herself for this weakness that her expression became cool and distant as it had been that morning. As she left the viscount to her husband's care so she might

61

change for dinner, even Mr. Biddles' keen brown eyes could not discern that anything untoward had happened between them, and he nodded his relief.

As he ushered the viscount into his library for some wine and conversation, he was able to speak jovially, glad that his Patsy had such good sense, for there was no denying it, this lord was a mighty tall and handsome young man, with an assured air of rank and a polished address. He did not care if it was his wife's lovely face alone that drew him to the hall as long as she kept him at a distance. He chuckled to himself. Patsy knew what would happen if she did not, for he had told her many times, and she knew as well that no amount of tears or pleading would make him change his mind. He would ruin her father in an instant if she did not behave herself.

He had often wondered why she cared whether the old reprobate sank or prospered, after the way he had treated her, little knowing that she disliked her father now and it was only her word that made her remain his wife. Well he remembered her sick, white face when she had been forced to accept him against her will to save her father and her brothers from bankruptcy and prison, and how she had reacted to his first kiss. For a moment he had been sure she was going to faint in his avid clutching hands, but when he shook her a little and demanded her composure, she had controlled herself at once. Yes, little Patsy was too much under his thumb to show any rebellion at all, and in five years he liked to think he had molded her to his will and she was now completely tamed and compliant and had come to feel a measure of gratitude and affection for him as well.

He remembered also how haughty she had become when he warned her the first time about taking a lover or trying someday to leave him.

"There is no need to be insulting, Mr. Biddles," she had said, those violet eyes cold. "I assure you that having promised to be your wife, I shall keep my promise. I would remind you that I am a gentlewoman."

He had laughed then, a high whinny of derision. "Aye, you're a gentlewoman, all right, m'dearie, but you're also a Westerly. Never known a one of 'em, from your precious father to those two hell-born babes you call your brothers, to keep their word. Gentlemen, ha!"

Her face had paled, and she had lowered her eyes, until he

went and pinched her cheek. "There now, puss, never mind them. Just you behave as you ought and we shall deal famously together."

Now he pressed some of his excellent Canary on his noble guest and, taking a seat across the fireplace from him, dismissed his butler with a barked order to make himself scarce. Until his wife joined them, he asked the viscount's impressions of the estate, especially the Venetian bridge, but although the viscount was polite, the only words of praise he would utter was to say he had never seen anything quite so unique.

"Aye, that it is, all right! Damned unusual, I daresay," he beamed, forcing himself to be pleased with this meager compliment.

When his wife came in, she was wearing a simple afternoon gown of watered taffeta. Mr. Biddles, in full evening regalia, showed his temper at once.

"Here now, Patsy, why didn't you wear that white silk I had your maid put out for you? Aye, and the sapphire and diamond set I sent up from the vault as well?"

"But that would be much too formal for a simple dinner, Alvin, and the viscount would be uncomfortable, the only one in riding clothes," she reminded him, her head held high.

Her husband bridled, for he could never stand to be corrected, but fortunately the butler announced dinner just then, and he bounced up to lead them to the dining room.

"You will find we set a good table here, m'lord, in spite of Patsy's calling it simple," he boasted as they took their seats. "None of these skimpy two courses and paltry removes for the Alvin J. Biddles!"

The dinner was as elaborate as he promised. There was enough food for a dozen people and half a dozen wines as well, and to make matters worse, Mr. Biddles was a hearty trencherman who chewed and slurped with such eagerness that his face grew quite red with his exertions. Guy tried not to notice when his host asked him questions with his mouth full or waved his laden fork at him, but he had seldom enjoyed a table partner less.

As the first course was removed, he resigned himself to a long and tedious time, but before very long he realized that Mr. Biddles was angling for a return of his hospitality. He

could see, from the alert way she held her head, that Patricia
was aware of it too, and he sensed her distress even as he
parried every thrust.

No, he did not have his own rooms, he was staying with his
aunt, the Lady Sylvia Randolph of Great Pulteney Street. No,
she rarely entertained, for she was elderly and troubled with a
rheumatic complaint. Yes, it was too bad this must be so, but
since he was on a repairing lease in Bath, he rarely attended
parties. The evening of the cotillion ball had been an exception.
No, he did not think he would attend this week. He had
another engagement. Yes, his aunt made full use of the baths
and the Pump Room and could be found there most every
morning.

As this information escaped him, he realized he had made
a gaffe, and hastened to regain control of the situation by
saying that he was leaving Bath in a few days.

Mr. Biddles was successfully drawn off the scent. "Leaving
us so soon? Well, well, that's too bad! And where are you
going, m'lord? Can we not persuade you to remain? Patsy,
add your entreaties to mine, if you please," he bellowed
down the long table to where she sat opposite him.

Before she was forced to speak, Guy smiled at her and
then, turning to his host, he said, "Even Lady Patricia could
not prevail, for I am summoned by the Prince Regent himself,
sir. He is in Brighton, as I am sure you know."

Mr. Biddles had not known, but even his conceit would not
let him think m'lord would cry off when royalty beckoned,
and his heavy face settled into an expression of profound
discontent.

The viscount changed the subject by asking if Lady Patricia
enjoyed living near Bath and if she had ever visited any of the
other watering places throughout England. Mr. Biddles allowed them to wander from Royal Tunbridge Wells to
Leamington Spa and Harrogate before he took control of the
conversation once again.

"Here, you, Ames, more wine for the viscount. What are
you thinking of, idiot, to let his glass remain empty? And
bring me back that platter of fried oysters. Now, m'lord,
when do you go back to town? Will you be there for the Little
Season or do you travel to your own estates then? I would
enjoy seeing them, you know."

The viscount waved away the wine with a slight smile that

seemed to convey to the butler how much he sympathized with him. "I have no idea, sir. I rarely spend much time on my estates, preferring life in town, although River Court is a lovely place, situated as it is so close to the coast. It is on the river near Arundel and the South Downs can be an exhilarating place to ride. Sometimes I think nothing has changed since I was a boy growing up there—the same stone walls and turrets, the many-paned windows, the same orchards and fields, even the same thatched barns and winding country lanes. Change comes slowly to that part of the country, and River Court is very old, for it was built in the early seventeenth century and hardly improved since."

He smiled a little at his memories, and Lady Patricia saw in her mind's eye a warm old mansion, its comfortable large rooms echoing to the noise of a happy family, and the dogs and ponies and punts he must have enjoyed when he was a child. A home, she thought wistfully, a real home, not a mortgaged old castle, leaking and empty, or an overornate showplace complete with a Venetian bridge.

Before Mr. Biddles could repeat his bid for an invitation, Guy continued, "I doubt I will be at River Court for many months. I have been thinking of traveling abroad now that we are finally at peace. Italy can be delightful in the autumn."

Mr. Biddles was treated to a lengthy monologue on the Italian scene, and then the viscount began a discussion of European politics, leaving Mr. Biddles no opportunity to press his guest for a return invitation.

When Lady Patricia finally rose to leave them to their port, Guy stood up at once. "M'lady," he said, "I thank you for the sumptuous dinner, and you, sir, for having been so kind as to have invited me, but now, since I have a long ride back to Bath, I must be on my way. No, no, sir, no port, if you please. The wines at dinner were excellent, but since I am promised to friends this evening, I must make haste."

Mr. Biddles was forced to rise as well, his fat lower lip outthrust in his disappointment. "Be glad to welcome you anytime, my boy," he assured him, trying to recapture the advantage. "What a pity you have been called away, and just when we were on the way of becoming such fast friends. You must be sure to let us know when you return to Bath so you can eat your mutton with us again."

Mr. Biddles insisted on walking with him to the front door,

arm and arm in great camaraderie, while Lady Patricia went
before them, and he continued to chat while Guy waited for
his horse.

Those few minutes seemed endless, but at last Guy took
Lady Patricia's hand and raised it to his lips. The gentle kiss
he pressed there burned on her fingers, and his own lips
tingled from contact with her soft skin, although not a sign of
this showed on either face. Only their eyes met for a brief,
burning second.

"Farewell, m'lady," he murmured, and then, as if he did
not trust himself to say more, he turned and bowed to Mr.
Biddle and escaped the hall as quickly as he could.

Guy thought of her all the long miles home. He had no
engagement, but he had not been able to remain for another
moment. There was no chance that Mr. Biddles would ever
count Viscount Reading as his friend, or have him visit his
home again, for even if Patricia had not asked him to stay
away, he knew that if he could not see her alone without her
gross boor of a husband, he would rather not see her at all.

The memory of her kiss kept him company on his ride. So
sweet, as sweet as she was herself, and her lips as soft and
velvety as that ridiculous habit she had worn. And the feel of
her in his arms, the slender, gently curved body pressed
against his. He shook his head. Their one embrace was small
recompense for all the lonely times ahead, but somehow he
still did not think that fate would deny him his lady forever.
Somehow, someday, he would be able to call her his own.
He knew he would become discouraged at times while he
waited, and he feared that the vivid picture of her that now
burned so brightly would dim, but perhaps they would meet
again, not by design, but by accident. Perhaps he might see
her in London or when he visited his aunt. He wished it were
possible to write to her and receive her replies, but he had not
been able to think of any way to keep it from her husband,
and he would never put her in danger of facing the man's
wrath if he should find out they were conducting a secret
correspondence.

The miles disappeared beneath the gelding's hooves, and
after he reached the stables and gave his tired horse into a
groom's care, he walked around to his aunt's house. He knew
she was dining with friends this evening, and he was glad, for
now he could sit alone and think about Patricia, storing up his

memories. Tomorrow would be time enough to tell Aunt Sylvia what had happened, and time enough to make his plans to leave as well. Tonight he had to be alone.

Lady Patricia was thankful that Mr. Biddles, displeased as he was at the viscount's decamping, did not come to her rooms that night, although she found it hard to sleep even so. Her violet eyes stared up into the dark for hours, as if she could see Guy's face in the damask canopy: the strong planes of his lean cheeks, his firm jaw, and most especially that well-formed mouth that looked so sculptured and yet felt so warm and alive.

Now she knew he loved her and she was disturbed to find such an answering surge of affection for him in her own breast. She had never had any intention of falling into such a trap and had steeled herself against it from her early teens, for, as she had told him, the example of her father and brothers, and her husband's later behavior, had not inspired her with any yearning for entanglement with the male sex, nor any desire to put herself under their control. But Guy seemed different. Was it possible that there could be a love between a man and a woman that was not vile or evil or degrading? Could he really care for her that way, enough to want her and wait for her above all others? She turned on her side and plumped up her mussed pillows. But stay, perhaps she was being naïve to put all her trust into a single kiss and some fervent words, when, for all she knew, he might just be clever enough to trick her into an affair even yet? Perhaps he had a wager on her capitulation to his considerable charms. Her brothers had often bet on their success with various ladies, she remembered.

She sat straight up in bed in her agitation and stared ahead of her in the dark. Suddenly she saw his face, his gray eyes serious and his mouth unsmiling as he shook his head, as if to tell her she should not doubt him. "No, not Guy. Not ever Guy," she whispered, and as if these believing words comforted her, she lay down and slept at last.

Her maid woke her early with the intelligence that Mr. Biddles wished her to make haste and dress, for he intended to drive her into Bath to the Pump Room this morning, and as she sipped her chocolate, her eyes were narrowed in thought. So, he had not given up trying to force Guy to introduce him to his aunt and his friends, and this was just a ploy to make use of him before he left Bath. Her soft lips tightened, and when her husband bustled in to choose her gown and accessories, she was lying back on her pillows, the draperies still closed and her maid nowhere in sight.

"Here now, puss, didn't that stupid maid tell you you are to have a treat today? I have decided to drive you to Bath myself to change your library books and perhaps have a look in at the Pump Room. You know how you enjoy the orchestra. Come now, get up at once!"

Patricia looked at him and there was something in her eyes that made him pause. "I am afraid that will not be possible today, Alvin."

Mr. Biddles dropped the dressing gown he was holding out for her to the floor. "Not possible? Are you daring to defy me, Mrs. Biddles?" he asked, his face growing redder as his voice rose.

He called her that only when he was very angry, and for a moment her resolution failed, but then she remembered the quickly hidden disgust on Guy's face for her husband's company and table manners, and it gave her the courage to say, "I am not feeling well. Perhaps it was one of the sauces last evening that is making me feel so queasy. I spent a wretched night and a trip to Bath is out of the question."

Her husband's little brown eyes glared at her as he leaned closer over the bed, and she forced herself to lie still and not flinch away. "This comes on mighty sudden, dearie, now, don't it?" he asked. "Can it be that something *did* happen yesterday on your ride with the viscount that you have not told me about?"

He never took his shrewd eyes from her face as he reached out to grip her shoulder hard. Patricia made herself look as disdainful as possible.

"Of course not! You know I told you everything that happened after Lord Reading left."

He could see no sign of consciousness or guilt written on her face, and after a moment he let go of her shoulder and began to pace the room. Patricia watched him warily, wishing she could rub away the red marks his fingers had left on her skin.

Suddenly he stopped and pointed an accusing finger at her.

"But if nothing happened, as you claim, then *that* is the problem!"

He sounded so threatening that she could not help a tiny gasp. "Whatever can you mean, Alvin?" she asked, completely bewildered.

"I've watched you with the young man, Patsy, and you have never bothered to be either conciliatory or coquettish. No wonder he is called away, no wonder he does not know when he will return to Bath or when he will visit his estates again. You have discouraged him with your coldness. It is all your fault!"

She could only stare at him, and after a moment he resumed his pacing, saying loudly as he did so, "And you knew how much it meant to me to make a friend of him! But would you try and help? No, not even to regain your rightful place in the *ton*. You have always thought yourself above me, always held me cheap, as if someone like me had no right to aspire to you, never mind marry you and take possession of you."

Patricia slid farther down in bed, pulling the covers close to her chin like a small child, her violet eyes enormous.

"Well, let me tell you, my *fine* lady, I paid very well for the privilege! A fortune you cost me, all told, thousands and thousands of pounds, and I expect good value for my money, out of bed as well as in it. The next time we meet the viscount you will smile and charm him and you will be so agreeable to his wishes that he will want to seek you out every chance he gets."

He came to stand over her, his hands on his broad hips and his jowls shaking with his shouted orders. "Do I make myself clear, *Mrs*. Biddles?"

"But, Alvin," she exclaimed, unable to stop herself, "how can you ask this of me? You know you have warned me over and over what would happen if I played you false. You cannot possibly mean that . . . that now you want me to make love to the viscount?"

He had the grace to redden even more. "Who said anything about lovemaking?" he muttered, his eyes avoiding her horrified stare. "No, no, you mistake my meaning, Mrs. Biddles. There are ways for a woman to lead a man on without being unfaithful, ways to make him think her surrender is only a matter of time and so encourage him to continue his pursuit. And by that time, the viscount will have introduced us to so many of his noble friends, we will not need his assistance anymore and you may be as cold and distant as you please.''

Patricia looked at him as if she could not believe her ears, and he stooped to pick up her robe to avoid the accusation in her eyes. Smoothing it, he laid it across the chaise nearby, and the silence in the room continued until he said, ''Very well, today you are too ill to go to Bath. Stay in bed, then, for I shall expect a complete recovery in the morning. The viscount said he was leaving in a few days. Tomorrow will be plenty of time. Remember, Patsy, you will be dressed and ready to accompany me early tomorrow without fail. And when we meet him—and be sure we will—I expect a drastic change in your behavior or you will be made to regret it, I promise you.''

He glared at her for a long moment and then he marched from the room, slamming the door behind him.

Patricia lay back and closed her eyes, her stomach churning until she felt just as sick as she had claimed she did. The only thing she could be grateful for was that she could spend an entire day alone, for she was sure she would never have been able to remain composed in his company after what he had just ordered her to do.

Lady Sylvia was surprised when Guy joined her in the breakfast room that morning, for he was seldom abroad this early. Behind her welcoming smile she searched his face carefully for signs of disappointment or despair, but there was nothing to read there except a calm gravity he had never sported before, and when he told her about his visit to the Biddles', leaving nothing out, her heart began to ache for him. Gone was the careless rake, the dissolute care-for-nobody, and in his place had come this serious, steadfast man. It was clear that he was disappointed, but he accepted the lady's ultimatum that her marriage was not to be set aside lightly. Lady Sylvia felt a flicker of interest and admiration for Lady Patricia Biddles and wished she might meet her and get to know her. She wanted to be able to thank her for this new Guy, for even if time did cure him of his hopeless infatuation, perhaps the memory of her would be enough to change his ways permanently.

He interrupted her musings to announce he was off to Brighton in two days' time, and then he warned her that Mr. Biddles was bold and brassy enough to seek her patronage even without a direct introduction from her nephew, and how much he regretted he had let slip the time she always visited the Pump Room.

"My dear Guy, do not worry about me," she told him as she poured them both more coffee. "The likes of a Mr. Biddles cannot cut up my peace. I have given setdowns to encroaching mushrooms before."

He nodded, and then a frown creased his brow. "I wish you did not have to, however, for no doubt he will have Patricia with him, and she has suffered so many slights and snubs since her marriage, I hate to think she will be wounded once again, and by a woman whom I know would love her in other circumstances."

"Then I shall contrive to snub the one and encourage the other, although I beg you do not ask me how I am to accomplish that," his aunt replied, and Guy came to kiss her and call her his *chère tante* before he went off to make his excuses for the future parties he had promised to attend.

The next morning found Lady Sylvia and Miss Kincaid in their accustomed places in the Pump Room, and although the lady looked carefully at all the people assembled there, she could see no one resembling the horrid Mr. Biddles or his breathtaking wife, and she relaxed.

Guy had promised to join her in the Pump Room at noon, after spending an hour or so at Duffield's Library reading the foreign journals, and he was deep in their pages when he heard the loud voice of Mr. Biddles and felt himself clapped on the shoulder, to his profound disgust.

"Glad to see you've not left yet, my boy," Mr. Biddles exclaimed, taking the seat beside him and wiping his brow. "Patsy will be in alt to see you again, for she has been quite cast down and in the mopes at the thought of your departure."

He paused and Guy murmured, "Indeed?" in what he hoped was an indifferent voice.

"I should be quite jealous, m'lord, if I did not know her better," Mr. Biddles assured him. "She is around here somewhere, changing her book. These ladies with their constant reading! I tell her it will ruin her eyes, and for what purpose? Look at me, I say, never opened a book in my life

except account books, but I'd wager you'd have to go far to
find a man to beat Alvin J. Biddles.''

He paused and the viscount inclined his head as he rustled
the sheets of his journal, hoping the man would take the hint.
An elderly man across the table with a fierce white mustache
seemed to agree with him, for he was glaring at Mr. Biddles,
his forefinger to his lips. Catching sight of him, Mr. Biddles
continued without bothering to lower his voice, ''Thought we
might run into you in the Pump Room, m'lord. At least there
a man may have a pleasant conversation with his friends
without being shushed by old fogies.''

Guy watched the elderly gentleman rise to his feet, collect
his cane and hat, and stride away, no doubt to demand that
Mr. Duffield himself rid his premises of such a noisy bounder.
His lips twitched a little at the coming confrontation, but then
he heard other familiar voices and his hooded lids came down
to cover the dismay in his eyes.

''Dear James, thank you for your exquisite courtesy,''
Clorinda Mills was saying as his cousin held open the door
for her and her friend Miss Reed. Lord Williams came in
behind them, and his face lit up as he spotted the viscount.

''There's Guy! Your pardon, ladies, must speak to him at
once!''

He came forward, his hand outstretched, Mr. Debenham
and the ladies behind him, and Guy thought, Now I'm for it,
even as he rose and greeted them all, his eyes steady and his
face calm. He was aware that his new crony had risen as well
and was waiting expectantly.

''I have been told that men dislike to be interrupted while
they are deep in the journals, but I have never believed it,''
Clorinda remarked, her black eyes sparkling at Guy. ''What
can possibly be written there that is more, mmm, exciting than
one's intimate friends, after all?''

''Guy, you must come with me at once,'' Charlie interrupted,
his hand twitching the viscount's sleeve. ''Found a new tailor
in Guinea Lane of all places, and I like his way with a lapel,
but you and James must be the judge.''

''Lapels? You dragged me all the way up Milsom Street to
see a lapel?'' Mr. Debenham inquired lazily, his eyes going
from his cousin's face to the fat and florid countenance beside
him, whom he had no trouble identifying as Alvin Biddles.
The man favored him with a wink as if to join him in his

depreciation of such foppery, and James stiffened at the familiarity and turned away, his expression haughty.

"I declare, men are worse than women when it comes to finery, don't you agree, Janice?" Clorinda asked, never taking her eyes from Guy. She seemed to be the only one of the group who was unaware of his companion, even though he had now laid his hand on Guy's arm. Lord Williams looked perplexed at this intimacy, and Miss Reed astounded, and then a soft voice said, "If you would excuse me, sir," and Mr. Debenham stepped aside to allow Lady Patricia to join her husband. Guy's eyes went at once to her face under the brim of her bonnet of natural straw trimmed with a multitude of roses and moss-green veiling. She was wearing an elaborate silk gown, but even overdressed for the occasion, she looked so lovely that for a moment he could not control his delight at seeing her again. Clorinda Mills' plump little mouth fell open in astonishment as she looked from one to the other, and then her face grew grim.

"Alvin, I have finished. Shall we be on our way?" Patricia asked in a dignified voice that was quite at odds with her costume.

"I'm ashamed of you, my love," her husband replied, his brown eyes hard. "Here's Viscount Reading with me, and you act as if you've never seen him before, and after he spent the day with us at Biddles Hall, too! Say good morning at once or the viscount will think you have no manners."

"M'lord," Patricia said obediently, dropping a curtsy and trying to smile when she saw the threat in her husband's eyes.

"M'lady," Guy replied, and then, as Mr. Biddles broke in to say, "Do introduce us to your friends, my boy," he took a deep breath and performed the introductions all around. Mr. Biddles beamed and bowed, clapped Lord Williams on the shoulder, and smirked in admiration at the ladies. His wife bowed slightly, her eyes wary, and she did not have long to wait for the expected snub.

"Lady Patricia Biddles?" Clorinda drawled, as if she found the name incongruous. "How . . . how very unusual."

"She was Lady Patricia Westerly before our marriage, m'lady," Mr. Biddles hastened to explain. "Only daughter of the Marquess of Westerly."

Clorinda looked his wife carefully up and down, from the overtrimmed hat to the fussy afternoon gown she wore and the strands of large pearls at her throat, and she sniffed. "Biddles becomes her better," she pronounced, and then she turned her back. "James, be so good as to take me away from here. I am afraid Meyler's will have all my custom from now on. Unfortunately, one does have one's standards, after all."

Guy stepped forward, and the angry look on his friend's face, as well as Lady Patricia's sudden pallor, stirred Lord Williams' easy sympathy, and he was quick to intervene in this dangerous situation. Guy looked as if it would give him enormous pleasure to throttle Clorinda on the spot.

"I think we should all be off," Lord Williams said. "Our conversation seems to be bothering Mr. Duffield's patrons. Allow me to accompany you, Guy, and . . . and your friends."

Mr. Biddles beamed again and called him a capital fellow as the uneasy group moved to the door. Outside, James offered an arm each to Lady Mills and Miss Reed, his expression apologetic as he caught his cousin's eye, and then, without another word, he led the ladies away.

Mr. Biddles did not appear to notice the slight as he began to speak again. "Give me your arm to the Pump Room, Lord Williams, if you would be so kind," he begged. "The viscount can escort my pretty Patsy, for they are great friends, you know."

Lord Williams sought Guy's eye for instructions, completely bewildered now, and when he saw him holding out his arm to Lady Patricia, he took his cue from that and fell into step with her husband.

Conscious of Mr. Biddles' shrewd eyes watching them as they went on ahead, Guy said, "I would not have had that happen for the world, my dear. I am so sorry."

Lady Patricia shook her head. "Do not regard it, for I have been subjected to far worse," she said in an unsteady voice.

"To think that you, who are worth a thousand of her, should have been slighted by that strumpet," Guy added, his voice bitter.

She pressed his arm and his mouth became a hard line as she begged, "Please let us speak of something else, m'lord."

"Guy," he reminded her, bending his head to try to catch a glimpse of the pure profile that her overlarge hat was hiding. "In spite of Lady Mills, it is wonderful to see you again so unexpectedly, my dear."

She turned her head then and smiled up at him, a smile that dazzled and beckoned and seemed to tell him he was her sole delight. Guy was so stunned that he missed his step. As they went on down the street, he noticed that she had colored and lowered her eyelashes, and there was a set to her soft mouth and a decided tilt to her chin now, quite at odds with her alluring smile of a moment ago.

"What is this all about, Patricia?" he asked, his deep voice confused. "Heaven knows how much I want you to look at me like that always, but it is so out of character, besides being very dangerous, with your husband only a few paces behind us."

She did not speak for a moment, but then she admitted, "I did so at his instigation, Guy. I should not tell you perhaps, but unless I do, you may misinterpret my flirting. You see, he has decided that the reason you are going away is because of me."

"And so I am, my heart," Guy interrupted.

"Yes, but he thinks it is because I have been so cold to you that you have come to see there is no hope of getting me to agree to be your mistress, and now you are off to seek easier game. He has ordered me to try to attach you, to—"

She stopped as she felt the muscles in his arm where her hand rested tighten with his rage, and when she looked up into his face, it was to find it dark as thunder.

"Oh, do not look so, my dear," she implored, and after a moment, the dangerous light in his gray eyes faded.

"I should like to kill him," he remarked in a conversational tone that was all the more chilling for its calmness. He might have been discussing the weather, she thought, and she hurried on, "You do not understand. Please listen! He does not want me to surrender to you, if that is what you think. He only wants me to keep you here in Bath in hopes that I will, so he can use you."

"As he has dared to use you, Patricia?" he asked. "A slow form of death would be the most satisfactory, I think, for such a snake."

"Guy, please! You see how it has answered, for look what he has accomplished this morning. And even though he was snubbed by three of the party, he has captured you and Lord Williams."

"And now has the additional plum of being seen walking

the length of the street on a peer's arm, is that it?" Guy asked, his voice still outraged.

She nodded and then attempted a smile again, but this time it was a tremulous thing and quickly gone. "Please smile at me, Guy," she implored him. "It is so difficult to flirt if you will not cooperate, and when Mr. Biddles sees that angry face, he will know I am not carrying out his orders."

"Why are you so quick to obey him, Patricia?" Guy asked, but this time he smiled down at her in turn. "He did not threaten you in any way, did he? If that is the case, I cannot allow either your wedding vows or your scruples to stop me from taking you away from him at once."

She knew he meant exactly what he said, and she swallowed before she said with a light laugh, "No, indeed he did not. You forget how much he cares for me and how much he paid for me. He would never hurt me; it is just that my life would be so uncomfortable, living with his displeasure. I am sure you would not subject me to that fate, Guy."

"I would not subject you to anything that caused you a moment's loss of peace, my love," he murmured, his voice caressing. The light in his eyes was all that Mr. Biddles could have hoped for, and Patricia could not restrain a tiny gasp.

"How horrid this is," she remarked, "to have to order you to say these things, to beg for your smiles, to playact this way."

"I am not playacting, my dear, and neither, I hope, are you," he replied, putting his hand over hers where it rested so lightly on his arm, and pressing it. "And since we have your husband's blessing, let us forget him for the short time we have to be together."

He waited until she looked up at him, and when he saw the shy agreement in her eyes, he proceeded to make love to her all the way to the bottom of the street. His murmured words warmed her and caused her heart to beat rapidly in response, and she knew she would remember and cherish them always.

As they came into Union Street, he glanced back to see Mr. Biddles deep in conversation with a disconcerted Charlie, and slowed his pace.

"We are almost to the Pump Room and we have so little time left. I wish it were miles farther," he remarked.

Patricia laughed. "I am afraid I cannot agree with you.

This gown is most uncomfortable, being far too tight and ornate for walking.''

"Your husband chooses your gowns, does he not?" Guy asked, sensing that she wanted him to refrain from any more lovemaking.

"Of course he does. I hope you did not think I had such execrable taste?" she asked, her voice indignant.

There was a quiver of amusement in his voice as he replied, "How could I be sure? I did wonder if you yourself had not chosen that velvet habit, unable to resist the chance to look like one of the equestriennes at Astley's Amphitheater.''

He looked at her out the corner of his eye and saw her bridling, her mouth opening to protest, and he added quickly, "No, don't eat me, if you please, love! Of course I am teasing. I wish I had the dressing of you. I would deck you out in simple gowns that would not distract from your beauty, with only a few perfect jewels that would still take second place to your magnificent eyes.''

The eyes and another warm smile thanked him, and he said, "Of course not even Mr. Biddles' bad taste can detract from your quality—you are unique.''

They had reached the Pump Room, hard by the tall stone walls of the abbey, and he said, "I meant to excuse myself here, although I am pledged to meet my aunt, but after what you have told me, I think it would be best if I were to escort you inside and remain by your side for some time longer.''

"I wish you would not, Guy," she replied, a tiny frown creasing her brow. "Then you would be forced to introduce Mr. Biddles to your aunt, and I would not subject her to that. She is a resident of Bath, and Alvin will try to presume on the acquaintance even after you leave.''

"Alvin does not know the Lady Sylvia Randolph," he said dryly, and then he added as they reached the entrance and waited for the others to catch them up, "Besides, I cannot resist the opportunity to make you known to each other—my dear aunt and my dearest love.''

"Guy, hush," she whispered as her husband and Lord Williams came up to them.

"I have been telling Mr., er, Mr. Biddles that I have an engagement, Guy," Charlie said. "You must all excuse me. Your most obedient servant, ma'am; yours, sir. Till later, Guy.''

He swept them his elegant bow and Patricia smiled at him
for his kindness as Mr. Biddles exclaimed, "Now don't you
forget, Charlie, my boy, we will expect you at Biddles Hall
anytime you care to come. And when next we go to the
Assembly Rooms, I will be looking out for you, never fear!"

Lord Williams did not hesitate another moment, and stam-
mering his thanks, he scurried away. As Guy ushered the
Biddles into the Pump Room, he did not know whether to
applaud Mr. Biddles' singlemindedness or deplore his insensi-
tivity more in the tireless pursuit of his goal, and now he
listened with only half an ear to his satisfied crowing as he
looked about for his aunt.

She saw him at once, and his companions as well, and
exchanged a pregnant glance with him as he strolled toward
her, Lady Patricia still on his arm, and both of them followed
closely by a smiling older man whom no one would ever
mistake for anybody but a cit. Lady Sylvia took a deep breath
and sent her companion away. When Guy reached her, her
expression was cold and haughty and her eyebrows were
slightly raised as if she wondered at his choice of companions.

"*Chère tante*, may I introduce the Lady Patricia Biddles?"
he asked, his deep voice warm. Feeling a tug on his sleeve,
he looked down to see the lady's husband nodding his head at
his aunt, and he added with punctilious courtesy, "And Mr.
Biddles."

Patricia curtsied and would have spoken, but her husband
was before her. "Delighted! A great honor, ma'am! Alvin J.
Biddles of Biddles Hall, your most obedient servant, ma'am!"
he said as he bowed over his huge stomach.

Lady Sylvia stared at him for a moment, her face expres-
sionless, and then after only the tiniest of bows, she turned
away and held out her hand to Lady Patricia. "I am delighted
to make your acquaintance, Lady Patricia," she said warmly.
"Do take the seat beside me so we may enjoy a comfortable
coze." She saw Mr. Biddles sidling around the tall figure of
her nephew so he would once again be in her line of sight,
and she said, "Go and stroll about the room, Guy, and then
you may both fetch us a glass of the waters, if you would be
so kind."

Turning again to Patricia, who was now seated at her left,
she added, "I always drink three glasses as prescribed, in
spite of the fact that they taste so horrible."

Mr. Biddles opened his mouth to speak again, but Guy motioned him away, and he was forced to retreat, hoping that Patsy did not make a mull of this golden opportunity to become intimate with such an august member of the *ton*, at least until he could return and cement the friendship. At least, he thought as he hurried after Guy's retreating figure, I have m'lord here, and he is sure to make me known to his friends. I saw the way he looked at Patsy during the walk, and I wouldn't be a bit surprised if his plans didn't change and he remained in Bath, after all. Life had suddenly become very sweet to Alvin J. Biddles, and he savored his satisfaction as he kept close to the viscount's side so all could see the exalted company he kept.

As soon as the two men were out of earshot, Lady Sylvia dropped her formal manner as quickly as she had assumed it.

"We do not have much time, Lady Patricia, and so I must forgo the social preliminaries and get right to the heart of the matter. Know I am completely in my nephew's confidence; he has told me everything."

"Guy has told you about me?" Patricia asked, her eyes widening.

She is as beautiful as he claimed, and her eyes really are violet, Lady Sylvia thought as she patted the girl's hands to reassure her. "Yes, we are very close. His mother died when he was still just a young boy, and he looked to me to take her place. Please do not be distressed that he has confided in me, I beg you."

"Of course not, m'lady," Patricia answered, but there was a hint of doubt in her voice at the wisdom of this.

"I must tell you first, my child, how much I admire you. Your determination to honor your vows can inspire nothing but praise, especially since I know only too well how devastating my nephew can be."

"He is very handsome, isn't he, ma'am?" Lady Patricia asked, her voice even.

"More than just handsome. He is a complete charmer, his manners and conversation such that he has always had phenomenal luck with members of our sex. When he first told me of you, I was sure you were to be just the latest in a very long list of inamoratas."

"I thought that was his intention, too," Lady Patricia admitted, warming to this honest and likable older lady.

"He has convinced me, however, that this time—and for the very first time—he is in deadly earnest. This is no infatuation, no casual *amourette*, oh, no. He has been steadfast to you since the first time he saw you, and I confess I had not hoped to see such a change in him. From a sad and rackety here-and-therein, he has changed into a sober, determined man of purpose. I must thank you for that, my dear."

"But of what use is it, after all?" Lady Patricia asked, her violet eyes darkening now with distress. "I am married, and Guy knows I intend to continue faithful; indeed, it is of primary importance that I do nothing to upset Mr. Biddles. I . . . I do not know if he told you . . ."

Lady Sylvia squeezed her hand. "There is no need to explain, I understand. And I myself can see no way out of this bramble patch, but since Guy has formed what I sincerely believe to be a true and lasting connection, I can only pray that something will happen so his life will not become an endless desert of loneliness and disappointment."

Lady Patricia looked as if she were about to remark on this statement, and then she bit her lip and lowered her eyes to her hands, now clasped in her lap.

Lady Sylvia looked at her keenly for a moment, and then she glanced around the Pump Room. It was crowded with the elite of Bath, but she could see Guy and Mr. Biddles waiting for the attendant to pour them each a glass of the waters, and she said in quickened tones, "We have but little time left. Tell me, my dear, does your husband ever allow you to come to Bath alone?"

Lady Patricia looked up. "Yes, sometimes he does when he expects business callers from London or when I have some shopping to do."

"Excellent! I hope you will call on me then in Great Pulteney Street whenever you come alone. I would stand your friend as well as Guy's, and sometimes it helps to have another woman to talk to, my dear. You may be sure I would keep secret anything you chose to confide in me, even from Guy."

Her kind gray eyes were so like the viscount's that Patricia felt a lump in her throat. "Thank you for your concern, m'lady," she whispered. "I would be grateful, for it has been a very long time since I had a friend."

Lady Sylvia patted her hand again, and then spotting the

two men coming back to them, she changed the subject and her face grew haughty and cold once more. She noticed as Mr. Biddles handed his wife a brimming glass that he did not seem so pleased now, and wondered at it. She was not to know that he was upset because, although Guy had nodded to several people in their walk through the room, he had not paused to speak to anybody, nor had he introduced his companion to a single soul. Guy recognized Mr. Biddles' disappointment for what it was and smiled to himself. It was a pleasure to be able to deny him the one thing he so fervently sought, after the way he had used Patricia, although Guy would never burden even the most casual acquaintance with such a loathsome man in any case.

It was only a short time later that Lady Sylvia announced that she wished to leave, and Guy was quick to help her to her feet and give her his arm for support. Miss Kincaid appeared like magic on her other side, and although Mr. Biddles offered in a loud voice to hurry ahead and fetch her a sedan chair, the lady denied him coldly by saying that of course she always had one waiting.

At his expressions of joy in their newfound friendship, she looked amazed, and her voice was formal and distant as she bade him good-bye.

Guy bowed slightly, and then his eyes went to Patricia's face for one brief moment, but that was still long enough for her to read the ardent message and sad farewell there. Her heart began to race with a combination of joy for his love and sorrow that now they must be parted, perhaps forever.

She was careful to hide any show of these emotions behind a mask of composed indifference as they bade each other a formal good-bye under Mr. Biddles' watchful eye.

PART TWO

1815
Two Years Later

5

Two years later, almost to the day they had parted, Viscount Reading arrived at River Court. He had returned to England only a few weeks before after an extensive trip abroad, and although his first instinct was to post off to Bath as soon as he set foot ashore, he curbed his impetuosity and embarked on a series of visits to various members of the family before he retired to his estate. The long months that he and Patricia had been separated had taught him patience. It had not been an easy lesson to learn for a man who was used to taking what he wanted when he wanted it, without a moment's delay. When they had first been parted, it was almost as if he were trying to put an end to himself by daring fate with wilder and wilder escapades than he had ever engaged in, and sometimes, even now, he railed still against that fate for depriving him of the only woman he would ever love. The memory of her had not faded; if anything, their separation had made his love stronger. The sweet contours of her face were still the first thing that came to his mind when he woke each morning, and his last conscious thought at night was a prayer for her safety and well-being. Even in his sleep she was with him, for she appeared in his dreams over and over again.

When he had ridden away from Bath that spring morning two years prior, he had gone first to London, thinking that the ceaseless activity and throngs of people to be found there would distract him, but even though the Season was at its height and he had thrown himself into all manner of wild debaucheries, they had failed to divert him, and all the amusements he sought so unceasingly seemed only shallow and childish and brought him no relief.

James Debenham, at Lady Sylvia's urging when she saw the savage set of Guy's face, had accompanied him, but even with his obvious concern and gentle probing, he could not get

85

his cousin to confide in him. He did not know that Guy felt
that if he spoke of Patricia out loud, he would lose her, that
any reference about her to others would cause the vision of
her to slip away, and he was guarding his memories jealously.
She was his, his alone, and far too precious to share with
another.

James shook his head, but eventually he had to admit
defeat. Watching Guy's desperate activity, he thought that his
cousin was trying to forget the lady by ever-increasing
dissipation, but unless the man came to trust him as a confidant,
he knew he was helpless to aid him. The only thing he could
do was to watch over him to be sure he was in no danger of
doing himself an injury.

It was not long before Guy left town for Brighton, but even
this small fishing village that the Prince Regent had turned
into the *dernier cri* of resorts could not please him, nor the
company of his friends all vying for his attention cause him to
forget the raw agony of exile he was enduring.

One morning he woke in a strange bed, his head throbbing
and his mouth dry, with a raddled drab of a streetwalker by
his side, and he had no recollection of the events of the
previous evening that had brought him so low. Even in his
present condition, he was disgusted with himself and knew he
had to take himself in hand before it was too late.

In desperation he went to River Court alone for the rest of
the summer months. Many problems had arisen during his
absence, and perhaps this saved his sanity, for now he had
the benefit of hard work and long hours spent in the saddle
and at his desk as he strove to put the estate and the court in
good order again. He was able to sleep at night because he
was exhausted mentally and physically, and if he never smiled
and showed no interest in the activities of the neighborhood
gentry, to his tenants at least it was enough that m'lord was
home.

He oversaw the installation of a new roof for the west wing
of the court, and set in train a host of major improvements,
from a modern cook stove for the kitchens to new paneling in
the library to replace that damaged by dry rot. Around the
land as well he was quick to note the need for a drainage
ditch here, a new hedge there, and whitewash and thatching
for the cottages.

Sometimes he pretended he was readying the court to

receive his bride, making it a showcase for her grace and beauty, and for a few hours his mood would lighten as he pondered what she would like. In the rooms he decided were to be hers, he was meticulous in his choice of furnishings, sending back to the warehouse again and again anything that did not seem worthy of her. He considered for a long time before he selected overdrapes and bed hangings of pale-blue silk shot through with silver threads, and a carpet of dark-blue pile. To relieve this coolness, he chose deep apricot for the pillows and accessories, and had her dressing room hung in palest peach. Speculation was rife among the servants as to whom the new viscountess would be, but to their disappointment, no mistress appeared.

When everything was finished at last, it became Guy's habit to have the fire built up in her boudoir in the evenings, and he would sit in the large wing chair he had installed for his own use, staring at the smaller chair opposite and picturing her there, smiling at him over her embroidery, her violet eyes glowing and her chestnut curls aflame in the firelight.

But even these fantasies could not comfort him for long, and by October he was restless again. When the first autumn storms began to blow from the north across the Downs, he knew it was time for him to leave, and remembering his remarks to Mr. Biddles about the beauty of Italy in the fall, he made arrangements to go abroad as soon as possible. James, who stopped at the court from time to time, was easily persuaded to travel with him, and the two cousins did not see England again until the following spring.

Guy spent a few weeks in London then, and it was here that he saw Lady Patricia again, for the first time in almost a year. She was coming out the door of Grillon's Hotel on her husband's arm, and Guy, who had been strolling to his club on the opposite side of the street, stopped dead in his tracks to watch her with hungry eyes, glad he was concealed behind a parked hackney cab.

His heart beat strangely as he stared at her. She had not changed. Her chestnut hair still curled the same way around her brow, the delicate profile that she turned to Mr. Biddles was as pure as ever, and her large violet eyes were as clear and luminous as he remembered. She was wearing an elaborate gown and bonnet whose color he could not recall later, for it was only her face and gently curved figure that he saw.

If there was any difference in her that he could detect at all, it was in the resigned sadness of her expression, for in all the time he watched, not once did even the smallest smile brighten her face.

Guy drank her in, not daring to move, as he hoped the carriage they were so obviously awaiting would be further delayed. He spared a glance for Mr. Biddles when he saw Patricia move slightly away from him, and was astounded at the change in the man. He was older, true, his sideburns completely gray now, and he was much heavier, but the greatest change was in his expression. His red face showed no trace of joviality; instead, he wore a mighty frown, his pendulous jowls were set in permanent lines of discontent, and his thick brows were contracted above his narrowed eyes. Guy saw him speak to Patricia, a short, barked sentence, as he grasped her arm. She stood still immediately, her eyes lowered and her hands clasped before her while her husband bustled away to give the head porter what appeared to be a crushing scold from the pout that could be seen on his fat lower lip.

Now that she was momentarily alone, Guy stepped from behind the cab, and once again, as he had in the past, he willed her to look at him. When she raised her head to stare across the street, he saw one hand go to her heart, and her face pale with shock and surprise. He removed his beaver and bowed, and then he smiled at her, a smile into which he tried to put all his constancy and love, and his undiminished hopes for the future they might share one day.

He knew she understood, for her lips curled in a delighted answering smile before she turned away abruptly as Mr. Biddles came back to her side. Guy retreated behind the cab, cursing the necessity for such a hole-in-the-corner approach when he longed to stride across the cobblestones and take her in his arms. A few moments later, his heart sinking, he saw her enter a smart traveling carriage with her husband, and from the amount of baggage tied on the roof, he knew they were leaving London and that one brief glimpse of her was all he was to be allowed.

Guy remained in the city then for only a short time; Lord Williams invited him to join a party of friends at his ramshackle estate in the north of England, and he was glad to agree to be one of the party. If Patricia was not in London, it was all dust and ashes to him again. Besides, Charlie's house parties were famous for the unexpected surprises that occurred. In other, better-run establishments, a guest could be sure of a luxurious room, regular mealtimes, and every care taken for his comfort and amusement, but Lord Williams' staff was so poorly supervised that guests never knew when or even if dinner would be served, if there would be any fires lit to welcome them in their rooms, or indeed, any room prepared for them at all. Guy remembered one memorable occasion when some sixteen people had remained at the dinner table awaiting the dessert course for over half an hour, only to discover when the butler was finally dispatched to the kitchens that not only had the orange soufflé collapsed, so had the chef. He was facedown in it as a result of too much cooking sherry.

Then there was the time the chandelier in the drawing room fell to the floor in the middle of the night with what James called such a din of sounding brass and tinkling cymbal that he had sat bolt upright in bed, his heart pounding and sure the Last Judgment Day had arrived, and only too aware he was not at all prepared for it. There were also the multitude of leaks throughout the hall whenever it rained, armies of mice in the walls, and the tendency of the fireplaces to belch black smoke into all the rooms whenever the wind was from the north.

Guy sometimes wondered how Charlie ever got anyone to accept his invitations, but when he mentioned this to his cousin James, he was told that it was because everyone hated to miss the latest disaster or the opportunity to regale society with the story firsthand when London was reached safely once again.

At least, Guy told himself as he drove north with his valet, I will have a chance to fish and hunt if the weather is not too foul. April in Yorkshire was unpredictable, as he knew. But as it turned out, he found he was to be the hunter's quarry instead, for Charlie had included Clorinda Mills, *sans* husband, in the party.

Guy managed to hold her off for several days by disappearing to fish Charlie's well-stocked trout stream early every morning and by refusing to join the ladies' riding parties. Clorinda pouted and renewed her efforts. She had seldom been rebuffed by any man who caught her fancy, and she could not imagine failing with Guy Leighton. She had completely forgotten snubbing Lady Patricia Biddles in Bath and did not know that the viscount had not forgiven her for it, nor did he have any intention of taking her into his bed. And so, all her burning glances, all her suggestive remarks and low-cut gowns did not so much as draw a smile or a raised eyebrow. Guy listened to her politely when she managed to corner him, but was quick to excuse himself as soon as possible.

Clorinda's bosom bow, Janice Reed, twitted her about her failing charms, and stung, Clorinda renewed her efforts.

That evening, after the gentlemen rejoined the ladies in the drawing room after dinner, she beckoned Guy to her side. She was seated on a small sofa just big enough for two, he noticed. The tight, black silk gown she was wearing was so provocative that several of the other ladies had raised their eyebrows when she had first appeared.

Now she patted the seat beside her with a glittering smile, her half-exposed breasts swelling the taut fabric. Guy took the seat she indicated, his cool eyes never leaving her face, and she laid a hand on his arm and began to whisper in his ear.

She was much more direct this evening, her hints of the rapture Guy could expect from their coming liaison so blatant, that he was forced to drop his casual air and reply in kind.

"I fear you mistake my intentions, ma'am," he said in an indifferent voice, and when her eyes flew to his face in disbelief, he raised his hand to conceal a yawn. "I am sure your charms are everything you say, indeed, we have been treated to such a complete exposure this evening it is obvious, but I have no interest in them. May I drop a word of advice in your ear, Clorinda? You really should be more careful what you say to men. We think of ourselves as gentlemen, but when deliberately challenged, not all of us restrain ourselves as we should. Of course, I can assure you you have nothing to fear from me, but I cannot vouch for the others present. And rape is so unpleasant, is it not?"

He saw her face whiten with her fury as he removed her hand from his arm and excused himself. He knew very well that she could not tell anyone how he had rejected her, and so he was not concerned about any vindictive reprisals.

In the days that followed, he continued to treat her with a

polite indifference. This so infuriated her that she left the house party long before the other guests, and Guy was free to remember Patricia once again, quite undisturbed.

It was a long twelve months before he saw her again, however, but this time fate was kinder to him than it had been at their last meeting. His aunt had not been well that winter, and she begged him to come to her before he set out again on his ramblings, this time an extended tour of the countries that bordered the Aegean Sea. Although he had been assiduous in avoiding the spa all this time, now he knew he must return to his aunt no matter how it pained him to be so close to Patricia in miles, when for all the good it did them, he might as well be in Greece already.

Lady Sylvia had grown much frailer. Her hair was almost pure white now, and Guy hid his concern as he knelt beside her chair and took her gently in his arms to kiss.

She searched his face carefully with those keen gray eyes so like his own, and what she saw there caused her to sigh. "Still, Guy?" she asked as she motioned him to the tray of decanters and glasses so he could help himself.

"Always, *tante*, always," he replied without hesitation, and her eyes grew sad. She nodded when he asked her if she cared to join him in a glass of wine, and as he poured it for them, she was free to observe him. She could see that during the months since he had left Bath he had changed completely. True, he was as rugged and handsome as ever, but his demeanor now was stern rather than devil-may-care, and his infrequent smile never reached his cool, half-hooded eyes. He seemed much older, for there was about him an air of rigid self-control, the self-control of a man who had himself well in hand in spite of his unhappiness. She had heard about his earlier licentiousness and was glad he had found a way to conquer such behavior.

Still Lady Sylvia sighed. Over the long months of his absence, she had grown to know and love Lady Patricia, and there was no one she would have chosen as more suitable to be her nephew's bride if it had been at all possible. The resigned patience and sadness that she saw in his face was mirrored in Patricia's expression, and for these two dear people she felt nothing but grief that their ways in life must lie apart.

It had taken her a long time to get Patricia to confide in her freely, to tell her of her marriage, confess her problems, and finally admit her love for Guy, but when she did, all restraint disappeared. True to her promise, Lady Sylvia never relayed a whisper of these confidences to her nephew, no matter how she longed to do so, and invariably the only reference to Patricia in her letters was to say that she remained at Biddles Hall with her husband and continued well. Guy always inquired for her, but not once had he asked his aunt to remember him to the lady, nor had he sent any personal message for her in all those long months of separation.

Now as they drank their wine, Guy was careful to keep the conversation light. He told her of his travels, of the current London scene, and such family news as might interest her, but not once did he speak of the one person who was foremost in both their minds. Lady Sylvia thought he showed restraint beyond his years.

"I cannot stay with you for long this time, *chère tante*," he said finally, putting down his empty glass on the little cherry side table by his chair and rising to go to the long windows at the front, to stare down into the street. "I have promised James and Charlie I will join them in London in a week's time, and from there I must go to River Court for a few weeks before I leave for the Aegean. But stay! Can I not persuade you to join me there? The air that blows from the Downs is so refreshing it can do you nothing but good, and if you travel slowly, I do not think you will come to any harm." He paused abruptly, and his aunt saw him lean close to the panes, and then she heard him whisper, "Dear God, can it be possible?"

Before she could question him, Gregson knocked and entered to announce the Lady Patricia Biddles. He stood waiting, his wrinkled old face going in alarm from m'lord's half-stifled exclamation and sudden start to his mistress's look of distress.

Lady Sylvia spoke at last. "Guy?" she asked softly, "Shall I deny her?"

The viscount frowned, deep in thought. She could almost see the war that was raging in his head between his desire for another meeting and his conviction that this would be unwise.

And then he looked straight at her and said, "No, do not deny her, I beg you." She noticed his eyes were alight with anticipation, although his face seemed set in stone.

As he turned away to pace the room, she ordered her butler to admit the lady, and the old retainer bowed, his face still puzzled.

There was an uneasy silence in the drawing room until Patricia stepped inside, the small smile of greeting for her friend fading immediately as she saw Guy standing in the middle of the room, his gray eyes intent on her face.

For a moment, Lady Sylvia thought she was about to faint from the shock, and Guy must have thought so, too, for he hurried to her side, one arm going around her waist to support her.

"Come and sit down, Patricia," he said, his deep voice unsteady. "I am sorry if I startled you, and if you do not wish to see me, I will go away at once."

He led her to the chair across from his aunt's where he had been sitting, and waited for her reply. Not once had either of them taken their eyes from the other, and when Lady Sylvia saw the naked longing written on both their faces, she held her breath, hoping the girl's reply would be honest.

"Well, my heart, shall I leave you?" Guy prompted.

"No, please do not go," Patricia said, shaking her head with an air of decision, and he took up her hand and kissed it, visibly shaken, before he went to pour her some wine.

"Drink this, my dear, you need it," he ordered when he came back.

Patricia smiled her thanks, and then she forced herself to turn to her hostess. Lady Sylvia noticed that the slim white hand that held the wineglass was trembling a little.

"I would not have come if I had known you had your nephew with you, dear ma'am," she said, trying for a normality no one was feeling. "I am sure you have much to say to each other and a third party can be only an intrusion."

Lady Sylvia had been wondering what to do, and now she came to a sudden decision. "Help me up, Guy, if you would be so kind," she said, and as he hastened to do so and Patricia rose as well, she added, "I will have many opportunities to speak to my nephew, my dear, never fear, but this moment belongs to you. I will tell Gregson that you are not to be disturbed, and I shall not return for half an hour."

For a moment, Patricia looked as if she wanted to object to this plan, but then she lowered her eyes and nodded. She remained standing there staring at the carpet while her hostess made her slow way across the room on Guy's arm, but when she heard the drawing-room doors close behind her, she looked up to seek Guy's face. He was still standing just inside the doors, as if he were waiting for her permission to return to her side, and she had to smile at this air of hesitation that was so incongruous on his strong, decisive face.

At that he came back to her and took her in his arms as if she were some fragile, priceless thing he hardly dared to touch. He rested his hard cheek against her hair, his warm breath coming unevenly, and his hands on her yielding back gentle in their caress. Her own arms went up around his neck to bring him closer still, and for a long moment they stood together holding each other like two lost children.

At last he put her a little bit away from him to search her face. Patricia tried to smile through the tears that were sparkling in her eyes, but several drops spilled over and ran down her cheeks. She closed her eyes when she felt one large hand come up to wipe them away as he had done before.

"I am always crying when I am with you, Guy," she said in a broken whisper. "You will call me a watering pot."

He kept one arm around her as he led her to a sofa, and when they were both seated side by side, he took her hands in his, turning so he could look into her face.

"I shall never call you anything but my dearest love," he told her, his gray eyes warm and alive, and all the stern sadness gone from his face. "Tell me, are you well? Are you happy? You cannot know how I have longed to write to you so I could be sure your life continued smooth, but I did not dare to do even that and had to rely on my aunt's occasional references to you." He paused and then said savagely, "These last two years have been a living hell!"

"For me, too," she murmured, and his hands tightened on hers. "Yes, I am well, but I cannot claim happiness either. I shall say rather that I try to be content." She paused as if she would like to say more, and then she added in a brighter tone, "But tell me of yourself, Guy. Lady Sylvia keeps me posted on your comings and goings, but such news can only be the barest bones of your life."

"When I left you, I thought I would go mad," he replied, dropping her hands to run his through his dark-brown hair. "In fact, I did go mad for a little while, I think. I threw myself into every kind of excess and debauchery, no doubt trying to kill myself in my grief, but eventually the vision of your face recalled me to sanity, and I retired from society to River Court.''

"I know of your raking, Guy," she said quietly. "It bothered me when Mr. Biddles told me of it after one of his trips to town, for I was tempted to think I had been mistaken in you—''

"That I should ever have distressed you Patricia!" he exclaimed, a frown coming over his handsome face.

"You did not do so for long, my dear," she reassured him, and he took her hands in his again. "I soon came to see why you were behaving as you did, and although I regretted it, I understood. And then Mr. Biddles reported that you were seen no more in society, for you were traveling abroad. He wanted me to write to you when you returned and beg for an invitation to River Court, but I refused to do so.''

"If you could have come alone, there would have been no need to beg," Guy told her. "How I have wanted to show you my home and all my improvements.''

He wondered if telling her about the rooms he had designed for her would distress her, but then she remarked, a small smile playing on her lips, "I should not have come in any case unless you could promise me a Venetian bridge at the least, m'lord! You must remember that I am used to only the finest and most unusual estates, rich and pompous and ornate.''

Guy chuckled then and kissed her hand. "How disappointed you will be, love, when at last you come to River Court. It is only a gentleman's country manor compared to Biddles Hall.''

Patricia lowered her eyes to where their hands were entwined in her lap. "I shall never come there, Guy, and you know it as well as I do," she told him sadly. When he would have spoken, she hurried on, "You know we must go on as we have been doing; we have no choice. It is hard, and it does not grow any easier with time, but it is all we can do in the circumstances. Besides, you should be looking about for a wife to grace your home and bear your children, instead of wasting your life pursuing an impossible dream.''

"Patricia, look at me!" he commanded, his deep voice somber. When he saw those grave violet eyes searching his again, he took a deep breath and said in a quiet but positive voice, "You will come to River Court one day, of that I am sure, and I want you to believe it as strongly as I do myself. We will be together and I will have the great delight of calling you my wife, Patricia Leighton, Viscountess Reading. There can be no one else for me. Tell me you believe me, love!"

Patricia swallowed her first quick retort. If Guy wanted to hold fast to a fairy tale, it was not in her power to hurt him by denying it, but deep inside she did not think such happiness would ever be theirs to share. "I shall try to, Guy," was all she could promise him.

"Hold fast to that, love, and believe it, for it will come to pass," he told her, and the conviction in his voice showed her that this future happiness he clung to was the means that kept him sane.

The half-hour that Lady Sylvia had granted them sped by. Guy did not take her in his arms again, nor did he try to kiss her, and as much as she wanted his lovemaking, she respected his decision, for she knew if he made love to her, she would never be able to let him go, and she was sure he felt the same. Instead, their eyes made love for them, never leaving each other's face, and storing up each smile, each expression no matter how fleeting, against the cold separation that was soon to come.

It seemed no time at all and there was still so much to say when a knock came on the drawing-room door and Lady Sylvia was back. Guy helped her to her chair, and her wise old eyes searched both their faces. She was glad to see they were both in firm control of themselves, and although Patricia still looked unhappy and there were traces of tears on her cheeks, there was a new calmness on her face as well, and an air about both of them of renewed commitment, and she was glad she had given them this time together.

"Your sedan chair is at the door, my dear," she told Patricia, holding up her arms to kiss her good-bye. "I shall be looking forward to your next visit."

Patricia nodded and hugged her as she bade her good-bye, and then she turned to see Guy holding out his hand. She went to him, her head high and a smile on her lips that she hoped hid the anguish she was feeling at their parting. She saw his face was pale and stiff with the emotion he was repressing as well, and wondered when or if they would ever meet again.

"I shall see you to your chair, my dear," he said, taking her hand in his arm and leading her to the door.

"No, Guy, you must not!" she said, suddenly distraught. "I hire the chair to bring me here so Mr. Biddles will not learn of my friendship with your aunt, but I am never sure that my maid does not suspect where I go, although I bribe her with money and clothing. If she should see you with me and tell the coachman, all will be lost."

Guy frowned, but then he nodded. "Do not look so frightened, little one," he teased her. "In that case I shall not insist on it."

When they reached the drawing-room doors, she paused and looked once again into his eyes. "Good-bye, my dear Guy," she whispered. "Please take care of yourself."

He lifted her hand and kissed it again, his eyes still on her face. "This is only *au revoir*, love. Remember what I have told you. We will be together someday, I promise you."

She nodded as if she believed what he said, and then he reached out to grasp her arms as he kissed her cheek. She was sure she would break down if she had to remain another minute, and as if he sensed this from her trembling, he let her go.

She barely saw Gregson bowing as he opened the front door for her, and by the time she was seated in the sedan chair, she was having great difficulty containing her sobs, but when she was set down at Meyler & Sons, where she had ordered her coachman to fetch her, she had herself in control again. She went into the library to wait for her maid to return from her shopping, and a short time later she was bowling along in her carriage for the return to Midsomer Norton and Biddles Hall.

She tried to concentrate on the passing scenery, for she knew she could not think of Guy right now and remain composed, and she must do nothing to make her maid suspicious. She had to wait until she was alone in her room tonight, many hours away, before she dared to remember their meeting.

She was glad he had not persisted in questioning her further about her life now, for she would have had to tell him even more lies than she had already when she assured him

she was content with her lot. She was not content at all; she
was miserable, for in the two years since Guy had left Bath,
Mr. Biddles had changed dramatically, and not for the better.
Since Lord Williams had taken a hurried departure from Bath
the very afternoon he had been introduced to her husband,
and Guy had refused to be drawn into his trap either, Mr.
Biddles had been left without a single sponsor in his quest for
social acceptance, and this had embittered him.

He began to brood and endlessly bemoan the younger
men's departure, and then he had tried to plot a new course
involving Lady Sylvia. He attempted to engage her in conversation in the Pump Room in the weeks that followed, but she
treated him only to a cold formality at first and finally to a
royal setdown for his presumption that left him red-faced and
furious.

It was an easy step for him to begin to blame Patricia for
his failures, and she was subjected to his displeasure with her
behavior over and over again. He threatened and bullied her,
insisting she bestir herself and entrap some other lord, and
when she did not do so, he told her he was strongly of a mind
to send her noble father to a debtor's prison.

Patricia had heard from her maternal grandmother, the
Lady Eliza Darrow, that not only her father but both her
brothers as well had fallen into debt again, and Mr. Biddles
held new notes of theirs to hand, so he could do just that
anytime he chose. She could not help feeling angry and
betrayed. Wasn't it enough that she had saved them once, and
at such a cost? Would they never consider what all their
profligacy was doing to her?

And then she shrugged, her face bitter. When had they
ever, any one of them, thought of her feelings? Her father
had not even thanked her for her sacrifice when she married
Alvin Biddles. Instead, he had pretended the man was the
epitome of her fondest dream, and outside of a few teasing
remarks from Harry, and a lewd snicker from John, her
brothers had not done so either. Her eyes grew stormy as she
remembered.

She had come to Lady Sylvia's today in something very
like desperation, for Mr. Biddles was growing more persistent in his demands that she find some peer to dangle after
her. He even insisted she visit Bath alone twice a week, in
the hope that she would catch someone's eye. Today she had

made up her mind to confess this new development to her friend and ask her advice, until the sight of Guy banished all such problems from her mind.

But tonight she knew Mr. Biddles would question her all through dinner, oblivious to the smirking footmen and disgusted butler. Had anyone followed her while she was shopping? Perhaps she had spoken to some noble gentleman in the library or the Assembly Rooms? And when she would return a denial to his eager queries, as she always did, he would grow cross and shout at her, his fat red face furious with his anger.

He was nowhere near as considerate of her as he had been in the early days of their marriage, and sometimes he grabbed her and shook her so hard that the marks of his fingers lingered for days. She knew it was only a matter of time before he struck her; indeed, only this past week he had raised his hand to do so, only to control himself with a visible effort when he saw the scorn and disdain in her eyes.

She was glad now she had had no chance to tell her troubles to her friend, for she was sure Lady Sylvia would be so horrified that she would tell Guy, and if she did so, Patricia knew he would insist on removing her from Biddles Hall at once.

She stared out at the quarries they were passing with unseeing eyes. Much as she wished for that with all her heart, much as she longed to go to him any way she could, she knew it was for his own sake that he must never know. Guy Leighton, Viscount Reading, deserved someone better than the abused runaway wife of a hated moneylender, the scandal of a divorce proceeding, and the censure of his friends. No, she would keep her own counsel, and Guy and Lady Sylvia would never know. As for her father and her brothers, she found she did not care if Mr. Biddles called in their notes and ruined them. She had sacrificed all she was going to for them, ungrateful wretches that they were, and she had been snubbed so many times already that being treated as the daughter and sister of common felons could not disturb her further. No, her fortitude was all for Guy's sake, and for his sake alone.

Just as she suspected, Mr. Biddles was avid in his demands to know all about the events of the day, and when she denied meeting or even speaking to a single soul except for shopkeepers, his face reddened and the look of discontent that had become his normal expression settled on his features again.

Waving to a footman to refill his wineglass, he took up a large forkful of tripe and onions, and even while chewing it, began to read her a severe lecture.

"Aye, *Mrs.* Biddles, another wasted afternoon! But of course you are too *nice* to put yourself forward in any way, are you not, my dainty? There must have been many men who stared at you and wished for a further acquaintance, but even though you know it is my wish, you are too refined, too hoity-toity to lower yourself to help me to my aim."

He paused to take a breath and then he bellowed as his face turned purple, "Have a care, madam! My patience is not inexhaustible, and I can make you very sorry, very sorry indeed, my refined little lady, aye, and those worthless relatives of yours as well!"

"Mr. Biddles, the servants," she reminded him, trying to make her voice calm and remote. How I hate him, she thought as she stared at him until he lowered his eyes from her scornful face.

That night he came to her bed, something he had not done for some time, and his lovemaking was coarse and hateful, almost as if she were a prostitute. And, she thought with despair, since he paid for me, that is what I am. He seemed to be using his heavy, gross body to punish her for her refusal to do his bidding, and by the time he rolled off her at last, panting hard from his exertion, she had all she could do to keep the sobs of pain and humiliation from escaping her lips. She concentrated on remaining very still until he heaved himself out of bed to don his dressing gown and leave her. Not once had he spoken a single word.

As soon as he had gone, she went to her dressing room to wash and put some ointment on her bruises, sobbing a little now in her distress. When she was back in bed at last, wearing a clean nightgown, she felt somewhat more serene, and to forget her husband's hateful embrace, she began to wonder what Guy's lovemaking would be like. She remembered their only kiss, and how gentle and careful of her he had been, in spite of the desire that she had felt in the tense hardness of his body and on his insistent mouth, which had demanded from her an equal return of that passion he showed her so clearly.

How wonderful it would be to be able to respond to him with an abandon she could only imagine, how glorious to tell him how much she loved and wanted him, instead of having to school her face and body to the cold acceptance that was all she was able to summon when she was with her husband. But of course, she would never know the enchantment of making love with Guy.

She turned over on her side, trying not to cry in her despair again, and suddenly it occurred to her that not once had she ever told Guy she loved him, not even this afternoon when they had been alone. How could she have been so remiss? And then she smiled, alone there in the dark, as his face came to her mind and she seemed to hear his voice whispering, "Dear heart, I know you love me; you do not have to say it. It glows in your eyes and I return it tenfold."

I will tell him anyway, she promised herself as she closed her eyes at last. The very next chance I get, I will tell him.

She went to sleep dreaming of that future meeting, completely forgetting her fears that their love was destined to come to nothing, and that only this afternoon she had thought she would never know the happiness that he promised would be theirs.

6

Mr. Biddles had the grace to appear slightly ashamed of himself the following day, avoiding Patricia by shutting himself up in the library to deal with business matters all day, and not quite meeting her eye when they were forced by custom to dine together that evening. His conversation and tone of voice were mild, but this new attitude did not encourage her to think him changed in any way. No, in a short time, she knew, he would be back to his old ways, arguing and shouting at her and demanding that she do something—anything—to gain him the one thing he so dearly wanted that had persisted in eluding him up to now.

When she refused to go to Bath with him two days later, and used the cloudy day that might come on to rain as an excuse, he accepted it without an argument, to her relief. She knew there was every chance that she might run into Guy if she went to town, and although she longed to do so, it was not her intention to tell him of her love in the crowded Pump Room, or whisper it to him between the stacks of a library. Besides, if Mr. Biddles discovered he was back, he would take advantage of this to reopen his campaign, using Patricia as his lure. As intelligent and quick as Guy was, he would be sure to realize how Mr. Biddles had changed, and he would force her to leave her husband at once.

No, it was better they did not meet, even alone, she told herself, for she was still feeling so heartsore from her husband's treatment of her that she was not sure she would be able to keep it from Guy. Those intent gray eyes saw too deeply into her heart for comfort, and if he should detect any shadow in her eyes and question her, what might she not be forced to admit?

Fortunately, Mr. Biddles left for London the next day on business, and although he did not bother to tell her how long he would be gone, she was relieved to be free of him for even a short period of time.

Still, in order to avoid a confrontation with Guy, she did not call on Lady Sylvia for almost two weeks, and when she heard from the lady that he had left for town and was then going to River Court, she did not know whether to be happy that he had gone away ignorant of her plight, or sorry for herself at her loss.

"My dear," the older lady said in a compassionate voice, "I cannot tell you how sorry I am for both of you. I have always known that many things in life are not fair, but in your case fate has decreed a terrible problem from which there seems to be no escape."

Patricia took the cup of tea Lady Sylvia had poured for her, trying not to remember that just a short time before she had been sitting on this same sofa with Guy close beside her, holding her hands as if he never wished to let them go.

"There is no escape, I'm afraid," she said, her violet eyes sad. "I still hope that someday Guy will forget me for another, but . . ." Suddenly she stopped. "No, that is a lie, and I will not lie to myself or to you, dear friend, again. I do not want him to forget me; I cannot bear to think he might marry someone else, even though I know such thoughts are wrong of me. He should marry and have sons, but I am not so noble that I can pray he will."

"I doubt you will ever have to face his marriage to another. Guy is still deeply in love with you, even after two years, and I am convinced if he cannot have you, he will never set another in your place."

Patricia felt a fierce elation and could not speak for a moment, and then she said, "But even if I were to divorce my husband, I would not be the kind of wife Guy should have, and you know it, ma'am. Not after having been the wife of Alvin J. Biddles."

"I will be honest and admit I thought so, too, at one time, Patricia," Lady Sylvia said as she passed a plate of cakes to her guest. "But now I know there is no one I would rather see as Guy's viscountess. As for Mr. Biddles, it is of course unfortunate that you were forced to marry him, unfortunate that the scandal of his business practices should touch your life, but it has not changed you, that is very clear. You are still the same girl you were before you wed. You have not allowed your marriage to coarsen or cheapen you, but have kept yourself as fine as you were before. That is the woman Guy loves, as I do.''

Patricia smiled her thanks, but she could not help wondering if Lady Sylvia would feel the same way if she knew of Mr. Biddles' assault.

A week later her husband returned, and Patricia could see from his absentmindedness and perpetual frown that his business in London had not prospered. His few remarks were terse, and as she could not bring herself to ask him about it, having no desire to know what unethical stratagems he was up to now, their conversations were brief and stilted.

And then one afternoon a few days later, a caller arrived at Biddles Hall. Patricia heard the butler admit the man and the murmur of their voices in the hall, for she was arranging a large bouquet of flowers in the drawing room. There was silence for a few moments and she wondered why Ames did not bring the gentleman in to her, until she heard him say clearly, ''Mr. Biddles will see you now, m'lord.''

For a moment she stood very still, her heart beating fast, and the roses in her hands falling unheeded to the carpet. Surely Guy had not come back! She made herself go out to the hall as the butler came out of the library and closed the door behind him.

''A caller, Ames?'' she asked in what she hoped was a casual voice.

Ames had nothing but sympathy for Lady Patricia. She was a real lady, refined and elegant, and he was sorry that anyone so aristocratic had to be married to that gross lout he was forced to call his master. If the salary had not been excellent, he would have handed in his notice long ago. And so he smiled at her as he told her that Lord Granford had called to see Mr. Biddles on a matter of business. Patricia shrugged and returned to her flowers. He must be a relative of the wild young man who had threatened Mr. Biddles, and she was sure he was just another in the long list of men who owed Alvin money and who had come to Bath to get an extension on his loan. No one ever called except for that purpose.

After the bouquet was arranged to her satisfaction, she went to speak to the housekeeper and the cook, and then she ordered her horse saddled and summoned her maid to help her change into her habit.

The late May day was warm and sunny, and she intended
to stay away from the hall until it was time to dress for
dinner. As she always did, she went first to the spot along the
brook where Guy had told her of his love for the first time,
and after a few moments of quiet dreaming, she rode away
through the woods and across the fields to Midsomer Norton
and the Mendip Hills beyond.

She was surprised when she returned to the hall to find out
from the butler that Lord Granford had been persuaded to
remain for a few days' visit. This was most unusual, for
although Mr. Biddles invariably asked any member of the
peerage to be his guest, to a man they had always refused,
not even bothering in some cases to hide their disgust at the
invitation. She sighed when she saw the elaborate gown her
husband had chosen for her to wear, for she had always
disliked the extremely low neckline of the dark-blue silk, and
the sapphire set that was brought up to her room from the
vault was much too vulgar for her to approve. She donned the
required costume without a word, however, for she was
careful to accede to Alvin's wishes whenever she could, even
though his taste warred with her own.

When she entered the drawing room, she found her husband beaming in quite his old way, his fat hand resting on the
arm of a blond gentleman of about thirty years of age who
showed a remarkable resemblance to their earlier caller, though
his face was more lined with dissipation and his blue eyes
were colder. He did not seem at all concerned by his inappro-
priate riding breeches and boots, even when he saw his
hostess so lavishly attired, but as she came forward, his
indifferent eyes grew keener as he stared at her, taking out his
quizzing glass to look her up and down with a connoisseur's
eye.

"May I present my wife, the Lady Patricia, m'lord?" Mr.
Biddles asked in a tone of plummy satisfaction. "M'dear,
here is Louis Granford of Suffolk come to stay with us."

"M'lord," Patricia said in a formal voice, curtsying and
holding out her hand, her eyes growing indignant at his
continued, leisurely inspection of her person. She felt as if he
were undressing her garment by garment, and she concentrated on standing very straight and still.

"But, m'lady, what an unexpected treat, why, I had no

idea," he murmured as he took her hand and raised it to his lips for a lingering kiss.

Patricia wished she might snatch it away, but a quick glance at her husband showed him smiling and nodding, and her heart sank. Obviously Lord Granford was meant to be Mr. Biddles' latest means to gain success, using her as the sweetener of the scheme.

"Exquisite, sir," Lord Granford said finally, turning to his host. "You are to be congratulated on having such a beautiful wife. I do not think I have seen her equal in many a year."

He turned again to subject Patricia to another head-to-toe leer. "No, I am quite sure the lady is *sans pareil*. By that, of course, I mean she is peerless, sir, for I am sure you have no French."

"My thanks, m'lord," Mr. Biddles replied, ignoring the thrust as he poured his guest a glass of sherry. "Patsy is Lord Westerly's daughter. Are you acquainted with him?"

"I know him, of course, but I am more a contemporary of his son Harry. I shall be delighted to tell you all the news of your brother, m'lady, in case he has not written to you lately. Mmmm . . . well, perhaps not *all* his news."

Since Harry never wrote to her except to beg her to get Mr. Biddles to send him the odd hundred pounds, Patricia was forced to nod and try to look agreeable to such a treat.

By the time all the courses of the elaborate dinner and the various wines had been consumed, she was feeling very angry as well as very disturbed. Lord Granford had let her know, with many a *double entendre* and whispered aside in his light drawling tenor, just what he thought of her and her husband, and just what he wished he could do about the situation. His glance went often to the low neckline of her gown, openly admiring the display of her half-concealed, creamy breasts, and after looking at Mr. Biddles' delighted expression, Patricia could hardly force herself to make a show of eating, she was so disgusted.

It was obvious that her husband had captured his own candidate since Patricia refused to bring one home with her from Bath, and she knew that this time he would tolerate no opposition on her part. She would be forced into Lord Granford's company every waking moment, until Mr. Biddles was sure m'lord was besotted enough for him to use the man to gain his own aims. Patricia knew that Lord Granford was not the type to fall in love or even treat her with the respect due her station, and she could see that her indifference and coldness were merely serving to pique his interest. As she rose to leave the men to their port, she saw his eyes linger on her breasts as he assured her such loveliness would not be left alone for long.

She paced up and down the drawing room, pausing now and then to stare down into the flames of the fire the footman had lit to take away the slight chill of the evening. She did not have the slightest idea of what she was to do, and she knew she was treading a very narrow, dangerous path. On the one hand there was her husband, all complacent agreement to her having an affair with Lord Granford, and on the other there was the man himself, all eagerness to accept this unexpected but welcome form of country entertainment. Somehow she must hold him at arm's length without Mr. Biddles' knowledge. She wondered how long he would stay with them, hoping that at least his visit would be of short duration.

When the men came back to the drawing room, she was seated at the piano, softly playing a Chopin nocturne, and although Mr. Biddles did not care for music, this evening he allowed her to continue when Lord Granford expressed a wish to hear her play. Even so, it seemed an age before Ames came to remove the tea tray and she could go up to her rooms, leaving them to enjoy a last snifter of brandy. Mr. Biddles had been quick to make plans for her to take m'lord on a tour of the estate in the morning, and Lord Granford had shown himself all eagerness to fall in with the scheme.

She wore one of her most severely cut habits the next morning, but even covered to her collarbone, she felt naked again when Lord Granford's eyes raked her body. As he came to toss her into the saddle, she tried not to flinch when she felt his hands pressing her waist so intimately, and sliding up her leg above her riding boot as he pretended to adjust her stirrup.

As they rode away down the drive, Mr. Biddles waving to them cheerfully, she decided she must take a direct approach. "I fear you have been mistaken in me, m'lord," she began. "I do not expect or welcome these close attentions that you give me so unceasingly."

"Indeed?" Lord Granford queried in his light drawl. "But how can I stop enjoying such beauty, Lady Patricia, espe-

cially when I am bidden to the banquet by none other than
your husband himself?''

He chuckled as her face paled. ''You are caught on the
horns of a dilemma, are you not, sweetheart? As an obedient
wife you are forced to follow Mr. Biddles' lead no matter
what your own inclinations might be. Perhaps sometime you
will tell me why he is throwing you at my head; it is most
incomprehensible. But stay! Perhaps the man is at heart a
maquereau?''

Patricia refused to meet his eye, the elegant cameo of her
profile stiff with distaste. ''You are mistaken, sir,'' she
repeated, ''and I have no intention of allowing you any
further liberties. You have been warned.''

''We shall see, shall we not? I look forward to the outcome,''
he murmured, and then to her relief, he changed the subject
by asking her if she cared to canter.

For three long days and nights, Lord Granford remained at
Biddles Hall. Patricia kept him at bay with light, casual
conversation, a coldness of expression and scornful stares
when he dared too much, and a desperate game of hide-and-
seek whenever she was forced to it. Lord Granford might
look for her in the gardens to find she had gone to the kitchen
to confer with the cook, and if he came to her own rooms,
her maid was always in attendance. When they went out
riding, nothing he said could induce her to dismount. He
seemed more amused by these tactics than offended, for there
was a definite air of the hunter about him, an adversary who
knew he would succeed in the end, no matter how long she
fenced with him, and it made her uneasy. Mr. Biddles frowned
at her, his fat lip pouting at her reluctance to further the
affair, but with Lord Granford in residence, there was no way
for him to charge her directly to do as he wished. He even
refrained from coming to her room at night after his noble
guest had gone to his bed, perhaps fearing an untimely
interruption.

The last night before Lord Granford was to leave, Patricia
went up early, claiming a headache and trying to quiet the
uneasiness she felt still. By tomorrow he would be gone, so
why didn't she feel relief that her strategy had worked? she
wondered.

After she had dismissed her maid, she wandered over to
the large windows facing the terrace and opened one slightly

to breathe in the warm, scented air, and then she stiffened. She could smell the smoke of Mr. Biddles' cigarillo and hear his voice and that of his guest as they strolled up and down.

"Come now, Biddles, what is it you have to say to me?" Lord Granford was asking, his drawl impatient. "You forced me to remain here as your guest by hinting of an advantageous deal, but I warn you, I am off tomorrow. Out with it!"

"Aye, I have a deal for you, m'lord," her husband's gruff voice said slowly. "It is a proposition to both our advantage."

"How coarse of you to come right out with it, sir," Lord Granford replied. "I assure you it is not necessary; I understand you very well."

"How can that be when I have not told you of it yet?" a bewildered Mr. Biddles inquired. "But I know you will be glad of it when you hear it."

"Oh, I am more than glad, I assure you. Such a delicious plum would be difficult for any man to refuse."

Patricia held her breath and leaned closer to the window as her husband continued, "What I propose is this, m'lord. I will cancel your debt to me, aye, and the interest as well, if you will sponsor me in the *ton*. Mind now, I mean to get good value for my money, so do not be thinking you can chouse me out of it with a paltry dinner or two with your wild friends, or a visit to your estate with no one of importance invited."

There was silence for a moment, and then Lord Granford said, "You disappoint me, really you do. I thought you had something quite different in mind, something much more enticing. To this proposition, however, I can give you an immediate reply. The answer, Mr. Biddles, is an unequivocable no. I would not back you in the *ton* for all the money in England, not even if it were possible for me to do so. I may owe you a fortune, but someone like you cannot use even that to force my friendship. I would rather sponsor a toad."

"Here now!" Mr. Biddles exclaimed. "Watch what you say there or I will make it hard on you, sir! I can call in your notes, you know, anytime I like."

"I believe I still have a month to repay you?" Lord Granford asked as if he were not much interested in the reply.

There was a short pause, and then Mr. Biddles said more calmly, "You go away and think about what I have proposed,

and when you come back in thirty days, I will expect a more
agreeable reply.''

"I am forced, of course, to do as you say, but I beg you
not to order any Court dresses for your beautiful wife in the
interim. My reply will not change.''

"Aye, Patsy is beautiful, is she not, m'lord? I have seen
your eyes on her and I have no doubt you will be glad to
renew your acquaintance with her at least, perhaps even more
intimately then,'' Mr. Biddles crowed, his good humor restored.

"I am a rake and a scoundrel, sir, but even so, I am not
your equal,'' Lord Granford told him, his light drawl scornful.
"However, I must admit I am depraved enough to consider
this *new* offer seriously. I believe we understand each other.
Oh, one other thing. Keep well away from my brother Sidney.
At twenty-two he is still a member of the infantry and I do
not want to have to rescue him from your clutches, young
lobcock that he is. I leave at dawn, so give my regards and
my thanks for a pleasant stay to your wife. For now, I bid
you good-bye.''

Patricia heard him stride away as her husband called after
him, "Thirty days, m'lord, you have thirty days!'' Then she
heard him mutter to himself, "And when you return and
make love to Patsy, I'll blackmail you into sponsoring me—
aye, so I will, even if I have to have your younger brother
thrown into debtor's prison to force your hand.''

Patricia waited to hear no more, but ran back to her bed to
cower under the covers in horror.

It was a long time before she was able to sleep, and when
she came down late the following morning, it was to find that
Lord Granford had left the hall as planned. In order to avoid
her husband, she ordered the carriage to take her to Bath for
the day, and so she was not at the hall when her father, the
Marquess of Westerly, arrived unexpectedly that afternoon.
At least her absence spared her from having to hear him
begging his son-in-law for yet more money.

The marquess was some five years older than Mr. Biddles
and completely unlike him in any way. He was tall and
aristocratic and lean, but on his thin cheeks the life of un-
checked indulgence he had led was plain for all to see. The
whites of his faded blue eyes were yellow-tinged, and those
eyes were set in heavy, dark pouches, and the broken veins in
his hawklike nose were fiery red. His hands had developed a

noticeable tremor, and even though he had once been a fine-looking man, now only the wreck of his handsome youth remained.

Mr. Biddles received him in the library, sitting behind his massive desk and enjoying the plight of the Marquess of Westerly forced to stand before him and plead. For a change, his face wore a contented smile, although his little brown eyes were cold as he listened.

"Dammit, man, I must have more money," Lord Westerly concluded. "I'm about under the hatches, for the cards have gone against me this age, and the horse I was counting on to put all right was unplaced at the last moment at Newmarket. You see how it is."

"Aye, I see how it is, all right," Mr. Biddles sneered, "and I'll not throw good money after bad again, m'lord."

"But how can you allow a member of your family to be thrown into prison, sir?" the marquess demanded, wishing his son-in-law had the courtesy to ask him to sit down and to offer him some wine or brandy. His throat was growing dry with his supplications and his nervousness.

Mr. Biddles chuckled and clasped his fat hands before him on his desk. "You're not a member of my family, thank heavens," he said brutally. "You can go to the devil in a handbasket for all I care."

"But . . . but you are married to my daughter, Patricia," the marquess persisted. "Surely your affection for her must extend to her father."

"Well, now, m'lord, to be plain, my affection for the lady is not what it once was. No, indeed. I fear I made a bad mistake when I took her to wife, for I find she does not answer in the slightest."

"How can this be possible? You were mad to have her only seven years ago. In fact, you were so besotted that even the huge sum of money it cost you did not matter."

"Since then I have found out that the Lady Patricia is of no use to me. I have asked her time out of mind to help me gain the ranks of society, but she will not do it. So much for wifely obedience!"

Stunned, the marquess took a seat by the fireplace without permission and looked longingly at the decanters on the table nearby as he racked his brain for some answer to this unbelievable complaint. Of course Patricia could not bring the old

fool to popularity; no one could. Didn't the man realize that
he was offensive to anyone of rank, indeed, even to anyone
with the slightest bit of culture and refinement? He could
spend his entire fortune, but it would never win a moment's
acknowledgment from anyone in the *ton*.

"How can this be, Alvin?" he asked as if he were genu-
inely confused. "What has she refused to do? I am afraid I do
not understand."

"I have tried and tried to get her to dally with any number
of young men in the peerage, for I know that once she has
them entangled by her charms, they must, out of a desire to
be near her, promote my suit. Why, just these last few days I
had Lord Granford to stay, and he was mighty taken with her.
But did she encourage him? No, sir! Instead, she acts as if I
were some kind of lower being, and seems to feel I should be
grateful that she has even bestowed her hand to me. Let me
tell you, m'lord, I require more of a wife than just a pretty
widgeon wearing my jewels and gracing my table and my
bed."

Mr. Biddles' face was growing redder as he recalled his
grievances, and settling again into lines of discontent as he
continued, "But instead of missing her friends and her own
kind, she seems content to live retired from the world. Well,
I am not! It was not for the life of a country squire that I paid
you all those thousands, and now it is useless for you to ask
me for more. You, sir, are a rake and a gambler, a man of no
substance and little sense, and your precious daughter is a
failure and useless for my purpose. I made a bad bargain, one
of the few bad bargains in my lifetime, and remembering it
does not inspire me to open my purse again."

"Easily over the ground there, sir," the marquess implored,
his face white with indignation at this brutal speech. "Perhaps
if I spoke to her, it might recall her to her duties."

Mr. Biddles leaned forward, thinking hard. "Aye, that
might do the trick," he said slowly. "She must have some
sort of family feeling for you. After all, she did marry me at
your order. Maybe if her father tells her to do my bidding,
she might be more agreeable. Do what you can, and if there
is a marked change in the lady, I'll see you don't suffer for it
this time."

Biddles got up then and rang the bell to terminate the
interview, and when Ames arrived, he asked him to escort the

marquess upstairs and have the housekeeper prepare one of the guest bedrooms.

"And, Ames, tell Lady Patricia when she returns that she is to go to her father at once," he added as the butler was bowing the marquess from the room.

When Patricia came in some time later and learned that her father was waiting for her in the drawing room, she paused only to remove her hat and gloves before she went to him, feeling grateful that he had come and now would be able to save her from this new and disastrous problem. She tried not to think about the trouble he must be in to bring him here, and how much it would cost Mr. Biddles this time. She found him reading a journal, a half-empty decanter by his side and a full glass in his hand. He rose as she came forward to curtsy, her eyes wary as she noted the stern expression on his wasted face.

"You may kiss me, child," he ordered, and she complied lightly before she took the seat across from him.

"Whatever has brought you into the country, Papa?" she asked, her clear eyes never leaving his. "Can it be that you had a longing to see me again?"

"Of course I am delighted to see you, my dear, but you are well out of leading reins, and so I will not try to flummery you. I came to see Mr.—ah, Alvin, on a matter of business."

"In Dun Territory again, Papa?" she asked casually. "Or perhaps it is for Harry or John you have come to intercede? No, how silly of me. You never bother to seek their ends, being much too busy trying to accomplish your own."

"You have grown pert, Patricia," her father reprimanded her with a haughty stare. "Have a care or you will become known as a shrewish backbiter. My business with your husband is none of your concern. I find, however, I am required to be concerned about you."

"Indeed?" she murmured, looking amazed at this first bit of interest in her in seven years.

"Yes, I am most distressed to hear from your husband that you are not the conformable wife he had every right to expect."

"Do you mean I am not carrying out my part of the bargain, Papa?" she asked, her tone still light but now with an edge to it that Lord Westerly thought prudent to ignore. "But having bestowed my hand on Mr. Biddles, serving as

his wife and hostess, and never denying him his rights, I feel
I have more than complied with the terms of my marriage.''

"You have not obeyed him as you should, Patricia,'' her
father said before he tossed off his wine and poured himself
another glass.

"I see Alvin has spoken to you in some detail, sir. But
perhaps he did not make it plain exactly what he wished me
to do. No, he cannot have told you that, but I shall, for then I
am sure you will agree with me that obedience in this instance is not possible.''

She paused, and at her father's condescending nod, she
continued, "In the beginning when Mr. Biddles wished me to
attach some young peer, it was only to be a light flirtation.
Indeed, before we married he told me he would ruin you
without a qualm if he ever found out I was planning to leave
him or had taken a lover. Now, however, he has changed so
much that sometimes I think him insane! From a casual affair
of smiles and stolen kisses, he insists I sell myself by taking
some peer into my bed in exchange for his agreement to
sponsor Mr. Biddles' social ambitions. The latest candidate is
Lord Granford of Suffolk, who is to return here in a month
and collect his prize. Imagine, Papa! The Lady Patricia
Westerly, who is descended from Norman royalty, to be a
common demirep for the likes of Alvin J. Biddles, moneylender!''

She sounded so indignant that for a moment Lord Westerly
did not try to dissuade her. "Put like that, it does sound very
bad, Patricia," he said at last. "But you are unduly disturbed
and taking the affair much too seriously. I must beg you to
reconsider your hasty words. What Mr. Biddles is asking of
you is no more than most married women do, time out of
mind. It is quite in the accepted mode, you know, to take a
lover, or even several of them, and when a man gets to be
Alvin's age, he cannot expect a wife to produce his son
before she begins her philandering. Besides, after all these
years with him, you are entitled to indulge yourself. Why, I
never for a moment expected you to remain faithful to such as
he. And think how much you will enjoy liaisons with some
pretty beaux of your own station in life. Lord Granford, from
what I know of him, is a handsome man and sure to be an
accomplished lover. This shrinking modesty you parade is
absurd. What can it matter now? You are not a virginal miss,

but a married woman. Besides, Alvin will be pleased, and we can all go on more comfortably and serenely."

Patricia broke in then to say in disbelief, "Papa, you cannot mean it, not when I have told you how offensive such behavior is to me! Oh, say you will take my part and explain to Mr. Biddles why I cannot, I *will* not sink to such a low. Please, I beg you!"

"I would look a fool if I did, and I dislike playing the fool," her father replied coldly. "I expect your obedience to your husband in this and every other instance, daughter, just as I expected your obedience to me before your marriage."

Patricia rose to her feet, staring at her father as if she had never seen him clearly before. Her fists were clenched in the folds of her gown, and her violet eyes flashed her scorn and defiance, until his ravaged face flushed with a dimly admitted shame.

"I never thought I would ever hear such a thing from you," she said quickly, her voice bitter. "When you forced me to marry him, I was only a young girl, heartbroken that I must make such a distasteful sacrifice for your sake, but I am not nineteen now, Papa. No matter what you say, or what Alvin may do to me, I will have no part in such ill-bred, cold-blooded baseness."

"Control yourself, daughter!" the marquess thundered, in quite the old way that used to set her heart to fluttering with fear and make her quick to obey him. Now, she noted, the noisy order had no effect on her at all. He could thunder and bully all he liked, she was not bound even by ties of blood to make any more sacrifices for such a man. She had known all her life that he was unscrupulous, but she had not thought him dead to all honor, and she had tried to believe that, in his own way, he loved her. When she was small, he had treated her to a casual fondness, as long as she did not inconvenience him in any way, and she had tried hard to be a model daughter. Brought up by her nanny and a governess after her mother's death, and then sent away to school until she was of an age to benefit him by marrying money, she had seen very little of him, but through all those growing years she had held on to the belief that, deep inside, he loved her. Now she knew that he never had. He did not care what happened to her or how she might suffer; he only wished to use her, over and

over again, for his own advantage. What she had mistaken
for simple weakness was, in reality, evil.

She tried to compose herself as he said, ''That you are not
yourself is plain to see. I suggest you go and change for
dinner, since your husband still insists on an early repast. To
be sitting down to a hearty spread at five in the afternoon is
absurd, as I am sure you agree, but cits are not like us.''

He paused, as if wondering how the subject had changed
so dramatically, and then he added in a sterner voice, ''We
shall speak of this again, daughter, when you are not in such
a dangerous and disobedient mood. In the meantime, I suggest you reflect on your obligations, not only to your husband,
but to your father and your name as well.''

Patricia stared at him for a long moment, and then she
turned and left the room, for the first time in her life neglect-
ing her filial curtsy.

The marquess sighed and poured himself more wine before
he went to report to his son-in-law that he had made a
beginning, but that Patricia would need several more of his
fatherly lectures before she was brought to see reason.

His mouth thinned in a petulant line. He had no desire to
cool his heels at Biddles Hall, in company with that common
creature who had married his daughter, and little wish to
threaten or cajole the scornful puritan that his daughter had
turned out to be; in fact, he wondered how he could ever have
sired such a prude, but he was so desperate for money that he
knew he would have to remain for as long as it took to bring
Patricia to her senses.

7

The only time that Patricia had any peace in the days that followed was before noon, for her father considered the morning hours suitable only for servants, cits, and farmers. When he had been shaved and dressed at last, he would descend the stairs at a languid pace, greet the butler with a condescending nod, and then wander into the breakfast parlor, where he invariably began his day with a bumper of ale. During the afternoons, however, he followed his daughter around, renewing his campaign, until it was time to dress for dinner.

Some semblance of reluctance to discuss the affair openly before Patricia and her father stayed Mr. Biddles' tongue at the dinner table, and as the marquess never spoke of private matters before the servants, she was free there as well, although the effort to make innocuous conversation and eat her dinner under two pair of accusing eyes was a severe trial to her.

After dinner, Mr. Biddles went immediately to his library to leave the coast clear for the marquess, who, when he joined her in the drawing room, again subjected her to many a stern lecture on her willfulness, complete with loud threats that he interspersed with fervent, humble pleading that was so unlike him that it made her head spin. The marquess, who by this time of the day was always in his cups, often ended the evening by weeping into his brandy snifter, bemoaning the ingratitude of his only daughter in a sad, quavering voice, and then at last she was able to escape to bed.

She began to lose weight, for all her appetite had left her, and since she was having trouble sleeping and suffering disturbing dreams when she did so, she became so nervous that the slightest noise caused her to start up, her violet eyes dazed. One afternoon after she had been out driving with her father, all the while subjected to his ranting sermon, and was still stubborn in her refusal to consider Mr. Biddles' proposition, the marquess lost his temper. After she stepped down from the phaeton, he slapped her and then he shook her so hard that her bonnet fell off. When he let her go, she stumbled away from him, dizzy and confused, and slipped to the ground in a faint.

By the time she had been carried into the hall and revived with some difficulty, the marquess was disturbed, and even Mr. Biddles spoke of summoning a doctor if such an event should recur.

The letter that came the next day from her grandmother, Lady Eliza Darrow, was a welcome relief to Patricia. In it, the elderly lady wrote of her failing health and begged her to come for a long stay. Patricia, who was spending the day in bed after her unusual faint, reread this invitation with a tiny gleam of hope. She knew she would do anything to escape the hall for even a little while, but she saw no way she could gain permission to go unless she promised to comply with her husband's ultimatum when she returned. Since she had no intention of doing so, she stared out her window with unseeing eyes that were dark with misery at her helplessness.

All day she pondered the problem. She had to get away, for she felt as if her reason was leaving her, and she knew that the longer she remained at the hall and was browbeaten and manipulated by both men, the sooner she would break, and in a desire for any sort of peace, be tempted to give in to their demands.

At last she decided she would go down to dinner and at least mention the invitation, but she would not allow her maid to fuss over her toilette this evening, having no heart for such a show. When she came into the drawing room, her hair was severely arranged and her face pale. The marquess came to lead her to a chair, studying her carefully. Patricia had never been robust, even as a girl, but now she looked frail and on the edge of collapse. Her violet eyes were huge in her thin face, and he could see it was only a matter of time before she succumbed to a breakdown, either of nerves or of health. He did not feel at all ashamed of his own contribution to her condition, only regretful that she was not made of sterner stuff, for if she became ill she would be useless to help him out of his difficulties.

He poured her a glass of wine and made her finish it, telling her it would make her feel better, and he escorted her to the dining room himself, stressing the importance of making a good meal.

Patricia was not fooled by this sudden kindness. She had seen the dismayed look on his lined face when she came in, and knew his thoughts very well, and she tried not to shudder.

Over the turkey and ham fritters removed with an oyster pie, she mentioned her grandmother's invitation.

"I feel I should go to her, Alvin, for if she is ill, she needs me," she said as calmly as she could.

"And what good do you think you would be to her, Mrs. Biddles?" her husband sneered, waving his fork. "She's more likely to pop up out of her sickbed and insist you get into it, so worn to a thread as you appear. No, a visit is out of the question. Besides, such treats can only be granted to docile, agreeable wives."

Patricia bowed her head over her plate, disappointed even though she had fully expected such an answer, but then support came from an unexpected quarter.

"I think you ought to reconsider such a hasty decision, Alvin," the marquess said in his most top-lofty tone as he tried to avoid the sight of his son-in-law shoveling oyster pie into his mouth. "Patricia is not well, that is true, but a visit to her grandmother might do her a world of good." He nodded to where his daughter sat, her head lowered again and her face drooping in disappointment, as if to say, "What man would want her now?"

Mr. Biddles appeared much struck by this argument as the marquess continued, "And then, when she returns to the hall in a month or so, after having all that time to think and reconsider, I am sure she will be in a more amiable state of mind. Isn't that so, my dear?"

Patricia looked up to see Mr. Biddles regarding her with suspicion and doubt, and without a moment's hesitation, she said, "I shall certainly think of it, yes, for I find I need some time by myself for serious reflection."

"There, you see, Alvin. Sometimes a little space between husbands and wives does wonders, and it is most important that Patricia regain her health. Since Lady Darrow's estate is near Kingsfold, not too far south of London, I will be able to ride out every now and then and check on her health and, er other matters as well.''

"I'll not have her gone for a month." Mr. Biddles pouted, waving his empty wineglass at his butler. "No, if she does go—and mind you, I have not made up my mind to it—she must be back here in three weeks. Lord Granford returns then, you take my meaning, madam?''

Patricia nodded, not daring to look at him for fear the loathing in her eyes would cause the scheme to come to nothing.

"In that case, she should make haste," the marquess said evenly as he watched with avid eyes as the butler also refilled his glass with deep red claret. "Will it take you long to prepare for the journey, daughter?''

"No, I am sure I can be ready to travel in two days' time," Patricia said, her hands clasped tightly under the table. "I must write to Grandmother, of course, telling her of my arrival, and there are a few things I need to do here, but by Thursday I can be on my way.''

'Excellent,'' the marquess said as if the matter was all settled. "Can you spare a carriage, Alvin, or is she to go post chaise?''

"Of course I can spare a carriage, and one of the first stare, too. None of those nip-farthing hired vehicles for Alvin J. Biddles! And she shall take her maid and a footman with her, as well as the coachman. Lady Darrow shall see that a Biddles knows how to do things in the high kick of fashion,'' he bragged, and Patricia caught her breath in a little gasp of relief that the smoothness of her father's unlooked-for assistance had paved the way for her escape.

She barely heard his instructions and lectures that evening, for she was busy thinking of all she had to do. Besides setting her maid to packing and writing to her grandmother, she intended to write to Lady Sylvia as well, telling her where she was going and the obvious reason why, and thanking her for all her kindness. She knew she must be careful not to let anything slip of the true state of her affairs. She did not know if Guy had taken ship for the Aegean yet, and she did not want his aunt to write to him about her if he had not.

Even so, when Lady Sylvia received the letter early that Thursday morning, she frowned over it. Although she had never had one from her young friend before, this sounded so unlike Patricia that she was alarmed. It was so stiffly formal that even the words of gratitude for all the lady's goodness and friendship sounded wooden and contrived. Lady Sylvia tried to put her uneasiness from her mind, but when she continued to think of the letter off and on for most of the day, she knew she would have to write to Guy. She was sure there was something wrong, and he deserved to know. He had sent her a short note only this past week, saying he was remaining in England indefinitely, having canceled his tour of Greece, and although he did not explain his actions further, she was sure it had something to do with his feelings for Lady Patricia.

After she had written to him and given the letter to her companion to post, she thought to look in her atlas. Kingsfold, the village near Lady Darrow's estate, was not even a day's ride from River Court, being less than twenty-five miles across the Downs, an easy distance for Guy if he chose to visit the lady. She felt a twinge of alarm at what she had done. She did not want to make things more difficult for either one of them, and perhaps putting temptation in their way was not a kindness after all. At last she shrugged. They were adults, and they had behaved so well up to now that she must continue to trust that their good sense and restraint would continue as before.

Patricia set out early Thursday morning, trying to control her features so that nothing but a concern for her grandmother's health would be apparent as she bid her husband good-bye. Her father had made the supreme sacrifice of rising at eight so he could follow her carriage in his own phaeton, for he wanted to lose no time escaping from Biddles Hall, and to that end he had offered to see Patricia safely to the gates of Darrow Manor.

The marquess had acquired enough money from his son-in-law to stave off his most persistent creditors, in thanks for his assistance so far and in expectation of a successful conclusion, and he was feeling a bit more before with the world. He knew, however, that if Patricia did not return prepared to play the seductress, Mr. Biddles would not finance him further, and he was careful to reinforce all his previous arguments each evening in the inns where they stayed overnight to break their journey. Patricia bore it all much more patiently than she had in the past, for she knew she would be free of him in a short time.

In spite of his assurances to her husband that he would ride out and see her in Kingsfold, she was sure that once he regained the delights of London, the clubs and gambling hells, the cockfights and horse races—with a little money in his pocket, besides—he would be seen no more.

Then, too, she knew her grandmother had never cared for the man her daughter had married, for she had been quick to sever all relations with him at her death. The only time since then that she had so much as acknowledged his existence was in a strongly worded letter she had written when she learned he had betrothed Patricia to Mr. Biddles. Patricia had never seen that letter, but she had heard her father's thundering oaths and imprecations and seen how his face had grown white with rage at the old lady's assessment of his morals and character. Lady Darrow was well known to be a woman who called a spade a spade.

Although she knew her grandmother could not help her escape the marriage, it had warmed Patricia to know that she cared enough for her to take her degenerate son-in-law to task for what he planned to do. And although Lady Darrow was delighted to welcome her granddaughter, she would not receive the marquess at the manor any more than she would have Mr. Biddles, and he knew it. No, the Marquess of Westerly could be counted on to remain in town throughout her stay.

When Lady Darrow first saw Patricia, she was horrified at her appearance. Her granddaughter had always been slim, but now she was so slight that the bones in her delicate face were clearly visible. The skin that covered them was almost translucent in its paleness, and her violet eyes had lost their sparkle and were sad and resigned. Lady Darrow pretended to accept the girl's explanation that she had been trotting too hard and only needed a few days' rest to see her right again, but she was determined to find out why Patricia was so miserable.

Glad she had been able to placate her grandmother so easily, Patricia settled down at Kingsfold, and if she could not be happy, at least she was more content with her lot there. She fetched and carried for her grandmother, amused her with stories of Bath, read the latest romance aloud to her, and listened to all her ramblings about her ill health with perfect patience. She saw no one else and, outside of a few strolls around the grounds, remained secluded. Lady Darrow, who was in her early seventies, lived much retired from the world, and Patricia could only be glad that this was so, for she was not in the mood for parties or company. When she was alone, she spent the time thinking of Guy, trying to ignore the pressing problems in her own immediate future until such time as she was forced to deal with them. She knew this was cowardly, but she did not feel able to make any firm decisions until she had regained her strength.

Lady Darrow waited as patiently as she could for Patricia to open her budget, and as the days passed and the time for her to return to Biddles Hall came closer and closer, she began to think she would be forced to tax the girl with it directly.

And then one afternoon, only a week before her granddaughter was to leave, Lady Darrow's patience was rewarded. Patricia had been for a walk in the home woods, and when she came in, she found her grandmother in the salon, working on some needlepoint, which she was quick to put away.

"The walk has done you good, my dear," she said as she folded her canvas. "In fact, you are vastly improved from the pale thread that arrived here only two weeks ago. I wish you could stay longer."

Patricia flushed, but Lady Darrow did not notice, for she was searching for her copy of the romance they had been reading together every afternoon. "Now where did the dratted thing go?" she muttered, pushing her workbasket to one side and overturning a pile of yarn. "I am so anxious to discover what happens to poor little Deirdre and the wicked count in the next chapter, aren't you?"

Patricia took a deep breath and clasped her hands to hide their trembling. "If you would not mind, Grandmother, today I would like to tell you a true story, instead. It is a romance too, but the ending has yet to be written."

Lady Darrow looked at her keenly, her faded blue eyes intent in her round, rosy face. She was a short little dumpling of a woman who still wore the long side curls of her youth, and it was clear from her good-natured face that she had a kind heart.

She nodded and settled back in her chair, relieved she was to have her granddaughter's confidence at last.

"To begin, there was once a young lady who married at an early age, and much against her own wishes. It is not important to know why she was forced to do this—suffice it to say it was a matter of saving the family name."

Aha, thought Lady Darrow. The horrible Marquess of Westerly and Alvin J. Biddles, I'll be bound!

"The girl was not happy, of course, but she had made a promise and she was determined to keep it. For five long years she did. And then she met a man, a lord, who was everything she had ever dreamed of for a husband. He claimed that he fell in love with her at first sight."

Patricia paused as her grandmother, unable to help herself, sniffed. "I daresay," she remarked in a cross tone, "there is no such thing as love at first sight, child! Men will say anything to get their own way."

"It was not like that. When he discovered that she was married, he was in despair, for he did not want her to be his mistress, he really did want to marry her himself. He confessed his love, accepted her refusal to break her vows, and after only one kiss, he went away."

"How sad," Lady Darrow mourned, changing her mind about the young man's character at once.

"Yes, it was sad for both of them. They saw each other only twice in the next two years, both times by accident. The girl remained with her husband and he kept busy by traveling and estate work. But gradually, her life changed."

Here Patricia paused, and her grandmother leaned forward and asked, "What do you mean, 'changed'?"

For the first time Patricia looked away from Lady Darrow as she said, "Her marriage became impossible to her. Her husband's whole character altered and he began demanding things that she could not, in good conscience, do. She went away on a visit to try and think about her future, but no answers came to help her."

There was a short silence and then Lady Darrow said, "I do not think much of the tale, for there is no happy ending—certainly not if she returns to her husband or even if she leaves him to live estranged."

"Which course would you advise, ma'am?" Patricia asked.

"It would depend on what misery she was subjected to by her husband," the old lady said slowly, and then she sat up straighter as she ordered, "Now, my good girl, enough of these fairy tales. Out with it! What exactly has Mr. Biddles been up to, and who is your young lord?"

Without hesitation, Patricia admitted, "He is Guy Leighton, Viscount Reading of River Court near Arundel."

" 'Pon my soul! I knew his mother and father," Lady Darrow exclaimed. "What does he look like?"

Patricia's eyes grew soft, a fact her grandmother was quick to note. "He is tall and well built with dark hair and the most wonderful gray eyes, and he is very handsome."

"A paragon, to be sure. But come, my dear, you have not told me what Mr. Biddles has been doing to make you so ill, and this I must know."

The story was soon told, and although Patricia tried to censor the worst parts, her grandmother asked very astute questions that soon had her in full possession of the facts, up to and including Patricia's father's part in the affair.

"What horrible monsters!" Lady Darrow exclaimed in tones of loathing. "Of course there is no question of you returning to such a man, and as for your father, I shall give him a piece of my mind he will never forget. You shall remain here with me, my dear. Divorce is out of the question, of course, but nonetheless you will not live with Mr. Biddles ever again. I cannot like the arrangement, no woman of refinement could, and there will be endless speculation and gossip, but anything is better than spending one more second with that unscrupulous, unprincipled commoner."

Patricia felt as if a heavy weight had been lifted from her heart. Then Lady Darrow added, "Perhaps you should let Lord Reading know of your decision, my dear. It is only fair after all the time he has waited for you."

Patricia rose quickly from her chair. "No, no, dear ma'am! He must never know why I left Mr. Biddles, for he would kill him in a moment." Then her shoulders slumped and her voice grew sad. "It would be impossible, in any case, for he is on an extended tour of Greece and I do not know when he will return. I must be grateful, I suppose, that there is no chance he may discover the truth, no matter how I miss him."

At that moment, Guy was reading his aunt's letter. Lady Sylvia had sent it to River Court two weeks earlier, but he had been in London and then in Kent with James and Charlie and had only just arrived home.

As he read his aunt's disquieting words about Patricia, he

knew at last why he had canceled his trip. Every time he had
tried to make the final arrangements and book his passage, a
feeling of unease had come over him to the point that if he
had been a superstitious man, he would have posted back to
Bath at once.

He took the letter into his library while the bustle of
unpacking the chaise and carrying his baggage upstairs
continued, and after he had reread it, he went to the windows and stared out across the river and the Downs in the
direction of Kingsfold. She was there, on this soft June
evening, only a few miles away from him, and her husband
had not accompanied her. He groaned, his mouth setting in a
hard line. Much as he wanted to go to her, he knew he must
not. Instead of getting easier with time, each parting was
harder and more heartbreaking than before. Could he subject
them both to that only because he had a feeling she needed
him?

He paced up and down deep in thought. And yet, it was
not only his own uneasiness. His aunt thought she was in
trouble too. He smoothed out the page again. Yes, look
where she had written, "I know there must be something
wrong, for the letter I had from Patricia was so contrived and
stiff, it could not have been written by her if all was well.
Perhaps you will know what to do, Guy."

He nodded, his mind made up. He would set off at dawn
on horseback, with a saddlebag containing such clothing as
he would need if he had to remain overnight. He seemed to
remember that his mother had known Lady Darrow in a
casual way, so there should be no trouble about gaining admittance to the manor. He did not know how the old lady felt
about her granddaughter's marriage, but because of her previous acquaintance with his family, she would see nothing
wrong in Guy's visit. It would not matter if she did, he told
himself as he went back to the window again, for he was
determined to see Patricia by whatever means he had to
employ.

He arrived at Darrow Manor shortly after noon the following day, and he went to the stables, where he ordered his
horse rubbed down and watered before he strolled up the
gravel drive to the front door of the manor, a rambling old
country house made of rosy brick and set in pretty rose
gardens.

The old butler who admitted him to the hall shook his head and looked morose when Guy asked to see Lady Darrow. Taking the card Guy handed him, he said, "M'lady seldom receives visitors, m'lord, but I will go and inquire."

Guy amused himself in the interim by studying the family portraits with which the wide hall was lined. He had just decided that the young lady in the wide hoop skirts of the last century was no match for his Patricia even with her blond curls and blue eyes, when the butler returned, trying to hide a look of surprise.

"Lady Darrow will see you, m'lord," he announced in a disbelieving voice, and then he escorted Guy to a salon at the back of the house, called out his name in stentorian tones, and bowed himself away.

"How kind of you to receive a complete stranger, Lady Darrow," Guy said as he advanced into the room and then bowed to the plump old lady seated on a satin sofa who was peering at him intently.

"Not so much a stranger as you think, m'lord," she snorted, and then she waved her hand toward the chair opposite. "Sit down. You have come about Patricia, of course. Yes, she is visiting me, but she is not here at the moment. It is just as well; I would like a plain talk with you privately."

Here Lady Darrow straightened up and looked as severe as it was possible to do with her round, good-natured face, and Guy tried to hide his astonishment.

"Patricia has told you about me? About us?" he asked.

"Indeed she has, and a good many things besides," she added darkly, causing Guy to wonder if he was in for a trimming for daring to fall in love with the lady's grand-daughter. There was silence for a moment, and then Lady Darrow shook her head as if she had come to some negative decision, although all she said was "She told me you were on a long journey. How come you to be in Kingsfold?"

"I canceled my trip. Somehow I felt uneasy being away from England at this time," Guy admitted. "And then my aunt, Lady Sylvia Randolph, wrote to tell me Patricia was at Darrow Manor and she believed her to be in some kind of trouble. I could not resist coming to see for myself."

Lady Darrow nodded, not meeting his eyes for a moment, and then she said slowly, "Yes, Patricia has been ill, but she is vastly improved now, as you will see."

As Guy frowned and sat forward eagerly, she added, "Not quite yet, m'lord. You may join us for tea later if you would care to, but for now there are a few matters I wish to discuss with you, and I do not think it prudent for you to see Patricia alone."

Guy settled back into his chair, his feeling of anger at her managing ways changing to amusement when the old lady proceeded to inspect him from the top of his gleaming brown hair down to his equally gleaming boots. "Hmmph!" she said. "You are the complete beau, I see, and you have a look of your father. He was the handsomest man I think I have ever seen. I am inclined to believe that you do love Patricia, for you do not appear to be the kind of man who is accustomed to wait for anything he wants, and yet, according to my granddaughter, you have loved her for over two years."

Guy interrupted her musings. "You may believe that I love her very much, m'lady, so much so that I have decided I will marry no other. My problem of course is that I cannot convince her to leave her husband, distasteful and unprincipled though he may be. She has a very strong sense of her obligations and her duty."

"You would live with her without benefit of matrimony?" Lady Darrow asked sharply. "It is not to be thought of, sir. Why, every feeling must be offended."

Guy felt a flush stain his high cheekbones and he said in a harsh voice, "You mistake my meaning, ma'am. I wish her to divorce her husband and marry me."

"Divorce!" Lady Darrow whispered, now even more shocked. "Impossible! No Darrow has ever been embroiled in a sordid court proceeding."

Guy threw out his hands. "What are we to do, then, ma'am? Would you have us live our lives apart, waiting for Mr. Biddles' demise?"

"What I should say is that you should both forget this unhappy love affair, but it is obvious that course is not possible. And yet I cannot bear to see Patricia so miserable, her life empty and unfulfilled. What is to be done?"

She looked so distressed and confused that Guy hastened to calm her by saying, "Somehow, m'lady, our marriage will come to pass. I have thought so this age, for I cannot believe that fate would be so unkind as to deny me Patricia."

Lady Darrow swallowed another "hmmph!" Men, as she

had known for more years than she cared to think about, were air dreamers. What they wanted, they were sure would be given them, for they believed in fairy tales long after childhood. She hardly liked to call this to the young man's attention, though, for she found herself warming to him. He was not only handsome and devastating in his manner, he had behaved honorably up to this point, and that was to his credit.

In the face of the pleading in his fine gray eyes, she felt herself relenting. Two years was a very long time to be true to a dream, and she suddenly remembered a young lord of her own, and how impatient they had been in the weeks before their marriage. If it was right for William and herself, could it be wrong for these two? She recalled a certain glade in her father's woods and an unused keeper's cottage, and her old eyes grew distant with memory.

These daydreams were interrupted as Guy shifted in his chair, and she straightened her cap and tried to look disapproving. "Hmmph! I do not share your optimism, m'lord, but I find it impossible to deny you at least a few moments alone with Patricia. You will find her on the path through the home woods where I sent her to walk in the fresh air."

Guy rose with alacrity and bowed over her hand. "Thank you, ma'am," he said, his warm smile lighting his face.

She rapped his hand. "As if you would have gone away without seeing her! You do not fool me for a moment, Lord Reading, and so I will have your promise first, if you please."

Guy looked inquiring as she ordered, "It must be a short visit. I shall expect my granddaughter to return to the house in half an hour."

For a moment she thought he would argue the point, but he controlled himself and agreed to her condition.

Outside, he hurried until he reached the woods and started down the well-trodden path that wound through it. Patricia was nowhere in sight, and remembering the short time they would have to be together, he was tempted to call out to her, but then, as he came around a bend in the path, he saw her a little way ahead. She was sitting on a sunlit patch of grass, her head bent over her folded arms, which rested on her drawn-up knees, and her whole posture was one of unhappiness and deep despair.

"Patricia," he called softly so as not to startle her.

She raised her head, but she did not look in his direction,

and when he saw the little smile of disbelief on her lips and the way she shook her head, he called again more urgently, before he went to her.

As he covered the ground between them, she looked his way, and he was shocked at her frail appearance, but then her violet eyes lit up with joy and welcome, and he forgot everything else as he knelt beside her and took her in his arms.

"Guy, my dear," she murmured, "are you really here? I was just thinking of you, so perhaps you are only a dream that I conjured up, after all."

He took her face between his hands and stared down at her, his gray eyes dark with worry. He was about to question her when she put her arms around his neck as naturally as if she did it every day, and raised her face for his kiss.

Her lips were as soft and velvety as he remembered, but now there was no hesitation, only an eager, warm desire for his kiss that made his head spin. He felt her hands caress his neck before they moved to entwine themselves in his dark hair, and he drew her closer still, his own strong hands stroking her slender back. Their kiss deepened and grew more compelling and abandoned, and it was some time before Guy reluctantly raised his head and looked down into her face again. Her eyes were closed, the sunlight glittering in the thick chestnut lashes, touching them with gold; and her face was so pale and still that if he had not seen the little smile playing over her lips, and felt the rise and fall of her breasts as they lay crushed against his chest, he might have thought her in a faint. He stared at her, memorizing her loveliness anew, and then she opened her eyes and they widened with her delight at his nearness.

"My dearest, how wonderful to have you with me," she whispered. "I have missed you so much."

"And I you, my heart," he replied, his voice unsteady, and then he bent and kissed her lightly before he sat down beside her and drew her back into his arms again, her head resting on his chest, his strong arms cradling her close. She sighed and for a moment there was no sound but the beating of their hearts and the soft whisper of the breeze in the leaves above them.

After a moment he asked, "And now, my darling, perhaps you will tell me how you came to be in such a fragile state?"

His tone of voice was normal again, but Patricia could hear the distress behind his demand. She knew she could not tell him the truth, and her mind was searching for an answer when he added, "When I saw you in Bath only a few weeks ago, you were not so thin, so pale. Have you been so ill, then?"

"Yes, I was," she lied, grateful for this clue as she lowered her eyelashes so he could not read anything in her eyes. "That is the reason I have been allowed to visit my grandmother. I am quite recovered now, Guy, and feeling better every day."

"What manner of illness would cause you to lose so much weight and bring about this ethereal air? Besides, when I first saw you sitting here, you were the very picture of despair. What else is wrong?"

His stern voice demanded an answer, and she said quickly, "The doctor said it was a severe case of influenza, but it is not kind of you, sir, to point out how unattractive I am. If I looked despairing it was only that I was feeling tired. I know I am not in my best looks, but—"

His big hand came up to cover her mouth. "Hush, little one! You can never be anything but beautiful to me, but the bloom of health I have always associated with you is gone. You must be quick to regain it, if only for my sake. I could not bear to lose you."

"How did you know I was here, Guy?" she asked, anxious to change the subject.

"My Aunt Sylvia wrote to me after she received your letter. I did not have it to hand until yesterday, when I arrived at River Court, or I would have come to you before now. She was sure there was something wrong and asked me to find out what it could be, so I rode over this morning and made your grandmother's acquaintance. I am glad you told her about me, my heart, and glad you came so willingly into my arms."

Patricia picked a daisy from a clump nearby and twirled it in her hands, her head bent so all he could see was the top of her chestnut curls. "I thought you were on board ship bound for the Aegean, Guy, and I was so surprised to see you that I forgot myself and kissed you. I never meant to do so."

She felt the deep chuckle that began low in his chest and then he said, "I am not a bit sorry, and will not allow you to be so either. One kiss every two years is surely the epitome of abstinence. In fact, now that I have you in my arms at last, I intend to kiss you again.''

She was turned toward him as one finger came to tilt up her chin. He saw that her violet eyes were troubled, and her lips parted to protest, but he did not allow her to speak before he covered her lips with his own.

"Guy, we must not," she whispered when at last he allowed her to speak again, but this time she looked up at him, her eyes still glowing with the desire he made her feel, in spite of her cautious words, and he caught his breath at their beauty.

"My heart, after all this lonely time, I could not help myself. I know I promised you I would accept your decision to remain true to your vows. Forgive me.''

His voice was bitter and sad as he put her away from him and rose to his feet to pace the grass. Patricia stared at his strong back, seeing the way his broad shoulders slumped a little in his despair and how his hands clenched into fists as he strove to control himself. When he turned to face her, his expression was so bleak that she knew suddenly what she must do. Remaining married to Mr. Biddles and true to any of her vows to the man was a travesty of honor. Her husband wanted her to take a lord for a lover, and so she would, but not at all in the way he expected. She would divorce him, and then she would marry Guy. She got up and ran to him, putting an urgent hand on his arm as she said, "No, Guy, I do not ask you to accept my marriage anymore. You must not apologize for your love, nor will I deny my love for you. Perhaps in the eyes of the world our actions will be considered improper and we will be reviled and scorned, but I find I do not care very much what the world thinks. Such a love as we share cannot be wrong, nor should we have to remain apart forever.''

"Patricia," he whispered, "do you mean it?"

"Of course I do, my dear, for I see how wrong now I have been these past two years," she said, her eyes fervent and honest. "Why should we torture ourselves because of convention's demands? I love you and want you as much as you love and want me.''

Guy looked as if he had been given a priceless gift he had thought forever out of his reach. He drew in an eager breath, his gray eyes blazing, and she nodded as if she could read the question in his mind.

"Yes, I will divorce him at once," she said simply, her eyes never leaving his. He took her hand and kissed it, and then he stepped away from her. Her eyes grew puzzled and he could see that his refusal to take her back into his arms and make love to her had confused her. He hastened to press the hand he still held as he looked deep into her eyes.

"My dearest, as much as I want to make love to you here and now, a few stolen moments are not enough for the woman who is to become Viscountess Reading. Your grandmother has only permitted me to see you for a short time, and I promised to obey her ultimatum . . . this time! Tell me, how long before you are supposed to leave the manor?"

"I am expected in Bath no later than the twenty-eighth," she said, her voice subdued.

"And today is only the nineteenth! My love, if I come and stay at the inn at Kingsfold, will you ride out with me every day? We have so many plans to make, and besides, I must see you as often as possible. I give you warning, however, that I have no intention of allowing you to return to Biddles Hall. I intend to persuade you to remain here with your grandmother until such time as we can marry, and I can be very persuasive."

Patricia looked up at that dear, handsome face. All the lines of self-control and denial were gone, and he looked just as he had when he first told her of his love in the woods near the Venetian bridge, young and fervent and eager. She nodded, unable to speak for a moment until she had some semblance of control over her emotions.

He hugged her to him, but she noticed how careful he was to be gentle, and her lips curled in a little smile. Someday soon she would take great delight in showing him she was not as fragile as he seemed to think. And then, held close to his heart, she felt a pang of disquiet.

"But, Guy, how can we meet? Even if my grandmother can be won over, there is still my maid as well as the footman and coachman Mr. Biddles insisted come with me. It would be most unwise if they were to become suspicious."

He held her away from him so he could look into her face. "We must resort to trickery, of course, but it will be for the last time, love, that I can promise you."

Patricia stared up at him. The lean planes of his face and jaw were set in determination, and that sculptured mouth was taut above the strong column of his throat. Her eyes went from his broad shoulders to his narrow waist, down his slim hips and long muscled legs, and she was surprised at the warm tingle of desire that started deep inside her and spread over her body in waves until it reached her fingers and toes. Just looking at him made her feel warm and helpless and unable to solve any of their problems.

"Patricia," he said softly, one eyebrow quirked, "if you look at me like that, I cannot answer for my actions or my promise to your grandmother. Remember, I am only mortal."

She blushed and he laughed at her before he asked, "Could you explain our plans to your grandmother? Would it distress her to know you are meeting me, still a married woman?"

Patricia thought for a moment, pulling the petals from the daisy she held as she did so, and resolutely not allowing herself to drown in his eyes again. "No," she said slowly at last, "I do not think it will upset her after she has time to consider. She is what you call 'a good 'un,' in spite of her age and infirmity. But what of the servants, Guy? I am sure they all spy for Mr. Biddles and he must not learn that you were here with me. He would not hesitate to name you in the divorce and try to ruin you. I could not bear it!"

"Do not be distressed, Patricia. He cannot harm either one of us. But if the servants' presence disturbs you, send 'em away on a holiday. They will not think a thing of it, for you have little use for them here, living as secluded as you do."

Patricia smiled. "How devious you are, love. I never thought it of you, but I can see your plan might work. Tell me, where shall we meet, and when?"

Guy came back and drew her down onto the grass again, one muscled arm holding her tight to his side. "How I wish I could take you to River Court tomorrow! Someone as fine as you are, Patricia, should not be subjected to hole-in-the-corner, clandestine meetings."

She smiled and pressed his arm, comforted that he was so concerned about her feelings. "Much as I long to see your home, Guy, I would rather not go there while I am still Mrs. Biddles."

"You will see it soon enough, and when you do, you will

be my wife in name as well as the wife of my heart, I promise you.''

This fervent statement called for another recess from making plans, but at last Patricia sighed and sat up to reach for her bonnet. ''I must get back to the house or Grandmother will have the servants out to search for us,'' she said reluctantly.

As they strolled back through the woods, they arranged to meet at the bottom of the drive at ten in the morning in two days' time. ''If you are not there, Patricia, I will return at the same time the following day, but try not to disappoint me.''

Her eyes promised she would not, and just before the woods opened up to the lawn and gardens, he took her in his arms and kissed her again. ''No parting between us is ever easy, but this one at least I can bear, for in only a short time we will be together again,'' he said softly. ''My excuses to Lady Darrow, but I know I could not sit in her drawing room calmly sipping tea and engaging in polite conversation—not after what you have just promised me. I will see you in two days, my love!''

Patricia rested her head on his broad chest for a brief moment, and then she ran away across the lawn as if she did not dare to stay another moment.

Guy watched her until she reached the terrace steps and turned to blow him a kiss, and then, with a lighter heart than he had had for two years, he went to reclaim his horse for the ride home.

8

Everything went smoothly and exactly as they had planned, almost as if fate had relented at last. Patricia's maid was delighted to have a chance to visit her sister near London, and the footman and coachman, who had been cooling their heels for the entire visit, were glad of this unexpected bonus of three days' holiday. By the following morning they had all left Kingsfold and Patricia began to breathe more easily.

She had had only a few bad moments with her grandmother. When she told her that Guy had left the manor without staying for tea, the old lady looked affronted, but then, when Patricia announced she was giving her servants leave until such time as she had to return to Bath, Lady Darrow's expression changed to one of profound suspicion. Patricia attempted to explain her meetings with Guy and her plan to divorce Mr. Biddles and marry him, but before she could do so in any detail, Lady Darrow raised an imperious hand.

"I do not care to hear anything about it, Patricia, since I suppose there is nothing I can say that will dissuade you from this disastrous course of action," she said in her most rigid, disapproving voice.

Patricia shook her head. "No, I am quite determined, ma'am," she said in a calm voice. "I am sorry if you feel that what we are going to do is wrong, but not even your censure can keep me from marrying Guy at long last. I love him very much, and we have waited for each other for such a long time. And now that Mr. Biddles has shown his true colors, I feel no reluctance to break my vows. Please try to understand and say you do not condemn us."

For a moment Lady Darrow looked into her serious eyes, noting her air of firm purpose, and she knew there was nothing she could do to change her granddaughter's mind. Deep inside, she admitted to herself she did not even care to try, for in spite of her revulsion for the scandal of divorce touching the family, she was strongly sympathetic to their plight. But all she said in answer was "How can I condemn what I have no intention of knowing, my girl? Of course I quite agree with you that it would be rude not to ride out with your dear schoolfriend, especially since she lives so close by. I wonder we did not think of it sooner."

Patricia's smile was pure happiness and she kissed her grandmother with so much feeling that she knocked the lady's silk cap askew.

The first morning she was to meet Guy, she woke at dawn, and for a long time she lay in bed, conjuring up that dear face and powerful body and remembering his kisses and murmured words of love. She wondered if he was at the inn now, only a few miles away, perhaps, like her, still abed and dreaming of her and their meeting.

At breakfast, her eye on the butler's back as he adjusted a sputtering spirit lamp, Lady Darrow remarked, "How kind of Lady Whitton to send her grooms with her daughter's riding party, child. Be sure and say everything that is proper to her. I am so glad you have this opportunity to be with some lively young people after spending so much time alone with me, even if it is only for these last few days."

Patricia assured her she would do the pretty, her eyes dancing with merriment, for Lady Darrow looked as if she completely believed the situation she had invented to save face.

Guy was already waiting for her at the gate when she arrived shortly before ten, and after exchanging a smile that showed all their delight at being together, they rode off side by side in the bright June sunlight. Patricia had been worried that they might meet someone who knew her, but now that she was with Guy at last, she relaxed, for she felt as if they were both wrapped in a cloak of invisibility. She was amused when Guy would not let her gallop or even canter for long stretches, and when they had been riding only for about half an hour, he suggested they rest for a while, and pulled up his horse beside a wide brook.

Patricia was not in the least tired, but she agreed and slipped down into his arms when he came to help her dismount. He did not put her down but held her close against the long hard length of him, his hands tight on her waist as he bent his head and kissed her. His sun-warmed lips were firm and ardent and all-consuming, and together they were lost in that kiss until Patricia's mare turned her head and nudged them, as if to ask what strange manner of doings these were. Guy set her down then and released her to go and tie the horses to some bushes nearby, and Patricia strolled to a large willow tree that hung over the brook and sank down in the shade on the soft grass beneath it. When Guy came to join her, she was quick to cease her contemplation of the brook as she frowned at him in mock reproof.

"I must protest, m'lord," she said in a severe voice. "You are treating me like an invalid indeed. Such a short ride, and at such a gentle pace—for shame! I am not so delicate as that."

Guy thought she did indeed look better than she had two days ago, but still he was alarmed at her fragility, and the haunted look that lurked deep in her violet eyes, behind their gay sparkle at his nearness.

"I intend always to take the greatest care of you, m'lady, so you had better resign yourself to it," he promised, sitting down beside her and pulling her close against his chest. He was determined to find out the reason for the shadows in her eyes, for he knew influenza would not leave such lingering horror behind it; there must be something more that Patricia had not told him.

But although he probed ever so gently, she turned away all his questions with a casual reply or a careless laugh, and soon he gave up the quest when he sensed she did not want to remember. He had never seen her so merry, or so free in her manner, and her gaiety was so infectious that only a few minutes later he was caught up in the game. He was painfully aware that their meetings had been few and their private moments hurried and quickly over, and now that he had the time and the leisure, he wanted to show her how much he respected her as well as loved her. Lady Patricia Westerly would have the courtship she had always deserved, even though it meant he must wait until their marriage before he made them one. He smiled to himself. Such forbearance would have stunned his friends, and no one in society would have believed he intended to be so restrained and honorable, but now, like Patricia, he found he cared little what the *haut ton* thought.

And so, as the horses grazed in the grass nearby, and the tender branches of the willow tree bent down as if to hide them from sight in a private green world of their own, he did not kiss her or make love to her in such a way that would cause him to forget this vow. He could see the sweet acquiescence in her eyes and feel her tacit consent to anything he cared to initiate in the way she melted against him and caressed his face, but he had his desires firmly under control.

He picked up her left hand then and held it, his brooding eyes staring down at Mr. Biddles' ostentatious wedding band, and when Patricia followed his glance, a question in her eyes, he looked back at her, his face set and serious before he turned away. All she could see was his chiseled profile as he said a little stiffly, "I would ask you, love, to remove your wedding band. From this moment on you are not Mr. Biddles' wife, you are my fiancée, as you were meant to be all along."

As Patricia gladly removed the ornate band, he reached into the pocket of his riding coat and drew out a small velvet box, and her eyes widened as he opened it to disclose a large square-cut diamond ring, the central stone surrounded by rubies and diamond chips.

"This is the Leighton betrothal ring, Patricia," he said as he slipped it on her finger and then took up her hand to kiss. "It is yours, now and for always."

Patricia admired the flashing stones. "It is beautiful, Guy," she whispered, almost as if she were in church. Then she realized that that was just what she felt like, as if they were consecrating their pledge to each other there in the shifting patterns of light and shadow of the willow, while somewhere in a field nearby, a linnet sang the Gloria.

She leaned closer to him and raised her face. He bent down and slowly kissed her lips, a gentle kiss that showed her he felt the solemnity of the moment too, although from the possessiveness that he exhibited, there was no doubt in her mind he was setting this seal on her to mark her as his bride-to-be.

As she tucked Mr. Biddles' ring away in the pocket of her habit, he said, "I am sorry the ring is set with rubies, even though I know the impossibility of finding any sapphires that would be half as beautiful as your eyes. Know I will be looking out for them as soon as I return to town, however."

Patricia was subdued now as she gazed at her ring, for she was unable to quell a little feeling of shyness. Always, from the first time Guy had told her of his love, she had known how serious a commitment he felt, but in giving her the Leighton betrothal ring now, he had demonstrated anew his devotion. She felt a lump in her throat as she vowed silently that she would do her best to be worthy of that love.

Guy would not allow such solemnity to last, and covered her face and lips with light, teasing kisses until she protested she must catch her breath, and then he began to ask her about her childhood and family, her school days and her interests. Patricia was open with her answers now as she had never been when speaking of her marriage, and she seemed to feel there was nothing amiss in the life she described to him. Guy, secretly appalled, thought otherwise. It was plain that she had never had a chance to enjoy a normal childhood or adolescence. After the death of her mother and her father's consequent neglect, she had been raised by servants or abandoned in various schools, so up to and including her disastrous marriage, she had never known fun or laughter or the joy of a close, loving family. Guy vowed he would make it up to her if it took the rest of his life to do so.

He had brought some bread and cheese and cider with him in his saddlebags, and eventually he went to fetch it. When he returned, he found Patricia had fallen asleep, and after he had put the cider in the brook to cool, he sat down close to her where he could watch her face and the gentle rise and fall of her breasts. Besides the soft chuckle of the brook and the drone of bees somewhere nearby, there was no other sound to be heard, and he felt as if they were the only two people in the world and was content to have it so.

Patricia slept for an hour, and then at last those thick chestnut lashes opened and her violet eyes widened when she saw him beside her, patiently waiting. She sat up and leaned toward him to reach for his hand.

"Guy, you should not have let me doze off. We have so little time together I would not waste it sleeping. Why, I—"

"No time with you is ever wasted, love," he assured her. "Besides, soon we will have all our lives to spend together, and of that time a great many hours must be passed in sleep. But of course that will be even more wonderful, for I will have you in my arms."

He watched her eyes grow dreamy as she contemplated this picture, and he went to fetch the cider before he said too much of the delights they would share together.

They ate their country luncheon and Patricia fed the last bits of bread to some eager sparrows. Guy sprawled beside her, hands behind his head as he watched her trying to coax the birds to take some crumbs from her hand. The long afternoon passed quickly, in conversation and laughter, for now it was Patricia's turn to ask him about his past, where he had been and what he had done. Guy told her of it fully, trying to paint a picture for her of the kind of life he hoped they would share. At last, seeing the position of the sun, he sighed and rose and stretched before he held out a hand to pull her to her feet.

"Come, my lazy lady, we must be off or your grandmother will surely deny me the pleasure of your company tomorrow."

He took her in his arms, unable to resist kissing her again, more passionately now. "Do you know how much I adore you, my love? And how much I long to have this time before we can be married pass quickly?" he asked in a deep, husky voice, his warm breath stirring the tendrils of chestnut hair that had escaped her chignon.

Patricia nodded, brimming over with happiness, and then she smiled. "I honor you for it, my dear," she whispered, and he smiled in relief that she understood his motives.

They went to the horses then, Patricia held tight to his side by one strong arm as they made arrangements for tomorrow's meeting. When Guy asked her if she would care to drive out in his phaeton, instead of riding, she was quick to agree. "That way, my heart, I can have you close to me all day," he said as he tossed her into the saddle with a broad grin.

"I shall try very hard not to fall asleep, sir," she said demurely. "How distressing if I should repeat today's nap and tumble into the dusty road."

Guy eyed her across his horse's broad back as he prepared to mount, and one eyebrow rose. "Think you to inform me that my company is boring, ma'am? I shall be on my mettle, never fear."

Patricia laughed and wheeled the mare, and Guy drew his horse alongside for the ride back to Darrow Manor.

The following days continued the happy pattern they had set with this first excursion. When Patricia remembered them

later, they seemed to blend into each other like a kaleido-
scope of impressions: the feel of his lips, his warm, caressing
hands that never showed more ardor than would have been
permissible with a young girl in her first Season, the constant
care and concern he had for her, and especially his smile and
the light that came into his gray eyes when he looked at her.

Patricia found herself watching the changing expressions
on his handsome face with a love she never imagined she
could feel. Sometimes he was serious and determined, and
sometimes lighthearted and devil-may-care, but most of all
she remembered the warm, intent dark glance that told her of
his love and caused her heart to beat alarmingly, stirring that
warm tingle deep in her body she was beginning to associate
with his disturbing nearness.

When he took her out in the phaeton, it was almost as hot
as a day in August, and when Patricia saw a quiet millpond,
some miles from Crawley, she begged him to stop for a while.
When Guy lifted her down, he could see the beads of perspiration on her brow under her broad-brimmed hat, and he begged
her to rest in the shade while he attended to his team. When
he came back to her, he found that she had removed her
sandals and stockings and was seated on the bank, dabbling
her feet in the cool water, her skirts held to one side as she
splashed, and looking about two and ten as she did so. He
tried not to dwell on the sight, but when at last they went
back to the phaeton, Patricia swinging her hat by its ribbons
and still carrying her sandals and hose in her other hand, he
could not resist taking her in his arms and kissing her, she
was so beautiful with the bright sunlight touching her hair
with fiery highlights. Patricia kissed him back, her lips as
eager and demanding as his own, and both of them were
completely unaware of a smart open landau that was bowling
toward them, heading in the direction of Brighton. Some
intuition caused Guy to raise his head at last, and he found
himself looking directly into Clorinda Mills' furious, indignant face as the landau, driven by her husband, drew abreast
and passed.

He was glad that Patricia's face was buried in his coat,
although he knew both Lord and Lady Mills had seen her
plainly and knew very well the identity of the lady he held so
close in his arms. He cursed silently. Clorinda would make
trouble if she could, for he knew she had never forgiven him

for not succumbing to her charms. To have actual proof that
he preferred another woman would be too much for one with
her vindictive nature. He wondered why they were there, for
the Season was still in full swing, and the Prince Regent was
not expected to take up residence in the Royal Pavilion until
the end of the month.

Suppressing his worries, he lifted Patricia to the seat of the
phaeton and ordered her to put on her hose and sandals again.
"You look the complete urchin, madam," he scolded. "And
though it pains me to have to mention it, you now sport
several freckles on your nose."

Patricia only laughed, but as he sprang to his seat and took
the reins from her hands, she bent to do his bidding. Guy
glanced sideways as she pulled her stockings over those
slender, shapely legs, and the sight made him forget Clorinda
Mills at once.

The only time they disagreed during those days was on the
subject of Patricia's determination to return to Bath. In vain,
Guy argued that there was no need for her to leave the safety
of her grandmother's house, for he would be delighted to see
Mr. Biddles himself to explain the situation. Patricia knew he
was trying to shield her, but still she insisted that it was her
place to go.

"I will never spend another night under his roof, Guy, but
I must go back to Bath and tell Mr. Biddles so myself. I
would never be so cowardly as to allow you to do that
chore."

When he protested still and told her he feared she might be
in danger of the man's wrath, she laughed at him. "I plan to
ask Lady Sylvia to go with me. Perhaps she would even be so
kind as to allow me to stay with her. What do you think?"

Feeling easier, Guy promised to write to his aunt at once,
apprising her of both their arrivals, for even if Patricia insisted
on seeing her loathsome husband without his support, he
could not be easy unless he was nearby to assist her if
necessary.

They sat close together holding hands as they made their
plans. Guy knew that Patricia wanted to spare him the indig-
nity of being named correspondent in the *crim. cons.* case,
for she would not allow him to take her to Bath himself,
insisting on going back with Mr. Biddles' servants as planned,
and finally he agreed. Although he was sure Mr. Biddles

would have no trouble finding out his part in this, especially now that they had been seen by Lady Mills, secretly he hoped Patricia would not have to face a charge of adultery, for he was sure that Parliament would grant any lady of high degree a divorce from Alvin J. Biddles just on the grounds of mental cruelty alone.

The days raced by and it seemed no time at all before Patricia was preparing to leave Darrow Manor. Often she wished she had the power to make the clock stand still so she could prolong their meetings, for never had four days seemed so short. Late every afternoon when she came in to kiss her grandmother, Lady Darrow was glad she had not stood in the way of the lovers' trysts, for her granddaughter's face and eyes glowed with luminous happiness, although all she said, almost brusquely, was that if Patricia did not want the world to know what she had been up to, and most especially her own servants, she would cultivate a more sober expression at once.

Patricia tried to school her features to her usual placid acceptance, although she could not help dreaming of Guy, reliving the time they had spent together, and then, in spite of her caution, her eyes would grow soft. She had never imagined there could be such happiness, or thought to know the surge of joy she felt when he smiled at her or kissed her and held her close.

The last day, as they rode back to Kingsfold, it was almost in silence, but it was the silence of two people so perfectly attuned to each other that they did not have to speak to communicate. Sometimes Patricia would look at that dear, chiseled profile with its strong jaw and lean cheeks, and Guy would turn for a moment and kiss her with his eyes.

When they were only a few miles from the manor, she asked him to stop for a moment, and then she removed the Leighton betrothal ring and held it out to him.

"You must take it back now, Guy," she whispered, her voice composed in spite of the ache in her heart. "I shall never wear Mr. Biddles' ring again, but I cannot keep yours on my finger."

"No, I will not take it, love, for it is yours now," he replied just as quietly. "I know you cannot wear it openly as yet, but I wish you to put it on a chain around your neck. It will comfort me to know that not only is it in your possession, it is lying close to your heart. Will you keep it there for me until I can put it on your finger again for all time?''

He leaned forward and kissed her lips—a gentle, undemanding kiss that conveyed all his love and respect and confidence in their future—and she nodded her head, not daring to speak. And then he started his horse in motion again as if he did not dare prolong the agony of their parting. She looked with unseeing eyes at the familiar road ahead as the first few cottages of Kingsfold appeared in the distance. Guy had spoken then of their meeting in Bath, telling her he intended to put up at York House while she was with Lady Sylvia, and promising to call as soon as she sent word of her arrival.

He rode with her as far as the gates of the manor, and he did not linger over their farewell. Oddly, Patricia felt no need to mourn or to cry. Instead, she put up her chin and resolved to be a worthy partner for him. She would not succumb to depression or falter in her plan, and she would guard her feelings until she had told Mr. Biddles her decision.

As her carriage turned into the yard of the inn at Rushall where she and her servants would spend the night before traveling on to Bath the following day, she decided to spend the evening writing Mr. Biddles a letter.

She would have the coachman set her down in Great Pulteney Street with a pair of portmanteaus; her trunks could go on to Biddles Hall in company of the servants. She would send her maid with them, to deliver the letter. She had never liked the woman, for she knew she reported her every move to Mr. Biddles, so it would be no hardship to dispense with her services.

Unbeknownst to her, her maid was glancing slyly at her thoughtful face, wondering again what milady had been up to. She had learned from Lady Darrow's servants that Lady Patricia had changed her routine right after she herself had gone, and had absented herself on long rides and drives, and even though she had been told the story of the old schoolfriend, she was still suspicious. Why had the lady removed her wedding ring? The maid's sharp eyes had noticed its absence at once, and had seen the large diamond and ruby ring that now hung on a slender gold chain around milady's neck. Aha, she thought, there's something to do here or my name's not Betty Collins, and I shall 'ave to find out what it is for Mr. Biddles.

But all her sly questions and suggestions that the lady confide in her had gone unheeded, and on this last evening Patricia dismissed her early as well. In the morning, she seemed disinclined for conversation, but Betty only shrugged. Time enough when we are back at the hall, she thought to herself.

But when the carriage reached the streets of Bath that afternoon, Patricia rapped on the carriage roof, and the coachman stopped the team and slid open the trap to learn her orders. His eyebrows rose when she told him her direction, but he nodded, for he was another of Patricia's admirers who quite agreed with the butler that she was a fine lady who had to be pitied in her marriage.

As the coach started forward again, Patricia turned to find her maid staring at her in disbelief.

"We won't be goin' on to Biddles 'All, milady?" she asked, her voice incredulous. "But . . . but your 'usband expects us today."

"I will not be going on, but you will, Betty," Patricia said, her voice quiet and determined. "I wish you to deliver this letter to Mr. Biddles for me. I shall come out to the hall tomorrow, but for tonight I am going to stay with an old friend."

"Wot old friend?" Betty asked bluntly, and Patricia raised her brows.

"That is none of your concern. I would thank you to remember your place, for I shall not tolerate insolence from you."

Afraid she was about to lose a lucrative post, Betty retreated in a tangled flurry of words that Patricia neither heard nor heeded. In vain, Betty begged to be allowed to stay with her mistress, but Patricia denied her, telling her to hold her tongue and saying she would have no need of her services in such a careless voice that she angered the maid. Aye, but Mr. Biddles does, me foine lady, and we shall see 'oo pays the piper in the end, she thought, subsiding at last.

When the coachman pulled up before the impressive town house of honey-colored stone, and Gregson the butler came out to welcome the lady and direct the footman to carry in the portmanteaus she indicated, Betty began to feel somewhat better. Of course she would still have the chore of explaining her lady's absence to Mr. Biddles, but at least now she knew who this "special" friend was, for the old butler had announced that Lady Randolph was waiting for her in the drawing room. Perhaps it would not be so bad, after all, she thought as she lolled in solitary splendor in the luxurious coach for the last lap of the journey to Midsomer Norton. Surely Mr. Biddles would be delighted to learn that his wife had made the acquaintance of such an important society leader. Betty chuckled and put her feet up on the opposite seat, pretending that she was the wealthy owner of the coach as she dozed for the remainder of the drive.

Patricia entered the drawing room to find Lady Sylvia alone, for she had sent her companion away, and with a smile and a gay greeting she went to kneel beside her chair and kiss her wrinkled cheek. Lady Sylvia's eyes were still sharp and she did not miss the sparkle of happiness deep in those violet eyes, nor the air of determined assurance that made her seem so different. Where before there had been only a sad resignation, now there was the quiet confidence of a woman who knew how much she was loved and valued.

"Thank you for taking me in, ma'am," Patricia said as she rose to take the chair beside her hostess. "I could not bear to return to Biddles Hall a moment before I had to, and as for staying the night there, there was no way I could contemplate it with anything but distaste."

Lady Sylvia waved her hand. "It is nothing, child. I am delighted to welcome you," she said, but there was no answering smile on her face and Patricia thought she seemed troubled.

She did not look away from those gray eyes so like Guy's as she remarked, "I have the feeling I have disappointed you, ma'am, and I would not do so for the world, but I beg you to listen to me for a while and then I am sure you will understand."

Lady Sylvia inclined her head, and once again Patricia told the story of Mr. Biddles' startling change of personality and what he had demanded she do. By the time she reached the part where she became ill and had gone to visit her grandmother in Kingsfold, Lady Sylvia was looking disgusted and disdainful.

"Even such a horrid creature as Mr. Biddles was nowhere

near so depraved as that, two years ago. He must have gone
mad!'' she exclaimed in strong tones. ''But why on earth
didn't you tell me, my dear? I would have helped you to
escape him, and then there would have been no need for you
to involve Guy.''

''There was every need, ma'am,'' Patricia said in a quiet
voice, her eyes steady on her friend's face. ''Do you remember telling me once that although you did not want Guy to fall
in love with me at first, you had come to change your mind
and think I would be a worthy Viscountess Reading?''

''I remember,'' Lady Sylvia nodded.

''I hope you still feel the same way, ma'am, for I would
ask your blessing for us. I have come to Bath to tell Mr.
Biddles I want a divorce, and when that has been accomplished,
I am going to marry your nephew. I hope it will be with your
approval, but we intend to marry without it, if that is necessary.
I know now that there is nothing in the world more important
than our love, and after the way society has treated me in the
years since my marriage, I feel no hesitation or shame in
defying its codes. The *haut ton* is false and vain and arrogant;
our love is true and forgiving and kind. I cannot live without
it any longer.''

''And Guy feels as you do, Patricia? He will countenance
divorce?''

''He assures me that it does not matter; besides, I know
that he loves me as much as I love him,'' Patricia said, her
face lighting up with her memories and her eyes radiant.

Lady Sylvia thought she had never seen devotion written so
plain, and all her reservations disappeared. ''My dear child,
of course you both have my blessing,'' she said.

Patricia smiled her thanks, and then at the lady's request,
she went to pour them a glass of sherry.

When she had taken her seat again, Lady Sylvia said,
''Guy called on me this morning, all impatience for your
arrival, and I promised to send him word as soon as you
came. Ring the bell, my dear, and I will send a footman to
York House and ask him to join us for dinner.''

Instead of the anticipation for this reunion that she expected Patricia to show, she was surprised to see her frown as
she leaned forward, holding up an urgent hand. ''I beg you
will not, ma'am. I intend to drive out to Biddles Hall early
tomorrow, and if Guy knows I am here, I am sure he will

insist on going with me. I have no wish to embroil him in the matter, for Mr. Biddles is sure to be very angry and he will seek revenge on us both. I would spare Guy that at least, since I cannot spare him society's censure in the end.''

"Doesn't Guy know what Mr. Biddles was insisting you do, Patricia?'' Lady Sylvia asked, somewhat surprised.

"No, I let him think that I had just been ill and never told him, for I was afraid of what he might do. He told me once that Mr. Biddles deserved to die for something much less serious. If he learned of this new development, I know he would be so angry he would kill him in a fit of rage. No, please, ma'am, you must see we cannot let him know I am here until after I have seen Mr. Biddles and left him for good. Perhaps he will find out about Guy, or suspect him, although I have been as cautious and discreet as possible, and although we do not plan any more meetings, but he cannot be sure. There is no proof. But if Guy insists on accompanying me to Biddles Hall, our alliance will be only too plain. In his anger and revenge he will ruin Guy and take great delight in doing so in the most humiliating and abasing way he can find. He is . . . he is a terrible man.''

She folded her lips as if to stop herself from revealing any more, and Lady Sylvia nodded and agreed, even as she volunteered to join Patricia in the morning. "I admire you for your courage, but I could not be easy if you went out there alone, my dear,'' she said. "Mr. Biddles may try to keep you at the hall by force, but if I am with you with a pair of strong, young footmen to aid us, he will not be able to detain you against your will.''

Patricia was delighted to have her assistance, although she spoke somewhat doubtfully about the wisdom of exposing Lady Sylvia to Mr. Biddles' wrath, and the vulgar language she might be forced to hear, and for the first time since her arrival, her hostess laughed out loud.

"Dear child,'' she said when she could speak again, "as if I have not heard such words many times in my long life! You must not think because I am so old and frail that ranting and swear words will upset me. I hope he does lose control of himself to that extent, for then it will be my very great pleasure to tell him exactly what I think of him before we take our leave. And now, my dear, run away and rest; Gregson will show you to your room. I am going to write to

my solicitor in London, for we will need his services shortly.
And I will pen a note to Guy telling him we will expect him
for dinner tomorrow night. It can be delivered in the morning
after we have left for Biddles Hall.''

Patricia kissed her and left the drawing room, but she did
not lie down and rest in the pretty bedroom that was to be
hers. Instead, she went to the windows and stared out in the
direction of York House. It made her feel protected and more
confident to know that Guy was only a few streets away, and
yet at the same time relieved that she had succeeded in
sparing him any involvement in the problem she knew she
must face alone.

Lady Sylvia had ordered her carriage for ten, and true to
her word, she took her two footmen with her, riding in the
grooms' places on the back of the carriage. Patricia could not
help feeling a quiver of alarm. She had not mentioned the
purpose of her visit to Mr. Biddles in her letter, preferring to
face him when she told him, and she could not help feeling
alarmed when she thought how he would react. When Lady
Sylvia saw the way she twisted her hands in her lap, she
undertook to chat of other things—Guy's childhood and River
Court, a favorite dog of his and his first pony—and in this
way, when they arrived at the hall, Patricia was calm and
composed once again.

If the butler thought there was anything odd about his
mistress coming home accompanied by an older, crippled
lady and attended by two strange footmen, no sign of it
showed on his face as he ushered the party into the hall. Lady
Sylvia looked around at the ostentatious furniture and expensive decorations heavy with gilding, and sniffed in disdain.

"Where is Mr. Biddles, Ames?" Patricia asked as she
handed him her stole and gloves.

"He is in the library, m'lady," the butler replied.

Patricia nodded, and then he saw her take a deep, steady-
ing breath. "Escort Lady Randolph to the gold salon, if you
please, and bring her some refreshment," she ordered. Although Lady Sylvia demurred, Patricia ordered tea to be
served and instructed Ames to see to her comfort before she
put up her chin and went to the door of the library to knock.

Before very many minutes had passed, everyone in the
general vicinity of the library was aware that Mr. Biddles was
in a towering rage. A small upstairs maid paused on her way

up the stairs and clutched her duster in nervous hands at the
sound of his thundering voice; and Betty, Patricia's maid,
was drawn from the dressing room, where she had been
unpacking milady's gowns, to listen with her mouth ajar as
she hung over the banister. Ames stood stiffly in his place,
staring straight ahead of him with not a muscle twitching in
his face, but his two attendant footmen could not help exchanging uneasy glances, and one of them went so far as to
shuffle his feet before the butler frowned at him.

"Strumpet! Whore!" Mr. Biddles bellowed, and the housemaid gasped. "Who is the man? Come, now, I'll have it out
of you if I have to beat you senseless to get the information.
Sneaking around behind my back taking your own pleasure
with never a thought to my orders, and Lord Granford due
here tomorrow. What am I to say to him? That M'lady
Patricia has chosen another and our deal is off? No, no,
you'll not make such a fool of me, my girl."

There was a low murmur in response and then the sound of
breaking glass.

"I'll find out the man's name, never fear, for I know you
have lain with another, no matter how you deny it, and when
he is brought up on a charge of lewdness and adultery, he'll
sing another tune and forget the delights he has enjoyed in
your arms. Aye, and then I'll have you back here at the hall,
where I can punish you as you deserve. The 'dire mental
cruelty and anguish' that you claim you have suffered will be
as nothing compared to what I have planned for you."

Everyone held their breath as the soft voice of their mistress spoke again, at greater length. Out of the corner of his
eye, Ames saw Lady Randolph come to the door of the gold
salon on the arms of her footmen and whisper a few words to
them before she came into the hall to eavesdrop openly.

"And what of your father and brothers, madam?" Mr.
Biddles roared next. "I shall take the greatest pleasure in
ruining them, too! Aye, that gives you pause, now don't it?
The high-and-mighty Westerlys tossed into jail like common
felons and left to languish there for nonpayment of debt. I'll
wager you had not thought of that! Or do you rank your
charms so high that you think this new lover of yours will
save 'em? Coming it much too strong, *Mrs*. Biddles, for you
are in no way unique."

There followed a catalog of the lady's physical attributes

and lack of enthusiasm and expertise that had the housemaid white with shock, the footmen red with embarrassment, and even Ames looking offended. Lady Sylvia was the only one present who did not appéar affected by his coarseness.

He paused at last and once again came that soft but resolved voice. Her words, unlike Mr. Biddles' strident roars, could not be distinguished, but Ames could tell that although she did not raise her voice, she was as determined as her husband and that nothing he could say or threaten to do would dissuade her from her course.

Suddenly the door of the library opened and Patricia came back into the hall. Her color was high and her wide violet eyes angry, but she held her head high and attempted a smile when she saw Lady Sylvia and her footmen.

"Shall we be on our way, ma'am?" she asked, with only the slightest tremor in her voice. "My errand here has been discharged."

"No," Mr. Biddles screamed, rushing from the library to run and grab her by the arms, "it has not! You'll not run off now, my *fine* lady! Ha, 'lady' indeed! Trull—Jezebel—harlot! No, you are my wife and I order you to remain where I can deal with you. I'll beat some sense into you, you jade!"

He began to shake her then, and Lady Sylvia motioned to her servants. "Remove the Lady Patricia from that man's grasp, Henry, William," she ordered, and then she marched up to Mr. Biddles and poked him with her cane.

Infuriated, he spun around to stare at the tiny, redoubtable figure glaring up at him, her cane raised now as if to strike him. "Lady Randolph, you here?" he asked, noticing her for the first time.

Lady Sylvia thought Mr. Biddles looked most unwell. His fat face was almost purple in his rage and dripping with sweat, and he was drooling, his wet mouth open as he struggled to catch his breath.

"As you can see, but not for long. I am about to take my leave, as is the Lady Patricia. You cannot stop us, although it would give me a great deal of satisfaction if you tried," she said, her voice icy with contempt. "You, sir, are a commoner and no better than a gross procurer. I look forward to testifying as to your character after what I have heard this morning. How dare you call the Lady Patricia names after what *you* have attempted to get her to do?" she added.

Mr. Biddles' face grew even darker and his mouth fell open with shock. For the first time he was speechless at this unexpected accusation.

"If you offer any violence to either one of us, I shall have the Justice for the County and the High Sheriff here this afternoon, and I will have you taken up for assault," she said, and then she went to where Patricia was standing, guarded now by the two tall young men who wore her livery of silver and blue.

"M'lady, you do not understand," Mr. Biddles finally got out in a quieter tone, his hands outflung to plead with her. "You cannot know what my wife has told me, for a social leader like yourself could never condone divorce! There is no cause—the fault is all on her side. You are befriending a wanton and a whore, and if you persist in it, I'll make you sorry, too!"

The little housemaid dropped her duster and Betty almost fell over the banister in her shock. Divorce was the ultimate scandal, difficult and expensive to obtain, and although, as the daughter of a peer, Patricia's case would be heard in the House of Lords, it would require an act of Parliament to dissolve her marriage. And then, of course, she would be ruined forever.

Lady Sylvia did not deign to reply as she looked him up and down, her gaze rich with *hauteur* and distaste.

"You are mistaken, Mr. Biddles," Patricia said, and everyone turned toward her as she took a step forward. She had almost been forgotten in the excitement of Lady Sylvia's denouncement, but now she stared at the fat, ugly figure of her husband with hatred in her eyes. "I am none of the names you have called me, but you, sir, are worse, for you would have had your wife take lovers to further your own social ambitions. You are no better than the *maquereau* Lord Granford named you. I shall not spend another moment under your roof, and if you try to hurt my dear friend, I will kill you."

"Patricia, be careful what you say," Lady Sylvia gasped.

Patricia clenched her fists, her violet eyes dark with murderous intent, and then she seemed to recall herself. "Shall we be on our way, ma'am?" she asked. "Ames, my stole and gloves."

The butler hastened to bring the required items before he went to open the front door.

Mr. Biddles stood frozen on the spot, but as his wife and Lady Randolph passed through the door, he regained his voice and they could hear his bellowing threats and curses, all the veneer of gentility gone as he resorted to the gutter language of the London docks that he had learned as a child, even after they gained the safety of the carriage and the coachman had given his team the office to start.

PART THREE

1815
Summer

9

It took most of the drive back to Bath and several scoldings from Lady Sylvia before Patricia regained her composure. She had known the meeting was going to be difficult, but she had never suspected he would be so vile, so hateful to her elderly friend as well. In truth, she was more distraught for Lady Sylvia than she was for herself, but when she declared she would never have subjected the lady to such an ordeal if she had had any idea of the man's degeneracy and lust for revenge, Lady Sylvia waved her regrets aside.

"My dear Patricia," she said firmly as the carriage approached the outskirts of Bath once again, "kindly do not refine on it too much. The man is not worthy of our continued consideration. He is an animal. I assure you I have taken no hurt from this morning's expedition. In fact, now that I have seen his true colors *en personne*, I am delighted I was able to assist you to begin to free yourself from the connection. I beg you to be calm. No one but you and I and the servants know what has happened, and no one else will ever know. Guy can be told only the barest sketch of what really happened, for, as I know you realize, he would be sure to dash out there, *ventre à terre*, and run the horrible man through for daring to malign you so. My compliments, by the way, for your foresight in not allowing my nephew to accompany us. Now I understand your concern."

When Patricia would have continued to bemoan the experience, she was told to cut line. "You are to have a light luncheon with me, and then you are to go to your room and rest," Lady Sylvia ordered. "Guy will be with us for dinner, if indeed he can manage to restrain himself for as long as that, and I am sure you want to look your best."

This called for a change of subject, for the lady wisely thought to ask the girl what gown she intended to wear, and

157

from there it was only a short step to the many new clothes she would need to purchase now that she was no longer forced to don the garish overtrimmed gowns and ornate jewels her husband had formerly insisted she wear. Fortunately, Lady Darrow had given her granddaughter a generous amount of money, foreseeing her difficulties, and Patricia was well before with the world and looking forward to dressing only to please herself and Guy.

When that gentleman entered the drawing room that evening, his eager eyes swept first to Patricia, who was seated beside his aunt in a gown of palest lavender muslin. She had spent most of the afternoon removing the velvet knots and braids of ribbon and the heavy pearl beading that had adorned it, and now it was only a soft float of plain material with a round neck and tiny puffed sleeves. Guy did not miss the slender gold chain that disappeared in the low neckline of her gown and was her only jewel, and he smiled at her as he took up her left hand and kissed it, his strong fingers caressing her bare ring finger.

Lady Sylvia watched them indulgently for a moment, and then she brought Guy back to earth. "You will be delighted to learn, my dear nephew, that the deed is done," she said tartly. Guy had gone to take a seat across from the ladies where he could feast his eyes on Patricia, and at his look of inquiry, she added, "Patricia and I went out to the hall this morning, and Mr. Biddles has been informed of his wife's plans for a divorce."

At this, Guy leaned forward and frowned. "How can this be, *chère tante,* and why was I not informed? You knew that I meant to accompany you, Patricia."

Lady Sylvia snorted. "You would have been very much in the way, Guy. Besides, Mr. Biddles was unpleasant enough without adding your handsome presence and aristocratic air to fan the fire of his displeasure."

"He did not dare to touch you, did he, Patricia?" Guy asked, his face dark and thunderous.

Patricia tried to smile at him confidently, although her heart was beating rapidly at the lies she must tell. "Of course not, sir! As you can see, I am here and well. I should like to see the manner of man who would dare accost me while I am in your aunt's charge. Why, she was formidable."

They both looked at the little white-haired lady, hunched

over by her arthritis in her chair, and smiled as Lady Sylvia said indignantly, "So I should hope! I have never had any trouble dealing with the toads and mushrooms of this world. As if I could not give Alvin J. Biddles the setdown he so richly deserved . . . hmmph!"

She then told Guy she had written to her solicitor in London and asked him to call on her as soon as it could be arranged, so that the brief for a divorce could be prepared. "Of course, Patricia must stay with me until his arrival, for he will have a great many questions for you, my dear," she added. "As for you, Guy, I suggest you leave Bath. You will do a great deal of harm to the case if you are seen in constant attendance on the lady, and there is no need for your protection while I have her safe."

Guy looked as if he would like to argue the matter, but just then Gregson announced dinner, and he was forced to rise and take the ladies in. It was not until he rejoined them in the drawing room after his solitary glass of port that he was able to continue the argument.

"I take your point, Aunt, but I do not intend to leave Bath as yet," he said firmly.

Lady Sylvia looked a little haughty and he added, "I shall be the height of discretion, of course, and surely no one can take it amiss that I visit my dear aunt. And since there can be no balls or public entertainments for Patricia right now, no one will see us together."

Lady Sylvia argued, but Guy was adamant, and finally she had to be content with his promise to be circumspect. Patricia sat calmly while they discussed the matter, her eyes most often on Guy's handsome face, now earnest and determined above the spotless white of his cravat, or on his strong hands as they moved impatiently as he made his point, his gray eyes keen.

Lady Sylvia allowed them a moment alone at the end of the evening, and Guy took Patricia in his arms and kissed her until she was breathless. He drew his betrothal ring out of her gown and kissed it before he returned it to its hiding place, his eyes smoky with contained desire, and Patricia felt herself melting when his long fingers brushed her throat and breasts. She went up to bed on a cloud of happiness, sure that their troubles were well on the way to being resolved and confident that all was in train for their future together sometime soon.

True to his word, Guy called every day, but Lady Sylvia would not let him accompany them shopping, in spite of his pleas that he must have a say in Patricia's purchases. "You shall have all the say you like, dear nephew, after you are married. For now, you must trust my judgment and Patricia's. Or perhaps you doubt our ability to choose suitable gowns?" she asked, her voice so indignant at the implied insult that Patricia laughed out loud.

Guy was forced to retreat, for his aunt's taste was impeccable, and indeed in the days that followed and he saw Patricia dressed in the kind of gowns a gentlewoman should wear, and looking lovelier than ever, he had to approve.

His short visits to Patricia, almost always under the eyes of his aunt, were hard for them both, for Lady Sylvia would only allow him to stay the correct half-hour, and she refused to have him to dine every evening. After a week of this, Guy was becoming short-tempered and impatient. When his aunt left them at last one evening, saying she would expect Patricia upstairs in ten minutes, he growled with frustration. "This is intolerable, love!" he exclaimed. "She treats you like an aspirant to a nunnery, guarding you as close as any abbess would. I must see you alone."

He pulled her somewhat roughly into his arms and kissed her until Patricia was happy to agree to a little subterfuge, and a time was set for a ride the following morning.

"Tell Aunt Sylvia you are growing pale from want of exercise," he ordered, and Patricia laughed, knowing her face was rosy from his lovemaking. "Although we will dispense with your groom, we will be cautious and not ride toward any scenic spots that Bath society might frequent. No one will see us, on my word."

But even Viscount Reading could not order fate in this instance, and he was disturbed when they encountered Clorinda Mills driving with a party of friends as they cantered back to Bath in the early afternoon. She stared at them, her black eyes narrowing with her wish for revenge, and he saw her lean forward and whisper to her friend Janice Reed, who in turn pointed out the couple to a gentleman beside her in the carriage. Guy knew the news of his liaison with Mrs. Alvin J. Biddles would be all over Bath in a matter of hours.

Well, let it, he told himself stoutly. I have nothing to hide; in fact, I hate this sneaking about when I want to tell the whole world of my love for Patricia. Let the Bath quizzes chew it over with their tea and macaroons; it will be common knowledge before long, in any case.

Lady Sylvia was not at all pleased when she was apprised of this encounter, and refused to consider another outing. Her solicitor had been delayed on other business, but she looked for him within the week. The sooner we have all in train, the better, she thought, for lovers are so impatient. She sent Guy off with a lecture and orders to make himself scarce, and she was so displeased with him that he was surprised early the next morning when her footman delivered a note from her, asking him to come to Great Pulteney Street at once on a matter of some urgency.

Taking up his hat and cane, Guy strode over the bridge, the footman hurrying to keep up, and when Gregson admitted him and told him the ladies were in the drawing room, he would not allow the old man to make his stately way up the stairs and announce him, but took the flight alone, two steps at a time. A sense of foreboding told him that something was very wrong.

As he entered the room, Lady Sylvia looked up, and the relief on her strained, old face was palpable. Guy's eyes searched Patricia's face, and when he saw how white and frightened it was, he went to drop down beside her on the sofa and take up her cold hands to chafe.

"What is it, love? Why do you look that way?" he asked, his voice full of concern.

Patricia closed her eyes for a moment and swallowed, and he put his arms around her as she whispered. "It is Alvin . . . Mr. Biddles. He has been found shot in his library, murdered!"

Guy's brows snapped together in a fierce frown, and Lady Sylvia handed him a note. "This arrived only a short time ago from the hall, Guy. The butler sent it."

Guy read the sprawl rapidly. "But he says the man was shot yesterday afternoon. Why were we not apprised of it before this?"

"I imagine things were in a great uproar and there was much confusion." Lady Sylvia shrugged. "What is more, the Justice for the County had to be summoned and questions asked, since it appears the murderer got clean away. I do not see why the man is so urgent in his request that Patricia come back to the hall at once, but perhaps it might be the best thing. He was still her husband, after all.''

Guy looked down into Patricia's shocked face. ''Would it disturb you too much, my dear? I will be with you, of course.''

Lady Sylvia threw up her hands. ''Guy, you are impossible. Now that the man is dead, there is no need for a divorce, and after a year or so of mourning, no one will think a thing of it—well, not very much in any case—if you marry the widow quietly. But to tear out there now, showing by your every word and gesture how much you care for her, would only spur the rampant gossip that Bath is famous for. I beg you to remember Lady Mills! No, you will stay here and I shall go with Patricia. I have already ordered my maid to pack our things, and Wilma is preparing to attend us as well.''

Guy opened his mouth and then closed it thoughtfully. Aunt Sylvia was right. He would be circumspect no matter how he longed to be by Patricia's side through this ordeal. But convention be damned! On no account was he prepared to wait to marry her until she was out of black gloves; besides, the mere thought of anyone mourning Alvin J. Biddles was ludicrous. At his side, Patricia stirred and straightened up as she tried to smile at him.

''Lady Sylvia is right, Guy. It is my duty, I suppose, as his wife, to be at the hall to arrange the funeral and . . . and everything. Perhaps you could ride out someday to see your aunt, when things have quieted down a bit.''

Guy nodded. ''A letter to York House will reach me at any time, my dear. You have only to command me and I will be beside you.''

Lady Sylvia's maid knocked then and announced that the baggage had been loaded on the coach, and Miss Kincaid bustled in with the ladies' wraps and reticules. Guy ignored her as she helped his aunt, chatting breathlessly all the while, for he had taken Patricia into his arms.

''Courage, love,'' he said, his gray eyes warm and glowing as he tried to give her some of his own strength. ''In a short time this will all be over and then we can be together.''

He thought a shadow crossed her face, but she nodded before she went to join the others at Lady Sylvia's summons.

Guy escorted them to the carriage, and moments later they were on their way and he was left to walk back to York House wondering who, of all Mr. Biddles' many enemies, had finally been driven to commit this most heinous of crimes. He did not envy the authorities in the case, for surely the list of possible murderers would be long.

Miss Kincaid was incessant in her queries and shocked comments, and Patricia was beginning to wish it had not been necessary to bring her along when Lady Sylvia told her to hush. She subsided, but her little eyes were worried and her round face concerned.

Patricia noticed that the door knocker was already adorned with black crape when she entered the hall to find her butler, for once obvious in his relief. "M'lady! I am so glad you have returned home," he blurted out, his impassive calm gone.

Patricia tried to smile at him. "Thank you for writing me, Ames. Would you ask the housekeeper to see to rooms for Lady Sylvia and Miss Kincaid, and have some refreshments served at once?"

The butler waved a footman on the errand. "If . . . if I could see you privately for a moment, m'lady?" he asked, his hands in their white gloves clenched tightly by his side.

"Of course. Ah, there you are, Mrs. Keighly," she greeted the housekeeper as she bustled in from the back of the house. After relaying her orders, she asked her guests to go with the servant and she herself promised to join them shortly.

Lady Sylvia was glad to agree. The drive, at a faster pace than she was accustomed to, had taken its toll, and she was tired from the jolting and would be glad to rest.

Patricia turned absently toward the library and the butler coughed. "If you please, m'lady, not in there. Mr. Weems, the justice, has ordered that room closed until his investigation is complete. Perhaps the gold salon?"

Patricia nodded, glad to avoid the scene of the violence that had taken place only a short time before.

"Where is Mr. Biddles' body now, Ames?" she asked in a subdued voice.

"They have placed him in the small writing room at the back of the hall, ma'am," the butler told her as he opened the door of the salon and bowed her in.

Patricia did not sit down, but turned to face the man as she removed her gloves and placed them with her reticule on a small table. She noticed again that his usually calm face showed the strain of what he was undergoing, and his eyes darted nervously around, as if he thought someone might be listening. There was a sheen of perspiration on his high forehead as well, although the room was cool.

"What is it, Ames?" she asked as calmly as she could. "There is a great deal to attend to, and I must see to my guests."

"M'lady," the butler began, and then he paused to wipe his forehead before he spoke again. "M'lady, I thought to warn you at once. The justice has questioned all of us at the hall, and was quite astonished that you were not here, but staying just a few miles away in Bath when Mr. Biddles was shot. And although most of us tried to do our best for you, m'lady, that Betty Collins— Well, she says she's not about to hide any evidence, for she knows too much. Silly chit," he muttered.

"But what does she say she knows, Ames?" Patricia asked, trying to keep her voice level.

"She says, ma'am, that you were seeing someone else at Darrow Manor, and as we all heard Mr. Biddles talking about the divorce, and his words to you in the hall that day, her report has been believed. And unfortunately, we all had to confirm it when she told the justice that you had threatened to kill Mr. Biddles."

"I see," Patricia said slowly, and then she removed her stole and handed it to the butler. "Be so good as to have my things taken to my room, Ames."

The butler bowed, a little astonished at her coolness, and she added, "There is nothing whatever to worry about. I thank you for your concern, but of course I did not shoot Mr. Biddles; I was not even here. The notion is absurd. Betty is romanticizing to make herself important."

The butler looked doubtful. "Aye, it's true she'd like to put a spoke in your wheel, ma'am, she's that mad at you, for Mr. Biddles read her such a lecture after you left, all about how she didn't watch you careful enough, and he called her all sorts of names. I heard him! But she spoke up to him when he ordered her off the property without any of her year's wages or even a character. She told him he'd be glad of her evidence when the divorce case was heard, for she could testify to you seeing this other man, and . . . and other things as well. They spoke more quietly then, ma'am, and I couldn't hear anything else that was said, but that Betty came out of the library all smiles and simpers, like a kitten in the cream.'' He shook his head. ''It's a shame, m'lady, that's what it is.''

Patricia's mind was busy with this new development and there was a pause before she asked, ''When does the justice return, Ames? Perhaps I should send him a message telling him of my arrival, for I am sure he will wish to question me.''

''He said he would be back later this afternoon, m'lady. Shall you require a luncheon?''

''Just something light, I think. Before you see to it, be so good as to tell me exactly what did happen yesterday. Come, do not stand on ceremony. Sit down.''

She settled herself on a satin sofa and pointed to a chair nearby, and the butler obeyed, although he would only perch on the edge, twisting his hands absently in her stole as he did so. From his halting account she discovered that it had been late afternoon when he heard a loud retort from the library. Mr. Biddles had been in there alone for some time, working on business papers, and had left orders he was not to be disturbed. When Ames and the two footmen who were with him in the small room at the back of the hall where he sat when he was not on duty tried the door to the library, they found it locked, and it was some time before they were able to force it open. No one thought to go around the side of the hall and enter the room through the long French windows, and that was unfortunate, for they might well have surprised the killer. When they burst into the room, they discovered Mr. Biddles with half his head shot away, blood all over the rug, and the doors to the terrace wide open. Ames was reticent as he described the murder scene and Patricia, when she saw the way he swallowed and his Adam's apple rose and fell so rapidly, was glad for his restraint.

''Chairs were overturned and all the desk drawers were pulled out, ma'am, and his papers were lying about every which way. There must have been a struggle, but I didn't hear a thing,'' he added.

''Did they find the weapon, Ames?'' Patricia asked next.

The butler nodded, his face unhappy. ''Aye, m'lady. It was lying on the flags of the terrace just outside the doors.''

He seemed about to say more, but then Patricia spoke again. "And there was no sign of the murderer? You must have tried to find him."

Ames seemed glad that the subject of the gun had been closed. "I sent a message to the stables at once so the grooms could search, and the footmen went over the gardens, but there was no one to be found. We did discover where someone had tied a horse behind the gazebo, m'lady, but of horse and rider there was nary a trace." He waved his hand. "The property is so extensive, and the Home Woods so close to the hall, 'tis no wonder the man was able to escape, although Mr. Weems seemed to think we didn't try to find him very hard."

His face darkened and Patricia was quick to commend him. "I am sure you did everything you could under the circumstances. I shall tell the justice so myself."

She rose then and Ames was quick to follow suit. "Thank you for telling me all this, Ames," she said with her gentle smile. "I know this has all been most unpleasant for you, but I am glad you were here, and glad we have had this talk. Soon I must depend on your expertise, for I have no idea how funerals are conducted in a case like this, but thank you for seeing to the crape on the front door so promptly. And now, I do not want you to concern yourself further, but believe me when I tell you that all will be well."

She smiled reassuringly and left the room, so she did not see the worried look on her butler's face, nor the way he shook his head.

After a luncheon that was marked by many long pauses and disjointed conversations, she adjourned to the drawing room with Lady Sylvia to await the arrival of the justice. She was sorry her friend had not sent Miss Kincaid away, but she ignored her eager attention as she told them what Ames had said about the murder. Lady Sylvia listened carefully, only occasionally interjecting a question, and when she learned the name of the justice in the case, she snorted.

"Wilfred Weems, of course! I knew his family. He is a puffed-up stick, but I have never heard he is unfair. In any case, he shall not bully you, my dear, for I will be here to see that he does not."

She looked so fierce that a faint smile passed over Patricia's face. She had spent the remainder of the morning setting her house in order and seeing to her guests' comfort. There had been servants to listen to and to soothe, menus decided, and a long string of orders given, one of the first of which had been to tell Betty that her services as maid would no longer be required. The middle-aged woman had set her lips tightly when she learned she was to be replaced by a housemaid.

"That's as may be, m'lady," she said austerely, "and I am sure you can do as you want . . . for now. But send me off you will not, for I must tell you—"

Patricia had interrupted her. "There is no question of you being sent off, Betty. Of course your evidence will be required. No, you will remain here until the case is settled, but as soon as that occurs, I want you to be on your way. You may leave me."

The maid seemed about to speak, but at Patricia's raised eyebrows, she curtsied out of habit and left the room. Patricia began another list.

It was almost four when Ames came to announce that Mr. Weems had arrived.

"Show him in here, if you would, Ames," Patricia said. She had had time to control her features and her voice, and she looked calmly at the man who entered the drawing room.

Wilfred Weems was indeed the stick that Lady Sylvia had described, both physically and in his manner. Very tall and so thin he appeared emaciated, he had a long narrow face set on a skinny neck above bony, hunched shoulders, and piercing blue eyes that he opened very wide whenever he was astounded. He bowed deeply to the ladies, for he was first and foremost a snob, and then he began to offer his condolences for the lady's sad loss in a high, reedy voice. Dumbfounded, Patricia looked to Lady Sylvia for advice, and that lady was happy to assume control of the situation.

"That's enough of that, Wilfred! We know that you have learned that Lady Patricia's marriage was unhappy to the point that she was about to seek a divorce. There is no need for such mealymouthed pieties, for Mr. Biddles' demise— although, to be fair, one should regret the manner of it—is cause for celebration the length and breadth of England. Sit down!"

Startled, Mr. Weems subsided in a chair, folding his storklike legs beneath him. Patricia felt Lady Sylvia had been much too abrupt and unkind, and hastened to smooth the troubled waters.

"Can you tell us what happened, Mr. Weems?" she asked in a dignified voice. "I have heard from the servants, of course, but I would like to know what you, as an educated gentleman, think of it."

Mr. Weems' face sprouted a self-satisfied smirk before he remembered the situation and it settled into mournful lines once again.

"Quite right you should ask me, m'lady. I have gone through all the various accounts most thoroughly and made the following deductions." Here he paused and held up two skinny red hands. "You are not to suppose that it has been easy, m'lady, for asking ten people will get you ten different answers, and asking twenty solicits twenty more, but being a man with vast experience in sifting the facts, I was able to arrive at what I believe to be a true reckoning of the dastardly events—"

"Get on with it, man, do," Lady Sylvia muttered, shifting impatiently in her chair.

With one blue eye on this elderly termagant, Mr. Weems told much the same story that Ames had, although in greater and much more tiresome detail. When he was about to describe the body, he leaned forward eagerly, clasping one bony knee so hard that the knuckles on his red hands were white, and Lady Sylvia waved an imperious hand.

"It will not be necessary to tell us about the gore, Wilfred. Kindly remember that you are dealing with gentlewomen here," she said.

Humbly begging their ladyships' pardons, he resumed, and somewhat later he reached his peroration. "It is obvious that the murderer entered the hall through the French doors of the library," he said pompously. "The fact that he did not sound the knocker and apprise the butler of his visit shows his nefarious intent. No, the murderer came for one purpose, and one purpose only: to kill Mr. Biddles. Having done so, he took his leave the same way. There is only one problem, Lady Patricia, but it is a serious problem, indeed."

He paused for emphasis and shook his head dolefully, never taking his bright-blue eyes from hers.

"Yes, Mr. Weems?" she prompted. "A problem, you said?"

"I am afraid so, dear lady, but I am sure you can explain it to my satisfaction. You see, the weapon that was employed was your own pistol. Now, ma'am, if the murderer was not an intimate of the house and yet came with the express intent of killing Mr. Biddles, how could he be sure of finding a weapon already loaded and ready to hand?''

Patricia's look of astonishment was all that Lady Sylvia could wish for. "My pistol?" she asked in an innocent voice. "But I do not have one. Whatever can you mean?"

Mr. Weems' blue eyes were narrowed now and they never left her face. "Oh, come now, m'lady, I am sure you are mistaken. Isn't it a fact that Mr. Biddles insisted you learn to shoot for your own protection when you were first married, and isn't it true that he presented you with a silver chased pistol of your own? A very distinctive weapon, for it has your initial picked out with diamond chips on the handle.''

Patricia looked startled. "Why, yes, now that you mention it, he did, but I have not seen the gun for years. I told him that no matter how many robbers broke into the property I had no intention of shooting anyone.''

"One can certainly see why," Lady Sylvia said, looking around the ornate, ugly room. "One would be more apt to give them *carte blanche*, order wagons made ready, and hope they would take away the lot.''

Mr. Weems, who happened to think Biddles Hall very rich and impressive and the perfect gentleman's establishment, looked disbelieving, and then, as if he realized the conversation was getting away from him, he brought the ladies to order. "Was the gun kept in the library, Lady Patricia?" he asked sternly.

"I have no idea," Patricia replied, her voice cool now. "I have told you I have not seen it for years. Perhaps Mr. Biddles kept it in his desk. He very often had business callers from London, and some of them could become very unpleasant. You know, of course, that my husband was a moneylender and not universally admired? Just so. Perhaps he felt the need for protection, but I, I assure you, sir, did not.''

Mr. Weems leaned forward again and pointed a bony finger at her. "But how could the murderer know about the gun unless someone told him?" he asked in the manner of one playing his trump card.

"Surely you do not expect the Lady Patricia to know anything about that, Wilfred," Lady Sylvia interrupted. "Or perhaps you have it set in your mind that she hired someone to do away with her troublesome husband and thereby save herself the disgrace of a divorce?''

The justice seemed dumbstruck that the lady would expound his own pet theory so coolly, and his eyes opened wide. ''That has not as yet been established, m'lady,'' he said.

Lady Sylvia snorted. ''*Beñet*! And never will be! The Lady Patricia was with me at my home in Bath and has been ever since she arrived here from the east of England, where she has been visiting for some weeks. She has had no conversation with skulking villains or sly loose fish down on their luck, and I can testify to that. Besides, if she intended to rid the world of that monster, why would she put herself to the trouble of asking him for a divorce only a week ago? Such fustian! You had better find another tree to bark up, Wilfred.''

Mr. Weems looked affronted. ''All avenues will be investigated, m'lady, you may be sure. But I have been told, and on very good authority, that there is another man in the case, that the Lady Patricia is the mistress of another. Surely to win such beauty, and in the spirit of chivalry, the gentleman might take a hand in the case and rid her of her hateful husband.''

Patricia did not notice that Lady Sylvia was looking thoughtful, she was so frightened for Viscount Reading.

''You are insulting, sir,'' she said in a voice dripping with disdain. ''I have no lover. I suppose you have been listening to my maid, who is a woman with more hair than wit. Did she tell you these lies?''

Mr. Weems squirmed, but he answered promptly. ''I cannot divulge my sources until all is settled, m'lady. I shall leave you now but I must insist that you remain at Biddles Hall for the present time.''

Patricia looked astounded and rose, trying not to tremble. ''But of course I shall certainly do so, for there are the funeral arrangements to see to. I assume we may go forward with that event?''

Mr. Weems agreed to an immediate service and bowed deeply several times before he took his leave, saying he would return in the morning, when, he prayed, a night of reflection might recall some details to the lady's mind that she had not disclosed.

There was a long silence after he left the room, and then

Patricia ran to kneel beside Lady Sylvia's chair. "Dear ma'am, what shall I do?" she whispered. "I must not tell him about Guy, for you see how he suspects this unknown lover of mine."

Lady Sylvia thought hard for a moment. "No, we must keep Guy out of it at all costs, though I wish we could have his advice. However, even though it would be perfectly permissible for him to visit here to support his old aunt through such an unpleasant ordeal, one look at the two of you together and Mr. Weems would be leading Viscount Reading away to await the next Assizes in a cell! No, Patricia, we must keep Guy away from the hall."

10

To this end Lady Sylvia wrote a short note to her nephew and sent a footman to deliver it to York House before she went to change for dinner. She knew Guy, even in his new guise of patient suitor, and although he had told her he meant to be circumspect, she realized she must disarm him with frequent missives or he would be out at the hall whether they wanted it or not.

Guy was able to enjoy his excellent dinner much more after reading his aunt's words, for she had spoken only of an unknown assailant and told him Patricia was bearing up magnificently. With a long evening stretching before him, he thought to look in at the Assembly Rooms, not only for a little diversion, but to discover what Bath—gossip-loving, tattle-mongering little enclave that it was—was saying about Alvin J. Biddles' violent demise.

He had barely greeted one or two friends before the whispers came to his ears, and he noticed that several people were looking at him askance. Old General Cowles, his aunt's friend, colored up when he approached and was able only to cough and utter fragments of sentences before he excused himself and tottered away as fast as he could go.

"My dear, it is all too true! She was about to divorce the man, imagine!"

"No one can blame the lady. The man was a rotter!"

"Of course, as dear Clorinda has pointed out, he was as rich as Golden Ball, and she his sole heir. Is it any wonder . . ."

"Why ever is Lady Randolph supporting her? Even if, as I have heard, a certain viscount is *épris* there, why would she condone such a scandalous liaison?"

"And Lady Mills told me she saw her in Kent, with a gentleman we all know embracing her violently in broad daylight on the open road, and she was only half-clothed. My dear!''

"Midsomer Norton is such a short distance from Bath and the lady such an excellent horsewoman I hear tell . . . and of course, Biddles was shot with her own pistol.''

"Weems tells me an arrest is expected soon. Not a very difficult or subtle case, what?''

Guy's lips tightened as he moved around the room listening to these snatches of conversation. It was just as well that Lady Mills had another engagement that evening, or Mr. Justice Weems would have had another, albeit easier, murder to investigate. Guy realized now the truth of the old adage about a woman scorned, and wished he might leave the Assembly Rooms at once. To do so would only fan the scandal, of course, and so he remained, a smile on his handsome face as if he had not a care in the world.

He was able to defuse some of the rumors, but when he defended the Lady Patricia to a small group of gentlemen, little Sir Percy Fotheringay tittered. "Oh, stab me, sir! 'Tis no wonder that *you* champion her.''

Guy controlled himself with an effort, although he looked so thunderous that Sir Percy turned pale.

"May I say, sir, that we should all champion her? She is innocent until proven under English law, and as gentlemen, our sympathies must lie with the lady. We all knew of her husband and his reputation.''

"Hear, hear!'' Lord Crandell applauded, for he had once had dealings with Mr. Biddles that had kept him to the straight and narrow path of financial prudence ever since.

Guy was able then to expound the theory of the unknown assailant by pointing out that Biddles had more enemies than Napoleon, any one of whom would have been delighted to do the deed. "Surely there is a plethora of candidates,'' he concluded. "Besides, the lady has been visiting my aunt, who thinks highly of her, and she is seldom mistaken in her judgment of people. No, I feel for the poor girl to be chewed over this way when I am sure we will discover another is the killer.''

Thus Guy left a thoughtful group in his wake whenever he could, and he managed to discredit Clorinda a bit as well. He told Lady Helmsley and Miss Warrenstoke about the house party at Lord Williams' and those who had attended. Without mentioning her name directly again, he managed to give the impression that his refusal to make Lady Mills his latest mistress was causing her to malign him for revenge. As he pointed out to the two old quizzes, who were all agog at this delicious new *on dit*, a woman who had had countless lovers would not take rejection lightly. He added that he was sure the *ton* would disregard any malicious remarks that she might make, for, after all, her reputation was well known. He felt a small pang, for what he was doing was not the act of a gentleman, but he was able to restrain it. Clorinda's malice had more than freed him from any nice consideration for her reputation.

At last he took his leave and strode back to York House in a fit of temper that had his valet all thumbs. After he had been undressed, Guy sat down before the fire in his bedroom to think. He would ride out to Biddles Hall tomorrow and warn Patricia about the stories that were circulating—discretion be damned!

He also thought to write to his cousin James, begging him to come to Bath with all speed and bring Lord Williams with him, for he had great need of their assistance, and as he affixed his seal and wrote the direction, he felt easier. James was known as a loose screw, but no one had ever called him an out-and-outer, and there was no one he would rather have beside him in such difficulties as these. They would win through somehow, and Patricia would be Viscountess Reading at last.

Even with this comforting thought, his sleep was troubled that night and he was awake at dawn. It was still very early when he took the road to Midsomer Norton at a gallop. At the hall, Ames tried not to look disapproving at such an early caller as he told him austerely that the ladies were still at the breakfast table. Guy demanded to be taken there at once, and after only one quick look at his determined jaw and steely gray eyes, Ames agreed to do so.

Lady Sylvia's teaspoon clattered in her saucer when her tall nephew strode into the room, his eyes as always going first to Patricia's face. Afraid he was about to blurt out something indiscreet, she hurried into speech. "My dear Guy! How kind of you to come and bear me company, but there was no need for such haste, my dear. The funeral is not to take place until tomorrow."

Even to her own ears this sounded lame, for Guy was dressed in riding clothes, and although the dark-gray coat fit him superbly and his clinging breeches and high polished boots would excite the envy of anyone, it was hardly funeral attire, and she hastened to add, "But perhaps you were not aware there has been a death in the hall?"

Guy remembered his manners and bowed to both ladies, noticing Patricia's shocked look.

"My sincere sympathies, ma'am," he said, hoping to give her the clue. "I only learned of Mr. Biddles' demise when I visited the Assembly Rooms last evening, or I would have come out to extend my condolences yesterday. I am glad Lady Sylvia is with you to sustain you through this difficult time, and if there is anything I can do to help, you have only to command me."

Patricia thanked him gravely, and then asked the hovering Ames to bring the viscount a plate of breakfast. She managed to pour him a cup of coffee herself without trembling, and as Guy took the seat the butler was holding for him, he sent her a quick, admiring glance.

Ames eventually left the room, but until he did so, the three conversed as if Guy and Patricia were only the merest of acquaintances. Patricia managed to portray a formal, distant sobriety that Lady Sylvia silently applauded, for although she knew the butler was firmly on his mistress's side, he would not be able to refrain from gossiping if the true state of affairs was known. When the door closed behind him, however, all such pretense disappeared.

"How could you, Guy?" his aunt demanded. "I must have several more years in my dish, after all, for if I did not expire on the spot when you stamped in here with that speaking face, I am sure to withstand any shock for years to come."

Patricia smiled at him, and he picked up her hand and kissed it, his gray eyes caressing. "My heart," he murmured, "I have now discovered another facet of your charm and talent, for I have seldom seen such a superb acting performance even on the London stage."

And then he turned to include his aunt, and his face grew serious. "I came because of what I heard last evening. The news is all over Bath, and not only the news of Biddles' murder. Oh, no, the *ton* is naming names, for Lady Mills was quick to start the gossip. You will be as concerned as I when

I tell you that Patricia is suspected of murdering her husband for his fortune, or sending me to do so as her lover.''

"We will not be surprised at all," Patricia said. "Justice Weems was here yesterday to question me, and he intimated much the same.''

"You are very cool, love," Guy remarked, somewhat astonished.

"How else can I behave? I am sure the real murderer will be found, and although it is most uncomfortable to be suspected, Weems has no proof. Nor can he place either of us at the scene. However much I hoped to keep your name out of it, Guy, these tales of Lady Mills make the task most difficult. Will anyone believe us when she is so convincing in her story?''

"I have sent for my cousin James Debenham and for Charlie Williams, and I am sure they will be of assistance in our problem. Perhaps I will ask James to take Lady Mills in hand, since I do not dare approach her myself for fear of murdering her out of hand.''

Lady Sylvia chuckled and buttered another crumpet. "Yes, we must keep you away from the malicious Clorinda at all costs, and asking James to help was well thought on, Guy. Wasn't he once an *amoureux* of the lady's? He will know how to handle her to the best advantage, I am sure.''

"But why Lord Williams, Guy?" Patricia asked in a bewildered voice.

"I have often found Charlie to be invaluable in matters concerning society. We might set him to expounding several new theories concerning Mr. Biddles' death and thus draw the hounds off the scent. At any rate, he will lend us consequence, for his reputation is well known and he is always so impeccably turned out that people listen to him even when he is expounding nonsense of the first order. But Patricia''—here Guy took her hand and pressed it—''we must try and find out the identity of the murderer ourselves. I do not know this justice, but surely he would not continue to search the bush when he has, as he believes, two perfectly good birds in hand.''

"I shall take care of Wilfred Weems," Lady Sylvia said in a voice that boded ill for the gentleman's sense of self-esteem. "When I am through with him, he'll wish he had never stood for justice.''

"That reminds me, he is due at the hall this morning. Perhaps you had better leave at once, Guy," Patricia suggested, her violet eyes begging him to save himself a distressful encounter.

"I will make myself scarce, never fear, but leave you I will not. Try to get rid of the man before luncheon, and in the meantime I will ride to the village and speak to the vicar for you about the funeral service if you would like."

"The very thing!" Lady Sylvia exclaimed. "We meant to ask him to call, but this will relieve us of that chore. And I shall tell Wilfred that you are here to assist me and in courtesy, the Lady Patricia as well, for you were acquainted slightly with Mr. Biddles some years ago. It shall all be very open and aboveboard, and by acting as if it is nothing out of the common way, we will spike his guns."

She rose from the table and Guy hurried to hand her her cane. She looked into his handsome face for a moment, and what she saw there caused her to say, somewhat obscurely, "Yes, we will do very well now, even though it has not turned out at all as I thought. Come, Patricia, let us adjourn to the morning room and await the worthy Wilfred. Guy, we will deliver the latest report at luncheon."

Guy kissed Patricia's cheek and left the hall, avoiding any chance of meeting the justice's carriage by riding cross-country to the village church at Midsomer Norton.

Wilfred Weems was duly ushered into the morning room by a silent Ames and, after his usual extensive courtesies and deep bows, began his questioning of Patricia once again. He had tried very hard to persuade Lady Sylvia to leave the room while he did so, but this the lady had no intention of doing, and when he began to press her by insisting on privacy with Lady Patricia, she was quick to say in horrified tones, "How very immoral, Wilfred! Why, every feeling must be offended. You must consider the gossip that would arise among the staff if you were closeted here alone with the widow. I am quite sure you do not have any designs on the lady myself, but there are those who would not show such Christian charity if the fact were known. No, I shall stay in my role of *duègne* and make sure you behave yourself."

Mr. Weems' narrow face turned a brilliant scarlet, and for several minutes he was lost in a tangle of explanations and denials that made it difficult for both ladies to retain their composure.

But when at last he began his questioning, they discovered that he was much more intent on Patricia's trail today, and she could not help feeling a tremor of unease, although she was careful to act the part of an innocent, unconcerned lady.

"I must ask you first, madam, where you were the afternoon your husband met his untimely end?" Mr. Weems asked after taking a sheaf of papers out of his case and studying them for a moment.

Patricia's eyebrows rose. "Why, in Bath, of course, at Lady Randolph's house in Great Pulteney Street."

"You were there all day?" he asked, his high reedy voice sharp.

Patricia cocked her head to one side as she pretended to consider the question. "It is hard to remember," she said, trying to stall while she thought how she might best protect Guy. "Was that the day we went for the fitting at Mme. Thérèse's, ma'am?" she asked Lady Sylvia.

"No, I do not believe so, my dear. That was the day before, for I remember it came on to shower as we left the shop and you were concerned about your new bonnet. No, the morning of the day Mr. Biddles was killed you went out for a ride and met my nephew by chance as you were returning to Bath."

Her gray eyes were guileless and Patricia nodded. "Of course. It was a lovely day and Viscount Reading was kind enough to escort me home after my groom's horse threw a shoe. Even though there was only a short distance to go, he insisted. He is such a gentleman. And then, as you remember, ma'am, I spent the afternoon writing letters."

Lady Sylvia collaborated this and Mr. Weems made a few notes.

"Of course, you know Viscount Reading very well, don't you, Lady Patricia? One might almost say 'intimately'?" he asked next, the sly insinuation in his voice only thinly veiled.

"Not well at all," Patricia replied carelessly. "He did visit the hall once years ago when he first met my husband, but the acquaintance did not flourish. It is only my friendship with his aunt that has brought us into contact again."

"Such a dear, kind nephew," Lady Sylvia interposed. "Even now, if you can believe it, Wilfred, he has ridden to the vicar to arrange the funeral service as a favor to me, thus sparing Lady Patricia. He learned of Mr. Biddles' death last evening in Bath and was quick to ride out and lend us his aid.''

"Indeed?'' Mr. Weems asked as if he could not believe such folly.

"I have just said so,'' Lady Sylvia snapped.

Mr. Weems was obliged to change his tactics. "I see you wear no wedding ring, Lady Patricia. Yet surely Mr. Biddles must have given you a fine, expensive one. Where is it?''

Patricia considered her bare left hand. "I took it off some time ago when I decided to divorce my husband, and returned it to him when I came out to the hall to inform him of the fact. I suppose he put it back in the vault in the library, where he kept all my jewels, but I have no idea of its exact whereabouts.''

She shrugged and Mr. Weems pounced. "But there is another ring you wear, is that not so, dear lady? But not on your finger, oh, no. This ring you have hidden on a chain around your neck. Would you be so kind as to remove it for my inspection?''

Lady Sylvia pounded her cane on the floor. "This request passes all the bounds of propriety, Wilfred! Whatever the Lady Patricia wears around her neck can have no bearing on this case. I told you yesterday that you were barking up the wrong tree, but I see you persist in your folly even though the actual murderer is fast covering his tracks all this time. You are improvident as well as impertinent, sir.''

"*Chercher la femme*, Lady Sylvia, as everyone says,'' Mr. Weems persisted, his French accent atrocious.

"*I* never say it,'' Lady Sylvia shuddered, "and you would be wise to drop it from your list of *bon mots* immediately.''

"Is this the ring you wish to see, sir?'' Patricia's voice interrupted quietly, and the others turned to see her holding out a ruby and diamond band on a slender gold chain.

Wilfred leaped to his feet to inspect the band through his quizzing glass. "The very one! It has the look of a betrothal token. A singular place to wear such a ring, is it not, Lady Patricia? Unless, that is, there is some reason it must be hidden?''

Patricia's face was a little pale now as his skinny red hands fondled Guy's ring, and Lady Sylvia found herself uttering a silent prayer. "Not at all. It is a family ring, but I did not like to wear it before I left my husband, for he has a suspicious mind, much like yours, sir. He would never believe it was not a lover's gift and I preferred to avoid any more unpleasantness. Now, of course, I do not consider wearing jewelry appropriate, since I am a widow."

Reluctantly, Mr. Weems returned the ring, and after consulting his notes and peering intently at Patricia, he asked, "How did you feel on the morning that you came to see him about the divorce and your husband called you, er, called you a *cocotte*?"

Lady Sylvia snorted. "Not to put you to the blush, Wilfred, but since Mr. Biddles had no French either, he called her a whore, among other things. Of course Patricia was upset, and I was never more shocked in my life. I must tell you that I had hoped to be able to persuade the Lady Patricia to return to her husband, for the scandal and disgrace of a divorce could not be contemplated with anything but disgust by any woman of refinement, but after hearing what he said to her that morning, and seeing the way he shook her and threatened her with physical abuse of the most base sort, I could only agree with her that a divorce must be obtained without delay. As a gentleman, Wilfred, you can readily understand why I took her back to my house in Bath. There was no question of abandoning her to the man's cruelty. Mr. Biddles, besides being a very common commoner, was a dangerous out-and-outer."

"Just so, m'lady," Mr. Weems nodded, happy for once to have something he could agree to with the lady. "But even so, his murder must not go unpunished, no matter what his character. This is England." He turned to Patricia again. "Is it true that you threatened to kill him, m'lady?"

Patricia took a deep breath. "Yes, I did, after he began to abuse Lady Sylvia. I was very angry and distraught for my friend. Of course, I had no intention of carrying out such a threat, nor, in point of fact, did I do so."

Mr. Weems looked unconvinced at her ringing words and sadly shook his head. "We will leave that question for now. Perhaps you will tell me what you know about Mr. Biddles' will and who his heirs are? Or do you yourself inherit all?

What was the amount of the settlements Mr. Biddles made to your father at the time of your marriage?''

When Patricia said she could not answer these questions, for she did not know, and referred him to George Preebles, Mr. Biddles' solicitor, Mr. Weems smirked and chuckled as if he were sure she was dissembling. Lady Sylvia decided it was time she took a hand again.

"You have been questioning the lady for some time, Wilfred, and I am sure she must be tired of it. I know I am. Your suspicion that she is the murderess is obvious, and this whole thing is ridiculous. You have no proof, nor will you find any, for Patricia is not the one you seek. I suggest you continue your investigation in some other direction lest you be made to look the fool.''

Mr. Weems looked indignant, but before he could speak, Lady Sylvia continued, "When will the library be available? Mr. Preebles arrives tomorrow for the funeral, and I am sure he will wish to go through Mr. Biddles' papers so he may begin to set the estate in order. And if you are so anxious to discover the heirs, I suppose you had better attend the reading of the will.''

Mr. Weems assured her he had every intention of doing so, and she rose in dismissal. He had not meant to terminate the interview, but somehow he found himself on his feet, gathering up his papers and beginning his farewell bows.

With one last warning that he would return to the hall later in the afternoon to search the library again, and would expect both Lady Patricia and Viscount Reading to be available for any other questions that might occur to him, he bowed himself away.

"Whew!" Lady Sylvia said, sinking back in her chair and fanning herself with her handkerchief. She saw that Patricia was looking troubled, and gave her a gallant smile. "Yes, I can see you are beginning to picture yourself led away in chains to jail, aren't you, my good girl? Do not be such a chucklehead! You did very well this morning, and I do not believe the ring will cause any more speculation after your very believable explanation. That was the only time I was concerned for you, for I recognized the Leighton betrothal ring at once. Do take that Friday face away, my dear. It will upset Guy, and even if you are a widow, no one is going to believe you have been cast down in the slightest by Mr. Biddles' demise.''

Patricia tried to smile, but it was not one of her better efforts, and when Guy returned a few minutes later and found them together, he was troubled by the shadows on her face. Lady Sylvia waved him to the decanter.

"A glass of Mr. Biddles' excellent Canary, Guy? The wine cellar is the only thing I have been able to admire in this entire garish mansion. Pour one for me and for Patricia as well, for she has had a bad time of it this morning and could use the stimulant. However, I must tell you you would have been proud of her, for she acquitted herself nobly."

Over their wine, the morning's interview was discussed. When he learned that Mr. Weems wanted to question him that afternoon, Guy's face grew still and thoughtful as he ran his hand over his gleaming dark hair.

"Will you follow my lead this afternoon, my heart?" he asked, and Patricia was surprised to see the slight smile that played over his sculptured mouth. "And remember I don't mean a word of it?"

Mystified, she agreed as Ames announced luncheon was served. Miss Kincaid joined them then and chatted volubly throughout the meal, filling any little silences with comments about the weather, the gardens at Biddles Hall, and the Bath scene, and Patricia gave her a grateful smile that caused Miss Kincaid to smile and dimple with pleasure. Guy announced he would be returning to Bath later, for he expected Mr. Debenham and Lord Williams to arrive that evening, but he assured the ladies he would be back in good time the next morning to attend the funeral. He told them of the arrangements he had made for that event, and then they adjourned to the drawing room and privacy at last. Miss Kincaid sat down somewhat apart from the others and began to crochet.

Lady Sylvia took a seat near Patricia and took up her hand and patted it, but Guy paced up and down, stroking his chin in thought.

Suddenly he came to take a chair across from his aunt and he leaned toward Patricia as he said, "If only we could get into the library! I am sure there must be something there that would give us a clue to the murderer, for, as it is now, we know nothing."

"But we know a great deal, m'lord," Miss Kincaid chirped up, surprising everyone.

"Whatever do you mean, Wilma?" Lady Sylvia asked.

"Why, surely it is obvious if even poor little me can see it," her companion tittered. "Of course, the murderer was known to Mr. Biddles, for otherwise he would have rung for the butler if any stranger came in through the French doors. Since he did not, we can assume they were acquainted. I suspect the meeting had something to do with moneylending; it is obvious Mr. Biddles had few friends. Perhaps the visitor did not intend to kill, but he might have become upset by Mr. Biddles' manner. I understand he was not a warm or sympathetic man, and perhaps he taunted his visitor to the point that the man offered him physical harm. Mr. Biddles could have taken Lady Patricia's pistol from the desk to use in self-defense. The murderer must have wrenched it away, and in the struggle, the furniture was overturned and the papers were strewn around. When the gun went off and killed Mr. Biddles, the murderer panicked and ran away the same way he had come."

Lady Sylvia's mouth was wide open with surprise, Patricia looked admiring, and even Guy nodded in approval.

"However did you think of all this, Wilma?" Lady Sylvia asked, her voice bewildered.

Miss Kincaid blushed. "I have always been interested in the darker workings of the human mind, ma'am, and I have made a study of criminals. For example, did you know that the Edinburgh Stabber patterned his killings after Bill the Knife's technique?"

Lady Sylvia waved her hand. "Well, who would have thought it of you? Spare us Bill the Knife, though, Wilma, for we must consider the problem at hand."

"But, Miss Kincaid, how do you explain the locked door and the open desk drawers?" Guy asked, his voice respectful.

The companion thought for a moment. "If Mr. Biddles had not previously locked the door to be sure he would not be disturbed, perhaps the murderer was cooler than I thought. Instead of panicking, he could have gone to lock the door at once to give him the time to search the room. You see how this also points to a business arrangement? He had to recover the loan paper, for to leave it would incriminate him and make him a suspect."

"It all sounds so logical," Patricia admired.

Guy whirled suddenly. "Patricia, do you know the names of Mr. Biddles' debtors? If we could investigate them, it might lead to a stroke of luck."

Patricia shook her head in regret. "I do not know very many. You see, when we were first married, one of Mr. Biddles' clients came to the house one night to beg the return of his loan agreement, which he had forgotten to take after his last payment. Mr. Biddles refused to give it up, insisting he pay again, and a week later this Mr. Alderstoke committed suicide."

"How dastardly the man was!" Lady Sylvia exclaimed.

"After that, I did not care to know any more about my husband's business practices," Patricia apologized. "I quite see it was cowardly of me, but nothing I could do would make him change his methods, and so I stopped trying."

"Most understandable," Miss Kincaid said, her voice comforting.

"What about Lord Granford?" Lady Sylvia asked. "Didn't I hear Mr. Biddles mention his name the morning we were here, Patricia? Something about you making a fool of him by choosing another after he had made a deal with the man for your favors?"

"What?" Guy thundered, jumping to his feet.

Patricia's violet eyes begged him to control himself. "Yes, Lord Granford owed him a large sum of money, and it was due the first of this month. He was supposed to visit the hall then. I shall ask Ames if he ever came, and the names of any other visitors Mr. Biddles might have had."

"I would like to see you alone, Patricia, as soon as possible," Guy said, ignoring her last statement, and although his voice was quiet, his steely gray eyes were bleak.

"Was there anyone else, my dear?" Miss Kincaid prompted.

Patricia looked down at her hands to avoid Guy's angry face. "I don't think so, except for my father and brothers, of course," she said in a low, ashamed voice. "Oh, and some time ago Lord Granford's younger brother came and made such a fuss that Ames and the footmen had to remove him forcibly. That was after Alvin threatened to tell his father the amount of his debt, for at that time his father was a very sick man."

"I am feeling more in charity with your husband's murderer every moment, my dear," Lady Sylvia said. "What a horrible man Mr. Biddles was! But surely, in that case, the younger Mr. Granford should be investigated, too, don't you think so, Guy?"

There was no answer and she looked up to see him glowering at Patricia, his hands on his hips and his legs spread wide, and she sighed. "Come, Wilma, let us walk in the garden for a while. It is warm; I shall not need a wrap."

Miss Kincaid was quick to help her up and lead her to the door.

"I would not leave you, Patricia, but I can see that until Guy has a chance to question you, there will be no more sense to be had from him at all." Shaking her head, she left the room, shutting the door firmly behind her.

Patricia listened to the ticking of the clock and her own heartbeat for a long moment, her eyes searching Guy's angry face, and then he came and pulled her to her feet to face him as he demanded, "And now, madam, you will be so good as to explain this arrangement Mr. Biddles made that involved your favors?"

"Guy, please, please do not look that way. It is true that he tried to make such an arrangement, but I would not agree. I . . . I did not dare tell you that my continued refusal was the reason for my illness and my stay at Darrow Manor, for I knew you would kill Mr. Biddles, and I could not bear to bring such trouble to you. Please, my dear, do not be angry with me, I cannot endure it."

Her voice was a soft wail, and some of the fury faded from Guy's eyes as he took her into his arms. "It is all right, my heart, I am not angry with you. I could never be angry with you, but now I think I must know everything you have not told me before. Biddles is safely dead; unfortunately I cannot punish him further, no matter what you tell me."

Hesitating every now and then and sometimes stumbling over the words, Patricia told him what her life had been like in the two years since he had left Bath. Guy let her speak without interruption as he caressed her and held her close in his arms, and once he dropped a light kiss on her chestnut curls when he heard her voice break as she described her father's part and the way he had helped her husband to drive her almost out of her mind for money.

"I never did have influenza, Guy, but that was all I could

think of to tell you to account for my frailty. I meant to remain with my grandmother, for I thought you were in Greece; I never intended to come back to Biddles Hall. But then you came, and I found I could not stand to give you up again. And after all Alvin and my father had done to me, I did not feel I owed either one of them any further loyalty, so I agreed to divorce him and marry you. I know it was wrong of me, and weak, but I loved you so much and I had been so miserable . . .''

Her voice trailed away and she burrowed her face in his coat, trying not to cry and wondering if he would still want her now that he knew how she had lied to him.

Guy tipped up her chin with one strong finger and looked deep into her eyes, now sparkling with the tears she was trying so hard not to shed, his own face taut with emotion. ''My heart, you were very brave to endure such torture to save me from folly. I shall never forget it.''

He bent his head then and kissed her, his warm mouth moving with urgency on hers as he reveled in the soft surrender of her lips. When at last he could bear to stop for a moment, he whispered, ''But you must solemnly promise never to keep anything from me again, my own love.''

Patricia drew his head down to hers, and just before their lips met again, she whispered back, ''Never, I promise you, my dear,'' and then she lost herself in his passionate embrace, her hands caressing the lean planes of his face and the warm skin at the back of his neck.

As always, Lady Sylvia came back much too soon, and she peered at them before she nodded and said, ''Thank heavens!'' She took her seat and continued, ''Mr. Weems has arrived and is at present in the library. You will be glad to know that he accepted Wilma's offer of help with his search. He expects you both there in half an hour. Patricia, run away to your room and fasten your hair up. And may I suggest you wash your face? In very cold water?''

Patricia blushed as she put her hands to her tousled curls while Guy blew her a kiss, smiling as he did so.

When she came back, he was gone, but Lady Sylvia relayed a message. ''He said to remind you that you two are only the most casual of acquaintances, my dear, and that he will hold you to your promise not to believe a word he says, for in this case, the ends justify the means. I wonder what he has in mind? *L' homme mystérieux!*"

It seemed only a moment before Ames came to summon her to the library, and when she entered, it was to find Mr. Weems rising to bow to her from behind her late husband's massive mahogany desk and looking smug at this position of authority. Of Miss Kincaid there was no sign, and Guy had not made his appearance as yet.

"Come in, Lady Patricia, and sit down," Mr. Weems invited, and as she did so, Patricia was glad to see that all signs of disorder had been cleared away, although the Oriental rug had been replaced with a gold carpet she remembered used to adorn an upstairs sitting room. She tried not to dwell on the reason for this change as she spread her skirts and took the seat the justice indicated.

There was a knock on the door, and Guy strolled in without waiting to be invited. His hooded gray eyes were cold and bored, and after two slouching steps, he halted to take out his quizzing glass and subject their interrogator to a slow stare before he curled his lip and sneered. Patricia tried not to show her astonishment, for this was a Guy she had never seen before.

"M'lady, your humble servant," he said, his weary voice at odds with the elegant bow he swept her, which Mr. Weems would have given his soul to be able to copy.

He barely waited for Patricia's cool nod before the quizzing glass came up to inspect the man behind the desk again. "And Mr. Justice . . . er, Weems? Wil-fred Weems, I believe? How singular. I am, as I am sure you know, Guy Leighton, Viscount Reading."

He strolled over to a seat near the window and dropped down gracefully. "There are some questions, sir?" he asked, crossing one booted leg over the other and swinging it gently.

Mr. Weems seemed to recall himself as he took his seat again and shuffled some papers before him. "There are some questions indeed, m'lord, serious questions, for justice will not be denied."

"One sincerely hopes not. One never knows when one will have need of it oneself, after all, does one?" Guy murmured, taking out a snuff box and flicking it open with a practiced finger. After he had taken a pinch and sneezed into a large handkerchief, he said, "Well, my good man, what are these questions? I must tell you that newly arrived friends and an excellent dinner await me in Bath, so if you would be so kind as to make haste?''

Mr. Weems' face was growing red, and Patricia prayed that Guy knew what he was doing.

"I would ask you, sir, of your relationship with the Lady Patricia," he said sternly, his Adam's apple popping in his eagerness.

"My relationship? With Lady Patricia Biddles?" Guy repeated as if he were amazed by the suggestion. "Stab me, that is not what I thought you would ask!"

"I daresay," Mr. Weems said, "but I will have your answer nevertheless."

"You are quite sure you do not want to know where I was on the afternoon of the murder? Or inquire into my expertise with pistols?" Guy asked gently, as if he was much amused.

"First your relationship with the lady, m'lord," the justice asked, his thin, reedy voice rising now.

One of Guy's eyebrows rose as well. "I have none," he said baldly.

"Come, come, m'lord, we'll have none of that. 'Tis a well-known fact, substantiated by reliable witnesses, that you and the lady are lovers and have been for some time."

"You are mistaken, sir," the viscount said coolly. "I never make love before witnesses."

Patricia gasped and Mr. Weems colored up even more, and then he controlled himself with a visible effort. "Perhaps you would be so good as to tell me then about the afternoon you spent with Lady Patricia near the village of Crawley in Kent only a few weeks ago."

"Crawley, Crawley?" Guy mused, swinging his quizzing glass on its velvet ribbon slowly to and fro. "Was I in Crawley? Demned if I know! But you may be sure I was not there with the lady in question."

"You were identified, m'lord, embracing this lady beside a millpond one hot afternoon. Do you dare to deny it?"

"If it pleases you, I will admit to embracing any number of ladies beside any number of millponds, but I will never admit to embracing Lady Patricia Biddles. The very notion of my doing so would be impossible to contemplate for anyone who knows me."

Mr. Weems leaned his knobby red hands on the desk.

"You think to make mock of me, m'lord, but you will sing a different tune at the next Assizes."

"I do not intend to be in Bath for that length of time. If my aunt did not make her home here, I would never frequent it, for devoid as it is of any sophistication and refinement makes it a dead bore. Don't you agree with me, sir? When there is Paris and London and Rome in the world, who could support a lengthy stay in Bath?"

Mr. Weems went so far as to rap the desk like some beleaguered schoolmaster. "Come, sir, let us return to the point. Why is the idea of your embracing Lady Patricia impossible? She is a beautiful woman."

Guy turned and bowed to Patricia. "Most beautiful, but I never let such paltry considerations sway me. The world, as I am sure you must agree, sir, is full of beautiful women. Ah, me, yes." He blew a kiss out the window and sighed at his memories.

Patricia stole a glance at Mr. Weems and saw his red face was turning purple with suppressed rage.

"I will have a straight answer, m'lord! Do you deny any relationship with Lady Patricia, in spite of the sworn statements of witnesses?"

"I will admit a relationship, although not perhaps the way you mean it, for we have spoken several times. Why, on the very morning Mr. Biddles met his untimely end, I was forced to escort the lady back to my aunt's house. I have spoken to the Lady Sylvia many times about the ill-judged friendship she has with this lady, but since she chooses to ignore my warnings, as a gentleman I am forced to be polite to a guest of hers." He shrugged, as if washing his hands of such folly.

"And you would have me believe that a beautiful, fascinating, and seductive woman like Lady Patricia has not tempted you, m'lord? Coming it much too strong!"

"I see you are *épris* there yourself, sir. My best wishes for your every success. In regard to your question, I did not say she has not tempted me, but one has one's standards, after all. You must forgive my plain speaking, ma'am," he added, and Patricia lowered her eyes and nodded, suddenly aware of the way he was going, for she remembered Clorinda Mills' snub in the bookstore.

"If you do not give me a straight answer, and at once,

m'lord, I shall see you spend the night in jail,'' Mr. Weems said, his reedy voice cracking with his anger.

For the first time, this new, sneering Guy looked uncomfortable, and his gray eyes darted uneasily to Patricia's face.

"I would be delighted to explain it to you, sir, if we could be private," he said, his tone now almost pleading.

Mr. Weems preened. "You will explain it *now*, m'lord."

Guy sighed and rose to bow to Patricia. "As you insist. My humble apologies, ma'am. Remember, I did try to spare you."

Turning to the justice, he threw out his hands. "I am Viscount Reading, and as such, I have never made love to anyone but women of high degree. Anyone below the rank of lady is offensive to me."

"But . . . but she *is* a lady!"

"Lady Patricia *Biddles*," Guy corrected gently. "It is a technicality, to be sure, but one must never compromise one's high standards, not when there are so many beautiful countesses, marchionesses, and duchesses in the world."

Patricia put both hands to her throat, rising so rapidly that she almost upset her chair.

"Mr. Weems, you must excuse me," she said in a frozen, half-stifled voice, for she was trying very hard not to laugh. "I have never been so insulted in my life! I . . . I must retire."

"M'lady, if I had known . . ." Mr. Weems mourned, wringing his red hands and looking distraught.

They both turned to stare at the viscount and surprised him trying to hide a yawn as he gave Patricia another exquisite bow.

"M'lady, your most obedient servant . . . ma'am? Ma'am?"

But Patricia had swept out of the room, her head high, and then to the butler's surprise she ran up the stairs to her room and slammed the door behind her. No one would ever guess that she doubled up with laughter when she gained that sanctuary, both hands covering her mouth so not a giggle would betray her.

How had Guy dared?

11

Viscount Reading was only able to take leave of his aunt and her companion, for Lady Patricia was sequestered in her room. As he rode back to York House, a smile played over his handsome face. Mr. Weems had dismissed him with something very much like wonder, for he was such a high stickler himself, he could only look with awe at the niceness of m'lord's code of living, and Guy was pleased that his ploy had worked so well. Before he left, he had produced an unbreakable alibi for the time of the murder, and had taken the justice into his confidence as regards to Clorinda Mills' motives as well, leaving Mr. Weems to wonder how he could have been led so far astray by a woman's thirst for revenge.

Guy would not have been so pleased if he had known that his being crossed off the list of suspects only made Mr. Weems more positive that Lady Patricia was the guilty one, and as he was being driven back to his home, he determined to pursue her with even greater fervor in the days following the funeral. Since Mr. Weems considered himself a gentleman, he would not badger the lady at such a sad time. The fact that she would be feeling only elation when Mr. Biddles was buried, if she was indeed her husband's murderess, escaped him.

In the drawing room after dinner, Patricia told Lady Sylvia and Miss Kincaid what had happened in the library that afternoon, and both of them dissolved in helpless laughter in spite of Patricia's trying to shush them, afraid the servants would hear. The three of them went up to bed feeling better than they had for days.

At York House, Guy was greeted warmly by Lord Williams and his cousin, and as they sat and waited for the covers to be brought to his private parlor, and dinner served, he told them all about his long courtship of the Lady Patricia and the problems they now faced.

Charlie's round blue eyes were popping as he reached the end of his story, for although he could sympathize with Guy for falling in love with the lovely Patricia, her marriage to a commoner and his subsequent violent death made her completely ineligible and would cause nothing but scandal in the *ton*. And yet here was Guy determined to marry the woman. He shook his head as James said, "You appear to have extricated yourself very neatly, cuz. Since that is the case, why do you need us? Not that Charlie and I are not panting to assist you, I assure you, but I fail to see any way we can be of use."

The servants knocked then, and until the excellent dinner that Guy had ordered had been served and eaten with relish, especially by Lord Williams, conversation was general.

At last, the headwaiter bowed and left the gentlemen to their port, and Guy explained.

James' hooded eyelids drooped even more and a small smile played over his mouth when he learned he was to take Lady Mills in hand. "I shall be delighted, Guy, and you know, I think I can promise to ensure the lady's fervent cooperation. There is something that I know that even her oh-so-easy-going husband would find hard to ignore. As a gentleman, I cannot disclose it, even to you. Dear me, here I am prepared to stoop to blackmail. I fear my already low standards are descending to an even more subterranean level. But since it is in such a good cause, I will stifle any qualm."

"And what would you have me do, Guy?" Charlie asked as he selected several comfits from the silver dish before him.

When he learned he was to make himself highly visible in Bath and laugh heartily at the very idea of Patricia's guilt, all the while implying he had information that would clear the lady of any complicity in the murder and expounding several other more worthy avenues of investigation, he nodded, deep in thought.

"I rather think the yellow-striped waistcoat, the bottle-green superfine coat, and my new biscuit-colored pantaloons would strike the right note of carefree sincerity. Or do you favor a more somber hue? Perhaps the charcoal-gray coat from Weston, or . . ."

Guy begged him wear whatever he liked. For himself, he would be dressed in unrelieved black on the morrow, for he had a funeral to attend. "I daresay I will be the only mourner," he added. "It will be difficult to present a somber face after what Patricia has told me of the life the man made her lead. However, my attendance at his interment is merely to lend her my support and, I suppose, to make sure that devil is safely below ground at last."

"I shall go with you, cuz," James said. "After all, I would pay my respects to your future bride."

Guy's eyes lit up as he thanked him and called him a capital fellow, and Charlie was so struck by the happiness on his face that all his reservations disappeared at once, and he volunteered his presence as well.

"Of course, we shall not stay for the reading of the will," Guy told them. "I only hope Patricia angered him when she told him about the divorce to the point that he made a new one. Neither of us wants to have to touch his blood money."

The carriage carrying the three friends was at Biddles Hall at ten the following morning, but even so they were not the first mourners to arrive. Ames seemed bemused as he ushered Mr. Biddles' solicitor into the hall, for he was accompanied by a man and woman of very ordinary demeanor, both of whose eyes were big with wonder at the splendor of the hall.

"Mr. and Mrs. Alfred Biddles, Ames," Mr. Preebles announced. "My late client's nephew and his wife."

Ames bowed, eyeing the woman's cheap black cotton gloves and shabby cape, and the way the man clutched his top hat. Although he was dressed in full mourning, it was obvious that he had rented the outfit, for the striped trousers were too short and tight and the tailcoat pinched his shoulders. There was a look of Mr. Biddles about him, for he was short and stout and had the same brown eyes, but Ames could see his expression was much more benign. He left them whispering together as he went to inform Lady Patricia that guests had arrived.

When Ames brought them to the drawing room, where she was sitting with Lady Sylvia, Patricia did all she could to make them feel welcome, although she had never seen them in her life and had not realized Alvin even had a brother or a nephew, but conversation could not be said to flourish, and when Guy and his friends were announced, their impeccable attire seemed to strike even Mr. Preebles dumb. As for Mr. and Mrs. Biddles, they turned identically pale and could be seen to sit even closer together on the edge of a brocade sofa.

Guy did not notice, for his eyes were only on Patricia, her

delicate face and chestnut curls thrown into prominence by the black silk gown she wore, and the pride in his voice as he introduced her to James and Charlie made Lady Sylvia's throat grow tight.

At last the funeral carriages were announced, and the gentlemen left the room. Patricia was glad women never attended such services even as she wondered what she could possibly find to say to the shabby little mouse who looked ready to faint now that her husband's support had been withdrawn. Lady Sylvia came to her rescue.

"Patricia, my dear, order some tea, if you please. I always think a good cup of tea makes everything seem better, don't you, Mrs. Biddles? And you have had a long drive and it is such a sad occasion, too. I am sure you will feel more the thing for it."

As Patricia went to give the order, Mrs. Biddles smiled faintly for the first time. The old lady was kind and she had a look of her own Aunt Ada about her in spite of her grand black dress and jet jewelry.

"And then I think we will ask Wilma to read the burial service for us as well as some selections from the Bible," she continued, and Mrs. Biddles face lit up.

"That's right, that's 'ow—*h*ow it should be done," she whispered.

Patricia smiled at her friend as she passed the teacups, for Lady Sylvia was now deep in a discussion of the church Mrs. Biddles attended and whereabouts in London she lived. By the time the carriages bearing the gentlemen returned, the lady was feeling much more at her ease, and the others knew all about the small Methodist chapel she and her husband belonged to that was dedicated to helping the sick and destitute near the London docks.

After the men had partaken of the funeral meats, those not directly related took their leave. Guy came to bow to Patricia and murmur a few soft words. He thought she was looking strained this morning and pressed her hand with his own warm one as he said, "Courage, love. It will all be over soon."

Patricia's smile was faint. "I know, Guy. It is not that I mourn Alvin, but somehow I cannot help but feel regret for the way he lived his life, and the way he lost it."

"I shall ride out tomorrow, love, and you will be in my thoughts every moment until then."

With another bow, he stepped aside to allow James and Charlie to make their farewells. In the hall, they came upon Mr. Weems, just handing his hat to the butler, and he bowed when Guy introduced him to his friends.

"Come for the reading of the will, have you, Weems? You must not be too disappointed, for I really do not think Mr. Biddles can have left you anything."

Mr. Weems scowled as he prepared to follow the butler to the library. "I am only here in the execution of my duty, sir," he said stiffly.

"And to admire the lovely lady? No, no, do not deny it, sir. It was you, after all, who raved about her beauty and mentioned how fascinating and seductive you found her," Guy continued.

James raised an eyebrow at this baiting and Mr. Weems turned scarlet.

"Your jest is in bad taste, m'lord. And I'll have you know I am a married man with seven children," he said, and then he bowed again and followed the butler.

"Well, that's bowled you out, Guy," James murmured as they climbed into the carriage for the return to Bath. "But the Lady Patricia is indeed a beautiful and lovely woman. You are to be felicitated."

By now, Charlie had fallen under Patricia's gentle spell too, and he echoed these sentiments wholeheartedly, promising he would do everything in his power to help her.

It was a small party who gathered in the library to hear the reading of the will. Mr. Preebles took the seat behind the desk and looked at each one of them: the watchful Mr. Weems, Mr. and Mrs. Biddles, and of course, the Lady Patricia. He sighed and opened his case to withdraw the new will that had been witnessed only a few days ago, and began to read.

But the distasteful task he had to perform was not greeted by any hysteria or ugly scenes. When he read the clause that left Alvin Biddles' entire estate to his nephew, Lady Patricia smiled, a heartfelt smile of relief into which even Mr. Weems could read no duplicity. There followed a few small bequests to the servants, some men Patricia did not know as well as a lady called Bow Street Bella, and only at the end of the will was she acknowledged at all.

"And to Lady Patricia Westerly Biddles that was, I leave only her wedding band so that she might gaze on it for all her earthly life and be brought at last to a sense of shame for her treachery, her lack of obedience, and her willful pride."

Mr. Preebles darted a quick glance at the widow, whose hands were folded serenely in her lap, and she lifted her violet eyes to his and nodded in relief.

Mrs. Alfred Biddles hurried into speech. " 'Ere now, that's not right, Alfie! The leddy should have something more than that, no matter wot she done."

"That's the ticket, Mabel," Mr. Biddles said stoutly. "Never you fear, your Ladyship, we'll see you all right. Whatever are the likes of us to do with such a fortune and this big mansion?"

Patricia smiled as she rose. "Why, Mr. Biddles, I imagine you will find a very good use for your inheritance. Just think of all the ill, poor people that you can help now, the orphans and unwed mothers and disabled soldiers. I thank you, but I have no need of the money; in fact, I could not have accepted it if it had been left to me."

Mr. Weems' jaw dropped in shock, and Mr. and Mrs. Biddles sat staring straight ahead, their eyes shining as the enormity of the good they could do in the Lord's name became clear to them.

Mr. Preebles was delighted at the way things had turned out, and he opened the vault to give Patricia the wedding band she had hoped never to see again.

Tucking it into a pocket of her dress, she offered to show the Biddles the mansion and have rooms prepared for them. Mr. Biddles rose and bowed, his brown eyes soft. "Thank you for your kindness, your Ladyship, but Mabel and I are anxious to get back to London as soon as ever we can. We left the nippers with her mum, see, so we'll just be going along with that lawyer chappie. Now don't you feel you must 'urry to leave the 'all, for we won't be wantin' it. In fact, I intend to sell it if I can. It's too far from our church to be of any use to us, for the people wot we 'elps wouldn't want to live in the country. You just stay as long as you likes."

Patricia thanked him gravely, but said she had other plans. "What would you like me to do about the servants, Mr. Biddles?" she asked.

Arrangements were made to discharge them after she left, keeping only a skeleton staff as caretakers, and a short time later the Biddles, Mr. Preebles, and a strangely subdued and pensive Mr. Weems took their leave.

Patricia went to find Lady Sylvia, glad she did not have to entertain Mr. Biddles' relatives further, worthy though they might be, and the ladies spent a quiet evening and were early to bed.

Guy arrived the following morning as promised, and Ames escorted him to the gold salon, where the three ladies were seated with their needlework. He waited only until the door had closed behind the butler before he took Patricia in his arms and kissed her gently, his eyes searching her face. At her composed smile, he nodded his relief, although he hated the shadow still in her eyes and wondered why it lingered.

When he learned that Biddles had left his fortune to his nephew, and only the wedding band to Patricia, he uttered a heartfelt "Thank God!" but when he heard that Mr. Weems intended to call at the hall the following day, he frowned. Before he could speak, his aunt said, "There is no need for you to be here, Guy. You are well out of it, and between us, Patricia and I can handle the man. Tomorrow I am going to suggest he question my servants in Great Pulteney Street, for of course Patricia did not leave the house after your ride the day Mr. Biddles was shot. He will have to prove she hired an assassin, and since we know she did not, you have nothing to worry about."

Miss Kincaid, who had followed the conversation and squirming eagerly in her seat, now interrupted as if she could contain herself no longer. "There is something of much more importance that you can do, m'lord," she said. "When I was in the library helping Mr. Weems go over Mr. Biddles' papers, I noted a very curious fact."

Guy sat down next to Patricia as all eyes turned toward the lady who had already proved her astuteness.

"I remembered the name 'Granford' from Lady Patricia's conversation and looked for the two brothers' notes. There were any number of papers from Mr. Biddles' other debtors, but nothing pertaining to either Granford—not a letter, a note, or a loan. I find that most unusual and suspicious. Either Lord Granford discharged his debt and his brother's as well when he called here, or someone took the incriminating papers away."

"His killer, you mean?" Guy asked, his face intent and serious at this news.

As Miss Kincaid nodded, Patricia volunteered, "Ames told me that Lord Granford did call the day after I asked Mr. Biddles for a divorce, but he only stayed for an hour or so. There were no other callers before his death, most certainly not young Sidney Granford, for whom I asked especially."

"Excellent!" Miss Kincaid enthused. "If I might suggest it, m'lord, I think it would be wise for you to seek out these gentlemen and question them without delay."

Guy nodded, stroking his chin as he thought. "Lord Granford has rooms on Whitcomb Street in town. I am not acquainted with his brother, but his whereabouts should not be too difficult to discover." He turned to Patricia then. "Would it distress you if I left you for a few days, my dear? I agree with Miss Kincaid that this is a lead we must not ignore, and I do not think that turning over the information to Mr. Weems will produce the quick results that I myself can."

"I am going to be very busy, Guy. There is closing the hall to see to, and servants to dismiss, and since I want to be away from here as soon as I can, a great many domestic chores to do before that is possible. I should not say it, but right now you would only be very much in the way."

"That puts me in my place and dampens any pretensions that I might have, does it not?" Guy asked, but he smiled at her as he said it. "In that case, I shall leave for London this afternoon, but you may call on James or Charlie if you need assistance. They remain at York House, for they are busy with some commissions I gave them."

"Do not ask anything about it, Patricia. I am sure, knowing the three of them, it is something unsuitable," Lady Sylvia said as she rose to leave. "Come, Wilma, let us go out once more into the garden so Lord Reading can take his leave of Patricia."

As the two ladies reached the door, she added in an audible whisper, "I shall be so glad when I can stop popping in and out of gardens and drawing rooms, won't you, my dear? It does make one feel so . . . so unwanted."

Guy laughed, but as the door closed behind his aunt, he was eager to take Patricia into his arms.

Her response was as warm as ever, and yet there was something in her embrace, some little desperation, that had not been there before, and Guy looked deep into her eyes, his own a little puzzled. Then he shrugged mentally. No doubt he was reading things into her kiss because he hated so to leave her, even for only a few days. And perhaps she is upset by our coming separation, too, he thought, and he whispered in her ear, begging her to miss him as much as he would miss her.

"I shall, of course, but I will be too busy to fall into a sad decline, my dear Guy," she assured him, and then one hand came up and traced the contours of his lean, handsome face, almost as if she were trying to memorize it. When she saw him watching her so closely, she smiled a little before she lowered her eyes, and Guy held her close again for one last, prolonged farewell.

He was back at York House in an hour, ordering his valet to pack, and since neither James nor Charlie was in the inn, he wrote them both a short note explaining his absence and begging their kindness for his lady.

Even springing his teams, it was late in the afternoon, two days later, before he reached the outskirts of the metropolis, and he decided it would be better to wait and call on Lord Granford in the morning, when he was fresh. And so he changed his travel-dusty clothes, saw to the post that had accumulated in his absence, and strolled to Brooks Club to discover who might still be in town. He knew the Prince Regent had left for Brighton, and so he was not too surprised at the sparseness of the company, and after a hearty dinner and a few hands of cards, he went back to his rooms for a good night's sleep, for he knew he would need his wits about him on the morrow.

He arrived at Lord Granford's rooms in Whitcomb Street early the following morning, and was fortunate to find the gentleman in residence. Lord Granford's eyebrows rose when his visitor's name was announced, for although he knew Viscount Reading by sight, they had never moved in the same circles, but even so, he nodded to his man.

Guy found him in his sitting room, dressed except for his coat and cravat, as he lingered over the remains of his breakfast.

"Come in and tell me how I might serve you, m'lord." Lord Granford smiled cordially, but Guy noted that his smile never reached those cold blue eyes. "Some coffee, sir? Perhaps a mug of ale?"

Guy accepted the coffee and took the chair the manservant was holding out for him. He waited until he had left the room, and then he said, "It was good of you to see me, m'lord. Since we have never been particular friends, I am sure you are wondering at my errand. Not to put too fine a point on it, I am here in regards to Alvin J. Biddles' recent death."

Lord Granford put his cup down slowly, his narrowed eyes never leaving Guy's face. "Biddles is dead?" he asked in a wondering voice, and then he smiled broadly. "I did not know, and I can hardly contain my exultation, m'lord. You are a friend of mine indeed to bring me such news! But how did it happen? Did he die in a fit of apoplexy because someone managed to discharge his obligation at last?"

Guy noticed that he seemed overjoyed to hear the news, although he did not show any knowledge of the details of Biddles' demise, and his spirits plummeted. Surely, unless the man was a consummate actor, he could not have known anything about it.

"He was shot while working in his library, m'lord," Guy said.

Lord Granford paused in the act of wiping his mouth with his napkin. "Shot? Murdered, you mean?" he asked, his tone more interested now. "If I do not seem overly surprised, you must forgive me. The man had more enemies than anyone I know, for he was universally despised, and I, I must admit, was in the forefront of the ranks of those who hated him."

There was a short silence, and then he added, "You must forgive me, m'lord, but why do you come and tell me this news, welcome though it is? I am afraid I do not understand."

"You are known to have owed Mr. Biddles money, m'lord, as did your younger brother."

Lord Granford's pleasant look disappeared, and his eyes narrowed again. "I owed him money, that is true, but my brother Sidney has never had anything to do with the old reprobate, for I saw to that."

Guy sipped his coffee, his mind busy. "I am sorry to have to contradict you, m'lord, but he has owed Mr. Biddles money for over two years. Perhaps you can tell me where I can find your brother?"

Lord Granford rose to lean on the table, his manner threatening, and Guy stood up to face him. "I find such a request insulting, sir," he said, his voice as icy as his eyes. "May I ask in what capacity you are here and what right you have to question us?" He sneered a little. "Can it be that the mighty Viscount Reading has stooped to a career with the law? How very odd that would be.''

"I am here as a friend of the family, sir," Guy answered.

"Aha! Now I understand. Since no one would ever claim such a relationship with Mr. Biddles, it must be the luscious Lady Patricia you would befriend. I quite understand. I myself, you know, was very taken with her, very taken indeed. Did you know she was about to divorce the unprincipled Alvin, unfortunately before a certain business deal I had with her husband that involved her lovely self could be brought to fruition? I cannot tell you how disappointed I was at her defection.''

Guy clenched his fists, glad that the tablecloth hid them from sight as he strove to control his anger and his features. Lord Granford would never know how close to death he was just then.

"She is a beautiful woman, that is true," Guy remarked casually. "And she is a great friend of my aunt's, Lady Sylvia Randolph, as well. It is at her urging that I am investigating the crime, for the Justice for the County has made up his mind that Lady Patricia shot her husband. It was her pistol that was used, you see.''

Now Lord Granford smiled, easy again. "And who can blame her, poor honey, if she did shoot him? But we must hope the justice is wrong in his suppositions; it would be such a waste. In regards to myself, I called at Biddles Hall the first of July and I have not been in the vicinity since.''

He paused and straightened up to yawn before he rang the bell. "As for my brother, he has not left London since Christmas week. It would be useless to question him. And now you must excuse me, m'lord. A trifling matter of an appointment I have. When you see the Lady Patricia, do say everything that is polite for me, although one can hardly send her condolences at her loss. Show Viscount Reading out, Banners," he ordered the manservant who had come to stand behind Guy.

Guy was forced to bow and take his leave, but when he reached the street again, he only walked as far as the corner, and then he waited, half-hidden by some wrought-iron palings.

It was only a few minutes later that Lord Granford left his rooms, clapping his beaver on his blond hair as he strode away toward Trafalgar Square. Guy followed, at a discreet distance.

Lord Granford crossed the Strand and made his way to
Villiers Street. Fortunately traffic was heavy that morning
and there were plenty of people in the streets, although Granford
did not seem overly worried about being followed for he
never looked around. He entered a tall, narrow house halfway
down the block, and Guy turned away after carefully noting
the number.

An hour later he returned. The manservant who answered
his knock nodded when he asked for Mr. Sidney Granford,
and pointed up the stairs.

"Top o' the stairs, second door to your right, sir."

It was obvious that the younger man could not afford the
luxuries and amenities Lord Granford could. When he opened
the door, Guy saw that he was a younger copy of his brother.
He had the same blond hair, blue eyes, and loose-limbed
frame, although his eyes were worried and set in deep circles,
and the lines on his face were strongly marked, as if he had
not been sleeping well. When Guy introduced himself, he
tried at once to slam the door, but Guy pushed it open and
entered over his vehement protests.

"Here now, m'lord, what are you about to force your way in
here?" he asked in a high, nervous baritone.

"I have come to see you about the death of Alvin Biddles,
and that can come as no surprise to you, for I know your
brother was here just a short time ago. He no doubt told you
all about it. May I sit down?" he asked gently, and Mr.
Granford nodded, running a nervous hand through his hair.
Guy could see the faint sheen of perspiration on his brow,
although the young man soon had control of himself, for when
he sat down opposite his unwanted visitor, his demeanor was
cool.

"And if that is the case, why are you here?" Sidney asked,
trying for his older brother's sneer, and failing abominably.

"I came to discover if you know anything about the murder,
sir. You see, Mr. Biddles' wife is under a cloud, for it was
her own pistol that killed her husband. She was nowhere near
the hall at the time, but for lack of any other suspects, she is
being questioned and reviled by society. Surely you must
agree that that is an unenviable position for an innocent
gentlewoman?"

"I am sorry for her, of course, but what has that to do with
me?" Mr. Granford blustered.

"There is something that points to you or your brother in the case. I do not think it wise to disclose the information at this time, however. By the way, have you been in Midsomer Norton lately?"

"Certainly not! I have not left town for weeks," Mr. Granford exclaimed, but his eyes slid away from Guy's for a moment as he spoke, and his hands moved nervously until he clasped them to stop their trembling.

"Well, no doubt the authorities will have further questions for you, and it should be easy to check the inns in the vicinity or en route that might have enjoyed your patronage," Guy said casually as he rose. "Thank you for your time, sir. If you should change your mind about speaking to me, you may reach me at Number Fifteen, Jermyn Street, or at Brooks. I shall be in London for a few days before I return to lay my information before the justice in the case."

He bowed and went to the door, noting that Mr. Granford was chewing his thumbnail now and his blue eyes looked desperate.

Guy strolled back to his rooms, wondering if he had accomplished anything. Young Granford was obviously the prime suspect, and although that fact might have made him act as nervously as he had, it did not mean he was guilty, after all. Guy sighed. He would have to prove that the young man had been in Midsomer Norton at the time of Biddles' death. Perhaps the servant at his lodging house would know if he had been out of town at that time, and if Mr. Granford saw that he was still under suspicion, it might make him reckless. If he made a bolt for the Continent, Guy would have all the proof he needed.

But on the morrow, when he arrived at Villiers Street again, it was to find a crowd of people gathered before Mr. Granford's rooming house and two men carrying a blanket-shrouded body down the front steps. Guy pushed his way past the whispering crowd, all craning their necks to see, and went to question the constable in charge.

When he learned that the dead man was Sidney Granford and that he had taken his own life by what appeared to be a glass of poisoned wine, Guy explained his curiosity.

"I am Viscount Reading, and I have an interest in the case. Did Mr. Granford leave any letter?" he asked the constable.

"Aye, that he did, milord. He admitted he killed himself

because he was so afeared o' hangin' for the murder of some
gent down near Bath wot he said he shot. Claimed it's been
preyin' on his mind ever since, even though it was an accident.
Accordin' to him, this Mr. Biddles threatened him with a
gun, and in their struggle for it, it went off and killed him.
Would you be knowin' anything about that, milord?''

Guy admitted that he did, and he escorted the constable to
headquarters, where he told his story to the proper authorities.
He was sorry for young Granford, but at the same time he
could not help the elation he felt that Patricia had been
exonerated at last. He could hardly restrain himself from
riding to Bath at once to tell her the good news.

But he was forced to delay for another day while the
investigation was concluded, and when at last he left, driving
his racing curricle, he had in his jacket pocket a letter to Mr.
Justice Weems and a copy of Granford's suicide note.

He could not resist going directly to Biddles Hall, even
before he left his baggage and valet at York House, and he
was surprised to find the gate house empty and the first-floor
windows of the hall draped and shuttered.

He had to knock several times before the butler came to
admit him, looking flustered as he did so.

"Your pardon, my lord. There's only myself and a few
servants left, for Lady Patricia has gone away for good," he
explained.

Guy looked over his shoulder to see two men carrying a
large oil painting down the stairs, and his eyebrows rose, for
he could see that it was the full-length portrait of Patricia that
Mr. Biddles had bragged about so, and although her face and
figure in the lavender satin gown and lavish jewels were still
plain to see, the whole painting had been destroyed by deep,
savage cuts. At Guy's questioning look, the butler hastened
to explain.

"M'lady did that, sir. She said that she wanted it removed
from the hall, and to be sure that it was never seen again, she
slashed it with a kitchen knife. I'm sure I don't wonder at her
actions, m'lord, such misery as her life has always been here.
She ordered me to burn it."

He looked distressed at the task even so, and Guy hastened
to reassure him, even though he was disturbed at the magni-
tude of the destruction. "Quite right you should do so, Ames.
Lady Patricia wishes no reminders of her former marriage,

nor the agony of suspicion she has endured since Mr. Biddles' murder. You will be happy to learn that the case has been solved and it was the younger Mr. Granford who shot your late master. He killed himself in London and left a note confessing his part."

The butler's face brightened. "That's all right, m'lord, now the lady can be easy. It's been hard on her, poor lass, although I shouldn't say so."

Guy nodded and took his leave, sure he would find Patricia in Great Pulteney Street again. He took the time now to stop at York House and change his clothes, and to leave the evidence at Justice Weems' house before he went to join her, but when he entered his aunt's drawing room, it was to find her alone and looking somehow saddened and upset.

He blurted out the good news of Patricia's freedom from suspicion and she smiled her relief, but it was hardly her usual, warm smile.

"What is wrong, *chère tante*? And where is Patricia? I want to tell her at once."

"Sit down, Guy. She is not here, she left Bath this morning. Indeed, almost as soon as we quit Biddles Hall and after Justice Weems accepted her alibi for the afternoon of the murder, she decided to leave. But it was only after we attended services at the abbey yesterday evening that she told me her plans. Nothing I could say would persuade her to change her mind about going to her grandmother's—she would not even await your return."

Guy frowned, his eyes stern. "How could she go, Aunt, just like that, without a word to me?" he asked, as if he could hardly credit it.

"She left you a letter. You will find it in the drawer of the writing table."

Guy went to the delicately carved cherry table and took out a bulky packet. As he opened it, the Leighton betrothal ring fell into his hand, and he stared at it, his brows contracted.

For a long time there was silence in the drawing room, and Lady Sylvia watched him with apprehension. She saw the way his mouth hardened, the lean planes of his face grew taut with emotion, and his gray eyes became bleak and cold. At length he put the ring in his pocket without comment and read the letter. When he had finished it, he gripped the sheets tightly in a clenched fist, his eyes unseeing as he recalled the complete destruction of her portrait.

"What does she say, my dear? Where has she gone?" his aunt asked.

"You had better read it yourself," Guy said in a voice choked with emotion, and he handed her the sheets before he went to pour himself a glass of wine. In his distress, he tossed it off at once.

Lady Sylvia smoothed out the crumpled sheets, and as she read, her heart sank. Patricia had written to say good-bye, and to ask Guy not to try to find her or contact her again.

> I cannot marry you now, or at any time in the future. You have exchanged the stigma of choosing a divorced woman for a bride who was a suspected murderess, Guy, and that is much, much worse. I cannot allow you to make such a disastrous sacrifice, no matter how much we love each other. Your life would be ruined, for neither of us would ever be received again. I know the agony of society's banishment; I can never let you suffer such pain. Believe that I will always love you, my dear, and I will never forget you as long as I live, nor the wonderful gift of your love and devotion, which you gave me so freely. I can never thank you enough for that precious memory, nor for your support and endless kindness. Good-bye.
>
>   Patricia

Lady Sylvia felt her tears well up and spill over, and she raised her sad, old face to her nephew. To her surprise, he was smiling now, a little grimly to be sure, but smiling nevertheless.

When he saw her looking at him in such amazement, he said in a strong, determined voice, "You are not to be concerned or to worry, *chère tante*. I shall go after Patricia at once, and when I find her, possibly as soon as tomorrow, I shall claim her as my bride. There will be no nonsense about 'suspected murderesses' or 'disastrous sacrifices.' She will marry me, you'll see."

PART FOUR

River Court–1815,
London–1816

12

Guy spent several more minutes with his aunt, questioning her about the exact time Patricia had left town and in what manner she was traveling. He was relieved that she had hired a carriage complete with coachman and grooms, and a maid to lend her consequence for the journey.

As he strode quickly across the bridge on his way back to York House, he realized that there were several things that he must do before he went after his elusive bride, but even with the delay, he was sure he could catch her up before she reached Kingsfold. A lady traveling sedately by coach was no match for a driver of the viscount's ability, seated as he would be in his racing curricle behind a team of matchless horses.

Accordingly, he wrote several notes when he reached his rooms, sending them off at once by hired grooms, and then he went to make an important call on the local clergy. Even with the delay, he did not feel discouraged as his heart followed Patricia across the miles. Soon, he thought to himself, I will be with her soon.

For her part, Patricia held onto the strap of the carriage that was taking her to her grandmother's, and stared with unseeing eyes at the passing countryside. The maid she had hired noticed the grief and loss in her eyes, and her white, strained face, and wisely refrained from chattering.

Sad as she was, Patricia knew she had done the right thing in leaving Bath. She had known it since her final interview at Biddles Hall with Justice Wilfred Weems, an interview she had decided she would never relate to another soul, although she knew she would remember it always.

It had begun as all the others, with courtesies exchanged while Lady Sylvia fixed a firm eye on Patricia's questioner, but in a very few minutes, the elderly lady was called away.

A friend had driven out from Bath, and she had gone to receive her visitor in the morning room, thinking these final questions a mere formality. Patricia had been left to face the justice alone.

She noticed his air of profound suspicion and the way his bright blue eyes never left her face as he asked question after question. There was more than a trace of insolence in his manner, as if he had never really given up his idea of her as the primary suspect. Patricia answered him as coolly as she could, her courteous replies hiding the shrinking she felt at still being considered a murderess. To think that such a man as Wilfred Weems should treat her with sneers and barely veiled contempt, to think that even the servants' assurances that she had not left the house in Great Pulteney Street had not removed the stigma! He let her know, by some of his barked queries about her stay at her grandmother's, that he was sure she had hired an assassin. He accepted the fact that the viscount had not been involved, but surely she had found another to do the foul deed for her.

At last he shuffled his papers back into his case, his long, narrow face set in lines of mistrust and dislike. "I see there is no way to prove either your innocence or your guilt, m'lady," he sneered in a cold, angry voice. "I must accept this, er, this *alibi* of yours, but you may be sure I will continue the search for your accomplice."

At that, Patricia rose, her breathing unsteady, although not a sign of it showed in her flashing violet eyes and disdainful white face. "You are insulting, sir. I have told you I did not kill my husband, and since I know I did not hire an accomplice, I do not fear what any search of yours might reveal. And now, you must excuse me."

Her voice was so haughty that Mr. Weems found himself on his feet, making vague apologies as she went to summon the butler to show him out. After he had bowed himself away, Patricia sank down into a chair and gripped the arms tightly in her distress. It was plain to see that her innocence did not matter. If no murderer were ever found, she would continue to be suspected. And if a social snob like Wilfred Weems dared to treat her with such insolence, how not might society react? And not only to her, but to Guy as well?

As the carriage lumbered along, Patricia remembered how that thought had brought a sudden cry of agony that she had quickly muffled with a trembling fist, and how she had wept bitterly for some time.

Guy might think he loved her enough so that society's censure would not matter, but Patricia knew otherwise. After a few years, his resentment was sure to grow when he was still treated as a pariah, no invitations were ever extended to the pair of them, and he found himself lonely and universally scorned, even by his former friends. And if they had children, even if it did divert his mind for a while, sooner or later he would come to blame her, not only for his own exile, but for his hopeful family's as well.

Here, Patricia could not restrain a sob that she would never know the joy of holding Guy's son in her arms, and the maid shook her head as she handed her a handkerchief, sure the lady must be on her way to the funeral of her dearest friend. Patricia did not even notice her sympathetic gaze, for she was remembering that it was after Justice Weem's final visit that she had decided to destroy her portrait.

With the first slash of the knife through the ornate painted jewels and opulent satin on the heavy canvas, she had lost control of herself and been consumed by a frenzy. As she ripped, she told herself that never again would anyone look at this likeness and sneer at its owner. Never again would anyone be able to point to her as Mrs. Biddles. But when she was through and had dropped the knife to the floor, panting in her exhaustion and relief, she realized that that was who she would always be, no matter how many paintings she destroyed, and she dropped her face in her hands and wept again.

She had known even before Guy went to London what she should do, but she had tried to fight leaving him. It had taken Justice Weems to show her how she would always be regarded, yet still she made no move to leave Bath. In her mind were vague dreams of leaving the country, going somewhere they were not known—perhaps even changing their names. And then she had shaken her head and berated herself. Guy Leighton, Viscount Reading, was an Englishman. Not even for her would he leave his home, his country, and his responsibilities. If they married, they would remain here.

Yet, still, she put off going, and it was not until she accompanied Lady Sylvia to the abbey that she realized fully the terrible consequences of any marriage between them.

Even heavily veiled, she had been recognized in her black

mourning, and she could hear the whispers and exclamations all around until the choir drowned them out. And afterward, when she had followed Lady Sylvia up the aisle, she had seen how people turned their backs on her, both men and women, or pointed and denounced her. One woman had even gone so far as to cover her young daughter's eyes until she passed, and another swept her skirts to one side as if any contact with Patricia would contaminate her. James may have stilled Lady Mills' malicious tongue, but the damage had been done. Too many of Bath's elite subscribed to the old adage that where there's smoke, there's fire. No, she had been sentenced and condemned, and nothing would change that.

Lady Sylvia had not noticed this hateful reception in the abbey, for she had been attending to General Cowles, who was chatting with her eagerly in hopes he might return to her good graces after his snub of her nephew. In spite of her pleading that Patricia wait until Guy return from London, she had been unable to get her to change her mind. Patricia thanked her for her concern, but still she went away to write Guy a farewell note, to pack, and to ask Lady Sylvia's butler to see to the traveling arrangements.

Patricia knew that life with her grandmother would be quiet and uneventful, but she also knew it was all that was in store for her now. She hoped that in time she would be able to accept this haven with some degree of composure and resignation, even as she knew she would never be able to forget Guy. She was sure that he would be in her thoughts every day and that she would continue to pray for his well-being every night.

On the last morning before she reached Kingsfold, Patricia came down to find her carriage had not been brought around to the front yard of the inn. She sent her maid to find out the reason for this delay, in her abstraction missing the excited smirk the woman gave her as she curtsied and hurried away.

It was a lovely July day, and knowing she would be cooped up in a closed carriage and jounced and bounced for hours, Patricia took advantage of the delay to stroll down the road. She drew a deep breath of the fresh air, wishing her mood was more in tune with the cheerful songs of the birds and the riotous colors of the wildflowers that grew in profusion in the grassy verge.

Some little distance ahead of her she saw a curricle stopped by the side of the road, and although there was no driver nor groom in sight, she paused, not wishing to meet anyone. Accordingly, she turned to make her way back to the inn. She barely heard the rush of footsteps behind her, before she was caught up in a pair of strong arms. Her heart beat with wild fright for only a moment, for there close to her was Guy, his gray eyes blazing down at her and a grin creasing his handsome face:

"Thank you for allowing me the pleasure of your company, m'lady," he said formally as he covered the ground to the curricle in quick, impatient strides. "A delightful day for a ride, is it not?"

"Guy, put me down at once! What are you doing?" Patricia panted, pounding his chest with her fists.

"But I told you. I am taking you for a drive," he said as he deposited her in the curricle and climbed up beside her. Patricia was forced to slide along the seat to give him room, and he picked up the slack reins and clucked the team into motion before she could scramble down. She turned her head to see him smiling at her—that dear, familiar smile she loved—and her heart turned over.

For a moment, she sat silently, trying to put her tumultuous thoughts in order, then she put up her chin and, not looking at Guy, said, "You know the decision I made in Bath is irrevocable, so why are you here? You do not hope to change my mind on a short drive, do you?"

"Certainly not. I have no intention of attempting the impossible," Guy said, one corner of his mouth quirking a little in amusement.

Patricia did not notice, for she felt a stab of disappointment that he had accepted her ultimatum so calmly.

"No, I have quite another objective in mind," he continued. "You did not notice that there is no groom in attendance? Nor baggage? I bribed your maid and your coachman, you see. It is too bad that you have to figure in the piece as a runaway wife—I hope you will forgive me the duplicity. The coach is even now on its way to River Court." He paused, but Patricia only looked straight ahead and he had to say to her elegant profile, "But I have wonderful news, love! The younger Mr. Granford has confessed to Mr. Biddles' murder. You are no longer a suspect."

Now Patricia turned and stared at him, hope growing in her

violet eyes as he told her what had happened in London, ending by saying, "Now that the real murderer is known, and there was no divorce, you have become a fitting consort for even a duke. Alas, that you must settle for a mere viscount!"

He paused again, but still Patricia refused to speak, her face sad again. For a moment when she first heard the news, she had felt a wild elation before she realized that nothing had changed. The scandal would cling to both of them all their lives.

Guy ignored her stony silence and continued, "Our wedding will take place in Arundel this afternoon. It will be a private ceremony by special license. I have already sent to make arrangements with the vicar. And in the lifetime that we will spend together, I am sure I can convince you that our marriage is not the disaster you predict it will be, my darling, foolish Viscountess Reading-to-be."

"Take me to Kingsfold at once," Patricia commanded, finding her voice at last.

"No, we are going home—home to River Court," he replied, increasing the pace until she was forced to clutch the side of the seat as he took a corner at speed.

"I will not marry you, Guy! You cannot force me to do it!"

"You mistake the matter, Patricia. Kidnapped ladies always end up marrying their abductors. If you recall, they really have no say at all. You should know that from reading all those novels with your grandmother. And I *have* kidnapped you. Now, I can either keep you all night and ruin your reputation, or kiss you into complacency. Which would you prefer, love? I know which I would choose."

Again those gray eyes caressed her face, and she caught her breath.

"Since my reputation is ruined already, it does not signify," Patricia said bitterly. "You might keep me prisoner for years and no one would think a thing of it. Whatever sins the Lady Patricia Biddles commits can come as no surprise to anyone."

"Stop it at once!" Guy thundered in a harsh voice, and Patricia was so stunned, she fell silent, her eyes widening at the anger she had never heard in his voice before.

"I never want to hear such foolishness from you again, Patricia, do you hear me? It makes me very angry. Do not be imagining that society will never forget your late husband and

he manner of his death, or ever again blame you for it. The
murderer has confessed.''

Suddenly he pulled his team to a halt by the side of the
road and turned to her, his eyes dark with emotion and
determination. ''You must explain to me someday why you
were willing to face the scandal of divorce to marry me, but
refuse to consider it after the death of your husband set you
free. I do not understand it.''

She lowered her eyes and he commanded, ''Look at me!
Tell me you do not love me, assure me that you are happy to
be separated from me forever, promise me on your honor that
you do not want to marry me, and I will take you to Darrow
Manor now.''

There was silence for a moment, filled only with the sounds
of the horses and the clinking of their harness, and Patricia
stared at him.

''I cannot tell you that,'' she said at last, very quietly. At
once, all the deep frowning lines in Guy's face were gone and
his gray eyes blazed.

''Of course you cannot, because it would be a lie. Oh, this
nicety of behavior you practice and your wish to spare me is
all very fine, my dear, but I do not want to be spared, and
besides, there is nothing to spare me. I have no desire to
spend the rest of my life in loneliness and regret. You will
marry me this afternoon.''

He paused, but she did not speak, and seeing the trouble
and doubt still lurking in her eyes, he added more gently,
''You will see, my heart. I promise you that it will all come
right. I beg you to trust me, love.''

And then he leaned over and kissed her softly. His strong
hands still held the restless team, and she made no move to
touch him, so the only contact between them was their lips,
his demanding and hers surrendering. Patricia felt again that
tiny tingle begin deep inside her, and she sighed and gave up
what had turned out to be a very unequal struggle.

When he lifted his head, she said, ''Very well, I cannot
fight you any longer, Guy. I will marry you, but I hope you
will never come to regret it.''

''Idiot!'' He smiled, and then he transferred the reins to
one hand so he could reach into his driving coat and take out
the Leighton betrothal ring. He held it out until she raised her
left hand, and then he slipped it on her finger.

He looked deep into her eyes once more and then he nodded. "This is the last time we will become engaged, ma'am, for since our wedding follows so swiftly, I feel safe in assuming that my ring will stay on your finger where it belongs, now and forever."

He lifted the reins and started the team again, and Patricia stared at the road ahead with unseeing eyes. In spite of her inner happiness and her desire for him, she still felt a little *frisson* of unease. It was all very well for Guy to say that the *ton* did not matter, but she suspected that sooner or later they would have to pay, and pay dearly, for their present happiness. And then she put up her chin. I don't care, she thought, her violet eyes sparkling. I will marry him for I love him so much I cannot bear not to. I'll worry about the future later.

All through the brilliant July day they drove through the countryside, stopping at Billingshurst and Storrington to change the teams, and it was at this last stop that she saw Guy's grays being led from the inn stable and knew they were not far from home. Guy called for the innkeeper and demanded a private parlor and some refreshments for Viscountess Reading, and Patricia smiled as he lifted her down and escorted her into the inn.

"Viscountess Reading, indeed," she teased, "what a bouncer!"

"I could not resist saying it, love, and it is only such a little lie now," he replied.

Patricia was glad to drink some lemonade, but she was not at all hungry, and in a little while they set off across the South Downs, following the river to Arundel.

The ceremony in the village church seemed to take but a moment, and Patricia felt no regret that she was wed in a simple blue muslin gown and a wide-brimmed straw hat and that there were no flowers or music or wedding guests. With Guy beside her, his dark hair gleaming in the dusty motes of sunlight that came through the stained-glass windows, and his strong, warm hand holding hers, she needed nothing more.

She spoke the vows in her soft, gentle voice, watching Guy's face as she did so, and his gray eyes adored her as she did so. His own vows rang out in the empty church, and then his wedding band was on her finger and he was kissing her while the vicar, his wife, and the curate beamed and waited to lead them to the parish register to sign their names.

When the vicar's wife begged them to come to the manse for refreshments, Guy would not linger. "No, thank you, Mrs. Graham," he said as he helped Patricia to her seat in the curricle again. "We are for River Court. My viscountess has had a long drive today and I want to take her home."

Mr. Graham blessed them once more as they drove away, and a few miles farther on, Guy turned off the road between a pair of stone pillars and a wrought-iron gate and drove up a long gravel drive.

"Welcome to River Court," he said, his voice big with pride. "I cannot believe even now that you are here, where I have wanted to see you for so long—my wife, Patricia Leighton, Viscountess Reading."

Patricia looked about eagerly, noting the well-kept fields, mellow in the late-afternoon light, the tenant's cottages and orchards, the beech wood and the winding, slow-moving river, and as they came to a halt before the old brick mansion that was Guy's home, it was just as she had pictured it in her mind: warm, and welcoming, and beautiful.

13

Guy came around to help her down, his hands on her waist warm and supportive, and she took a deep breath. The air, even this many miles from the sea and heavily scented with summer flowers, still held a refreshing tang. There was a drone of bees and she could hear some doves cooing in a dovecote somewhere nearby, their contented sounds the perfect music for such a peaceful scene.

Guy introduced her as Viscountess Reading to his butler, and Petson bid her welcome to River Court as he ushered them up the steps to where his wife, the housekeeper, was curtsying and smiling. Patricia smiled in return when the good lady offered to show her her rooms and promised to be on the lookout for the coach and milady's baggage.

While Mrs. Petson took her over the rooms that were to be hers, Patricia could hear Guy next door, discussing the wines he wanted served at dinner with the butler and ordering champagne as well. Patricia looked around at the beautiful furniture and new hangings of pale-blue silk, and the many flower arrangements that covered every surface and turned the bedroom and salon into a bower, and she smiled. She sensed that Guy had decorated these rooms just for her, for everything was so fresh and new. She went to one of the windows and set it wide to catch the gentle breeze.

"Now, m'lady, you have only to ring and one of the maids—Sally's her name—will bring you hot water and unpack for you as soon as your trunks arrive," Mrs. Petson said. "Be sure and tell me if there is anything at all that you require."

She curtsied and left the room, and in a moment, Patricia heard Mr. Petson's slow steps going down the stairs. She leaned against the windowsill, admiring the setting until Guy came in and took her in his arms.

The kiss they shared, although as fervent as ever, somehow seemed different to Patricia. For the first time there was a feeling of freedom from any restrictions, an openness to their embrace, and she felt very married indeed. This feeling did not lessen when Guy took her out to stroll in the garden and beside the river until it was time to dress for dinner, nor did it change all through that festive meal. Guy looked at her face often, his own somehow solemn and too tightly controlled, although when Patricia began to wonder at this, she had only to look into those piercing gray eyes to find the eager lover waiting and watching her with so much longing, and she clasped her hands in her lap for a moment so he would not see them tremble. Their conversation was light and inconsequential as Mr. Petson hovered over the sideboard and directed the footmen as they served them.

Patricia wondered at Guy's restraint. He acted as if they had been married for years. She was not to know that her new husband had himself on a very firm leash. There was nothing he wanted more than to love her, but he wanted to make their wedding day and evening perfect in every way so no shadow would fall over this, their first lovemaking together. For his viscountess there would be no hasty tumble into bed, no breathless, quick release of passion; instead, he intended to woo her with all the powers he could summon to show her not only his love, but his respect for her as well, for surely that would vanquish all her doubts. He smiled a little as he toasted her silently with champagne when he saw the surprise and tiny reserve in her violet eyes, but still he did not change his manner.

After dinner, Patricia realized she could not remember a single thing she had eaten, nor had she tasted the wines that were served to complement the dishes, and she noticed Guy himself had no comment on the food. After a few, quiet words with the butler, he escorted her to the drawing room, for he had no wish to sit alone drinking port tonight. Patricia stood in the middle of the room, her hands clasped before her and her face still as Guy said, "Come out and stroll on the terrace, love. It is warm this evening and you will not need a wrap."

He led her to the French doors and then outside and put his arm around her as they walked up and down. Patricia sighed and rested her head against that comforting arm as she looked up at the stars—hundreds of them, it seemed—shining brightly above them. For a while they did not speak, and then Guy stopped and turned her to face him as he drew her into his arms. This time his kiss startled Patricia with its searching intensity and sensuality, but she was quick to return it with equal fervor.

"My heart," he murmured when he raised his head at last, but only to kiss the tendrils of chestnut hair that sprang from her forehead before he trailed his lips across her cheek and down her throat, leaving in their wake a score of tiny kisses. Patricia felt herself weakening with desire, her heart pounding and her breath coming in little gasps of delight. She put her arms around his neck and stood on tiptoe to bring her face close to his again, pressing against all the hard, lean length of his body as if she could never get close enough. She felt his demanding hands on her back and hips, and then she was caught in one strong arm while his other hand came up to caress her breasts as he bent his dark head, blotting out the stars as his lips possessed hers once again.

He put her away from him at last, and stepped back to admire her. "Shall we go up, Viscountess Reading?" he asked, his deep voice husky.

She nodded, one slender hand at her throat, and then she went to him and took his arm. "As you say, m'lord," she agreed, and they went back into the house and past the footmen on duty in the hall and began to climb the stairs. "I find the long drive and the fresh air have made me uncommon sleepy and I will be glad to go to bed."

Her eyes burned with smoky deep-purple fire and her lips parted when she saw the dangerous answering light in his own eyes, and then he pressed her hand where it lay on his arm.

"I have ordered you hot water for a bath, wife. I have no doubt you will be glad of it after the dust of the road."

"You are too kind, too thoughtful, sir," she murmured, and then he left her at the door of her rooms, only kissing her hand lightly before he moved to his own room.

Patricia found the little maid in the dressing room, pouring a last copper can of hot water into the tub. She allowed the girl to hang up her evening gown and brush out her hair until it hung in thick waves down her back, shining with coppery highlights, before she dismissed her.

"I shall ring when I want you in the morning, Sally. Leave the bath water until then, if you please," she said, and the maid curtsied and left her.

Patricia took off her shirt and her stockings, and fastening her hair into a knot on the top of her head and securing it with a ribbon, she sank into the hot, scented water. She leaned back and closed her eyes, remembering the feel of Guy's mouth, the lean planes of his face under her hands, and the powerful muscles of his body, and then she heard a slight sound at the door and opened her eyes to see him standing there as if she had just conjured him up, clad in shirt and breeches and rolling up his sleeves as he advanced into the dressing room. She sank down into the water until only her creamy shoulders were visible, her eyes wide.

She was speechless at his grin and then he explained, "Surely you wish your back scrubbed, my dear. Come now, sit up."

His eyes never left her face until she did so, and then he reached into the water for the soap and sponge and gently began to wash her back. "I could not wait another moment," he said easily. "I know I should have given you time to don a filmy nightgown, but since I intended to remove it at once, in any case, it seemed a waste of time. How lovely you are, just as I imagined. Your skin is like satin."

"Guy," she whispered, her eyes closed again as he laid her back on one arm and began to soap her breasts and belly. She felt his hand slide lower in the water and part her thighs, and as he lathered the triangle of chestnut hair and caressed her there, she thought she must die with her desire for him. The tiny tingle that his kiss always called forth was now a raging fire of longing, and she moaned.

Suddenly she was lifted from the tub and enveloped in a large, warm towel. The briskness with which he dried every inch of her brought her back to her senses and she was able to calm her breathing a little, but the fire came back in an instant when he dropped the towel and ran his hands over her shoulders to cup her breasts again, before he bent and kissed each erect pink nipple slowly and insistently. He reached up and pulled the ribbon from her hair, so the chestnut masses cascaded down her back, and he caught his breath as he wound his hands in them and kissed her, her naked body held close.

He picked her up in his arms then and carried her to the other room to lower her gently onto the bed. Patricia opened her eyes in distress when she felt a stir of cool air that told her he had left her, but she saw it was only so he could remove his clothes in a fever of impatience. His body is so lean and beautiful, she thought as she watched the long muscles under his smooth skin, and she admired his broad chest and narrow waist and the erect manhood that sprang from its nest of dark-brown curls between his powerful thighs. In a moment, he was stretched out beside her, to draw her close and hold her hard against him once again.

"How I want you, my heart," he said in a deep, ragged voice, his hands hungry in their caresses.

"And I you, love," she answered as her hips moved in a rhythm that told him the truth of her words. He rolled over and covered her body with his own, supporting most of his weight on his arms, his lips on hers again and his tongue warm and insistent as it explored her mouth, and then she felt his body pressing her deeper into the bed as his hands slipped behind her back to cup her buttocks and draw her up to meet him. She gasped against his mouth as he parted her and made them one, filling the secret, velvet core of her with a throbbing beat that grew slowly but steadily in intensity. Her own body was quick to answer his thrusts. From her very depths, waves of passion engulfed her, growing and becoming ever stronger, until she felt she was about to explode in a million tiny pieces, and she cried out in delight and surprise. At once, Guy abandoned his careful restraint and joined her in a shuddering release.

She opened her eyes when he laid his head on the pillow beside her, still enveloped by her body, his hands holding her tight, as if he could not bear to let her go, and she raised her own hand to wipe away the light gleam of sweat on his brow and smooth back the locks of brown hair that had fallen there. His eyes were closed and his well-cut mouth curved in a contented smile, and she felt such a surge of complete happiness that she had to dash away a few tears of joy.

At that moment he opened his eyes, worshiping her face and breasts as he said, "My dear wife at last. How wonderful you are."

"No, it is you who are wonderful, Guy," she whispered,

her eyes shining in the candlelight like two violet gems. "Wonderful and handsome, and, oh, so dearly loved!"

He bent and kissed her softly then, but when he lifted himself away from her, she cried out, "Oh, do not leave me yet!"

He hugged her a little. "Only for a short while. It would be a shame to crush you, my heart," he answered as he gathered her in his arms like a small child and cuddled her close. They lay there contented, each savoring what they had just experienced together. Patricia closed her eyes, a smile on her lips. So this was what marriage should be, she thought dreamily: a union of two people so attuned to each other, so perfectly matched, that their lovemaking was the final bond that truly united them. When Guy had joined his body to hers, she had been more than ready to receive him, and instead of the pain she had always felt before, now there was only a glorious fruition. She moved slightly, remembering, as she wondered how she could have been so stupid to deny them such happiness all this time, and she felt Guy's lips on her hair as one gentle hand traced the length of her spine up to the back of her neck and sent delicious shivers through her body.

"Yes, love?" he asked, his voice lazy and serene.

Patricia raised herself on her arms and leaned over him so she could look into his eyes. He lay back on the pillows, her own smile mirrored on his lips, and his eyes warm and full of love for her.

"Forgive me, Guy, for running away from you," she said in a small humble voice. "I did not know—I mean, I had no idea— Why, I have never . . ."

Guy laughed out loud at her tangled words, and then he brushed back the masses of chestnut curls that hung over her shoulders, the better to admire her before he pulled her down again into his arms. "You had better not run away from me ever again, madam," he growled, tightening those arms until she gasped and protested and promised she would never leave him.

For a while they lay there in the big bed, content to be together, and then Guy began to tell her his plans. Patricia was thrilled when he said he intended to take her abroad, for she had never had a chance to travel. She asked a score of questions about the clothes she would need, the places they would see, the route they would follow, and when they would leave.

"In a week or so, my heart," he told her, and then he added, "Besides, although we did not wait the customary year of your widowhood before we wed, not even the highest sticklers can fault us if we leave the country at once and are not seen in town all winter. Anyone who does not have ice water in his veins must agree that over two years is long enough for any man to wait for his bride. I am not made of stone, you know."

Patricia agreed in a demure voice that that was plain to see, and Guy kissed the tip of her nose and called her a minx before he went on, "And then, we can return in the spring, in time for the Season. How anxious I am to introduce you to all my friends and to let the rest of the *ton* as well see the good and beautiful wife that I have won."

Patricia felt a sudden coldness deep inside, and she could not restrain a shudder. Guy felt her trembling and, thinking she was cold, reached down to pull up the satin quilt. He covered them both before he took her in his arms and held her close to his hard chest again, and Patricia tried to forget London and society. Spring was a long time away; she did not have to think about it now.

Just before she fell asleep in his arms, for Guy held her as if he never wanted to let her go, Patricia caressed his broad shoulders and kissed the hollow of his throat. As she breathed in the clean, male scent of him, she realized that Guy was her husband now and she was his wife. No matter what society said, nor how they reviled them in the future, she would always be grateful that they were together, married, and lovers at last.

14

Viscount Reading and his bride returned to England in the middle of March, 1816, and they went immediately to River Court. Guy had suggested a short stay in London first so they could look at houses for the coming Season and Patricia could refurbish her wardrobe, but since they had come home via France, she had any number of stunning new outfits, and it was easy for her to dissuade him, especially since he was eager to see his lands again.

Spring was just beginning in southern England, and in spite of the misty rain that fell so regularly, it seemed wonderful to be home again. Home, in time to watch the first buds appear on the trees, the flowering of the tulips and daffodils in the garden that sloped down to the river, and to find a spot on the riverbank where Guy told her violets grew by the thousands.

Patricia had gone there with Guy one morning while he fished the Arun, and she was content to sit on a rug near the picnic basket watching him, that dark, well-shaped head and handsome face, the ripple of muscles as he cast his line, his strong hands when he reeled it in, and the way he braced against the current on powerful, long legs. She sighed and closed her eyes, smiling to herself. Marriage to Guy was so wonderful that sometimes she was sure she must be dreaming it, and then she would have to touch him to make sure he was real.

They had left from Portsmouth early in August and sailed directly to Greece, where Guy had shown her all the wonders of that ancient land: the Parthenon by moonlight, the colossal ruins and statues, as well as the noisy marketplaces and breathtaking views all through the hot, sunny days and fragrant nights. He had hired a yacht then so they could sail the Aegean, stopping at any island that took their fancy. Patricia bloomed. So far away from England and society, she was able to forget the scandal she knew awaited them on their return, for now there was only Guy, loving and adoring her as she loved and adored him.

She had learned many things about her new husband in the months of their honeymoon: how compassionate he could be when she became seasick in a storm in the Mediterranean, how commanding and cold when underlings disobeyed him, how impatient when he was thwarted, how tender to her always, and how much like a little boy when he fell ill himself from a chill and she insisted on nursing him.

Eventually they sailed to Italy, where there were new sights to see and new adventures to share, but although Patricia tried to concentrate only on the present, the day of their return to England grew ever nearer. She had loved Paris, the parks and the Seine, Notre-Dame, and Montmartre, though she protested at the way Guy lavished her with gowns and hats and fripperies. But he only laughed, saying he expected her to outshine every woman in the *ton* during the Season ahead, and for a moment she felt again that dark quiver of fear for what the future would bring.

She had more confidence now, of course, the confidence of a beloved wife whose unassailable position in her husband's life was clear and who was needed by him above all else; and once she was home again at River Court, she set about making the acquaintance of all the servants and tenants, the vicar and his wife, and the nearby neighbors. If she wondered at their complete, unquestioning acceptance of her, she told herself it was Viscountess Reading they smiled at, not Patricia Leighton, who had been Alvin J. Biddles' wife, little realizing that her kindness and gentle ways, her warm smile and concern endeared her to everyone who met her. Guy watched her, unable to hide his pride.

It was not long before both James and Charlie posted down to visit. Patricia was glad to see them, for she considered them as much her friends now as Guy's. Charlie was as funny as ever, and his tales of his latest houseparty had them all wiping their eyes one evening at the dinner table. James added an acerbic comment every now and then that just set the four of them off into fresh gales of laughter, until Patricia had to hold her aching sides.

"Enough, both of you!" she gasped. "I am so sorry I missed the fun, for I can imagine the expression on Sir

Harold's face when the canopy over his bed collapsed on him, or hear Miss Fartherington's screams when the cook's cat honored her with the results of his night's hunting by laying the dead mice on her slippers."

Charlie looked glum. "Yes, that was too bad. I am afraid Miss Fartherington will never come again, for she left the next morning and wouldn't even speak to me. Tch! *I* didn't put the mice there, don't know why she was angry with me."

At last Patricia rose to leave the three old friends to their port, and as her eyes sought Guy's, the wave of electricity that passed between them was so intense that even James could feel it. He raised an eyebrow. He had never seen Guy so happy and serene, and he envied him, remembering a lady he had known long ago. She was married to another now, but he wondered how different his life might have been if he had wed her as he had thought of doing once.

Before the men returned to London, Guy mentioned his plans for the Season, saying they would have to see about renting a suitable house. A shadow passed over Patricia's face, but she controlled it so quickly she was sure no one noticed.

"I shall be on the lookout for you, Guy," Charlie promised. "If anything worthwhile comes up, I'll send for you. Mustn't delay too long or all the good houses will be gone."

"Anywhere but St. James's Place," Guy told him later as the three sat in the library. "Patricia started her married life with the late unlamented Alvin there, and I would not remind her of it."

Charlie agreed, and James asked idly from the depths of a leather wing chair, "Is Patricia happy with this plan? Has she agreed to come to town, Guy?"

"Why, it has not been discussed. She has never said she would not," Guy answered, bending a suddenly serious eye on his cousin's face. "Why do you ask?"

"There was an expression on her face last evening— fleeting, to be sure, but very telling. I think she still fears the *ton*, fears what its reaction will be if you attempt to establish her, and of course, she fears most of all for you, that you will be snubbed as well."

"Nonsense!" Guy said strongly. "Patricia is not so foolish. Besides, that was all over with months ago and is long forgotten."

Charlie shook his head. "Don't know about that, Guy. After you left the country, you, and especially your new bride, were chewed over at every tea table from Perth to Land's End. M'mother told me it was the *on dit* of the century. Might have a harder time than you think."

Guy rubbed his chin, deep in thought. "We'll see," he said finally. "I may need your help once again, my friends, for I have no intention of remaining here in the country for the rest of my life, nor of hiding Patricia's light under a bushel. I want the *ton* to see her, to admire her, and to accept her, for she is too fine a person to be scorned. Somehow I'll find a way."

Neither James nor Charlie said another word, but after they returned to town, Guy found himself pondering what they had told him and planning his campaign. It was important that Patricia take her rightful place beside him, not for his sake but for hers. He wanted so badly to make it up to her for her previous ostracism.

And so he tried to get her to drive up to town with him when Charlie wrote to say he had found the perfect house in Grosvenor Square, but she refused. "No, you go without me if you would not mind, my dear. I have had it in mind to visit Grandmother Darrow, and this will be the perfect opportunity. I can go with you as far as Kingsfold, and when your business in London is finished, you can pick me up there on the return journey."

Guy agreed with this plan, although for a moment he looked at his wife carefully. When she looked up, a question in her clear, violet eyes, he shook himself. Surely he had only imagined that tiny shiver of alarm that passed over her features. Patricia was no coward, that he knew. James must be wrong.

But when they returned and settled down again at the court, he tried again. "I wish you would come and see the house, my heart. I know I have described it to you, but I would feel better if you yourself approved the rooms and furnishings."

Patricia smiled. They were seated in her sitting room on either side of the fire, just as Guy had pictured them so many times, Patricia busy with her needlework and he lounging in the big chair watching the firelight turn her hair to flame and silhouette that pure cameo profile.

"Now, Guy, you know whatever you choose is fine with me. Haven't I always agreed with you without question?" she asked demurely. "Besides, I intended to ask Lady Sylvia to come and stay. The gardens are a delight now, I know she would enjoy them."

Guy bit back a sharp retort. "I do not think it would be wise to invite her now, for we will be leaving for town shortly. I intend to go and stay on the first of May. You can be ready then?"

"Oh, please, not so soon as that," she begged, her voice breaking a little, and then she bent her head over her sewing so he could not see her eyes.

"Patricia, look at me," he commanded, and when she raised her head, he said more gently, "My dear, you really are afraid, aren't you? But putting off bearding the lion in his den will not placate him. Besides, you have blown things out of all proportion. No one will snub either one of us, you'll see."

Now that her secret was out, Patricia spoke more openly. "I hope you are right, Guy, but I cannot bear to think that you might have to endure what I did. We are so happy and content here, why do we have to go to town at all?"

"Because I am not content to remain a farmer all the year, Patricia," he replied, and she lowered her eyes again. "I want to see my friends, visit my clubs, hear the latest gossip, enjoy the new plays and operas. You loved Paris; surely London will amuse you as well. And most important, I want to show you off so everyone will admire your beauty and envy me my wife."

Patricia set her sewing down and went to sit on his knee and put her arms around his neck. "Well, sir, it is plain to see that I am boring you, for to be alone with me no longer suffices. How lowering! No, now you want clubs and friends and parties. Alas, how soon the bridal charms dim. I shall think familiarity does breed contempt."

"Idiot," he muttered as her slim hands caressed his hair and she bent closer to kiss his cheek. "As if I could ever tire of you!"

"Then let us stay at River Court, Guy," she pleaded, her hands moving down to undo his cravat and unbutton his shirt so she could slip her hands inside and play with the mat of dark-brown curls on his chest, pulling it lightly to tease him.

He bent his head and kissed her, and she opened her lips to lose herself in that demanding, familiar caress. When she lay back against his shoulder again, he whispered, "But we can make love in town, my heart. I know of no law to the contrary that the city fathers have passed. Much good it would do 'em if they did."

"Hmmm," Patricia answered, her hands busy again as they moved lower, and suddenly he stood up with her in his arms and carried her into the bedroom, all thoughts of a London Season gone from his mind, at least for now.

Nothing more was said about leaving the court on May first, but when Guy took her to visit the spot where the violets were just starting to bloom, and saw her kneeling among them to pick a bouquet, he came to a sudden decision. Her eyes, when she looked up at him, perfectly reflected their soft tints and he said gruffly, "I shall always think of violets as your flower, my heart. They were the first I ever gave you, and they are so like you—slender and beautiful, soft and sweet."

Patricia buried her face in her nosegay and inhaled their woody aroma, and Guy wished he might have her painted in this setting. It was a long time before they returned to the court that afternoon.

But as the days passed, Guy could not help but become impatient. Patricia always had a good reason why she could not leave for town today or tomorrow, and there was a sparkle and voluptuous roundness about her these days that kept him intrigued in spite of himself. Finally he wrote several long letters and posted them to London, and then, a few days later, when he joined Patricia in the breakfast room, he was dressed for traveling.

"I am off to London, my dear," he told her as he took his seat and Mr. Petson brought him a plate of sirloin and eggs. Patricia poured him a cup of coffee, her hand trembling a little. "For how long will you be gone, Guy?" she asked.

Guy pretended an interest in his food he did not really feel. "I have no idea. Perhaps a week, perhaps more. It depends on my business. If you would consent to come, ma'am, I would be glad to delay until you could be packed."

"No!" Patricia said, more sharply than she intended. "That is, I would not delay you, my dear. I shall miss you, of course," she added, one eye on the butler's back as he bent over the sideboard, and she blew her husband a kiss, her eyes teasing. Guy grinned back, for the night before had been a memorable one for both of them.

Assuring her that he would return as soon as possible, he put an arm around her waist as they strolled to the front door when Petson announced the phaeton was ready. Patricia went with her husband down the steps, but before they were in earshot of the groom, Guy stopped. "Be very good, little one, and I may bring you a surprise," he promised, his gray eyes intent on her face.

"Of course, Guy. I am always very good, as you yourself have told me so," she said demurely, reaching up to kiss him. "Perhaps I will have a surprise for you as well," she added, and he wondered at the mischief in her eyes.

A few moments later, he was tooling his team down the drive, turning back only to wave to his wife, whom he knew would watch from the steps until he was out of sight.

Somehow after his departure, Patricia was restless. The days passed very slowly, in spite of a meeting with the vicar about the Church Fair that was soon to take place, and visits to some of Guy's pensioners, which she had made one of her regular duties. She always enjoyed Mr. Simpson especially, for although he was very old and almost toothless, he always had a cheerful smile and told her many stories about life at the court when Guy was young. But now even his reminiscences did not suffice to cheer her. She wished Guy had not had to go up to town, not now when she was almost sure she was carrying his child.

When she had first suspected it, her immediate thought was one of great relief. Surely Guy would not insist on her appearance in town when he learned she was *enceinte*; no, it was the perfect excuse and she could be easy at last. But how she wished she could have told him before he left! Perhaps that was why she was feeling so depressed at his absence, she told herself as she tried to interest herself in arranging flowers for the drawing room or going over menus with the cook.

But two weeks passed and Guy did not come back and she could not help some feelings of anxiety. Perhaps he had decided to have his Season without her? Perhaps he had grown weary of her excuses and denials and had decided to stop pleading with her? Or perhaps he had come to realize, from something he had heard in town, that she was right and that she would never be accepted? She pounded her pillow in disgust at these very sensible conclusions and told herself she was behaving irrationally. Soon, soon Guy would be back, and then she would tell him about the baby and they would be happy again here at home.

He arrived the next day, driving up to the front of the court right after breakfast. Patricia flew down the steps to hug and kiss him, and for a moment they forgot the rest of the world in the joy of their reunion.

"I see you have missed me, wife," he said when he held her away from him so he could admire the way her muslin gown of pale-green molded her waist and clung to her breasts.

Patricia dropped him a little curtsy. "More than you know, husband. Oh, Guy, whatever took you so long? It has been ages since you left the court."

He chuckled, and putting that strong, familiar arm around her, he led her up the steps. "I will tell you all about it shortly. Now I want my breakfast, and then you are to put on your prettiest bonnet and cape, for I am going to take you for a drive, just the two of us."

His glance spoke volumes and she smiled, sure he was going to seek some quiet spot where they could be alone, for he could not wait until tonight to make love to her.

It was only an hour later when he helped her to her seat in the phaeton. He was not driving his grays, she noticed, but a strange team, but before she could ask why, he had sprung into his seat and taken up the reins, and they were off. Patricia leaned back, her eyes closed and a little smile playing over her lips as she savored her happiness. Everything was all right now, for Guy was home at last.

Several long minutes later, she opened her eyes and looked around. Guy was springing the team, and they thundered over a bridge and through a small hamlet at much too fast a pace. She wondered uneasily where they were, for the countryside was unfamiliar.

"Guy, where are we going?" she asked, foreboding filling her heart.

"We are going to London, right now, this very minute, my heart," he answered cheerfully, waving his whip to two barefoot boys and a mongrel dog who were trudging along the side of the road.

"Have you lost your mind? Going to London, indeed!

With no baggage and no instructions left with the staff at River Court? Stop teasing, Guy, and take me home at once."

"No, we are not going back," he answered, his gray eyes turning to her face for a brief moment. She noticed his jaw was set in stubborn lines, and that sculptured mouth was a firm, determined line. "I have made no secret of the fact that I intend to spend the Season in London, but I could see that this was the only way I was ever going to get you to come with me."

Patricia's eyes were blazing now. "You're mad! I won't go, I won't!"

"You really have no say in the matter, Patricia, for I have kidnapped you. It is well known that kidnappers never heed the pleading of their victims, as you should know from previous experience. No, to London you will go whether you want to or not."

"How could you do this, Guy?" she cried. "I will never forgive you."

"Oh, come now, my heart. My last kidnapping of you didn't turn out so badly, now did it?" he teased, and then he laughed out loud when she had no reply.

As they drove through the soft spring day, Guy only stopped long enough to change his teams and allow her time for a little refreshment, and he never left her side, but even so, it was late when he turned into Grosvenor Square and pulled up at a tall, imposing mansion that was lit from top to bottom. Patricia was silent now, for although she had begged and threatened and tried to reason with him by turns, nothing she said would change his mind, and at last she had settled back on her seat, her eyes stormy as she accepted the inevitable. She had not told him about the baby, for somehow she could not bring herself to use such wonderful news as a weapon.

As Guy lifted her down to the pavement, the door above them opened to show a tall butler bowing his welcome.

"This is Jeffries, my dear. I am sure you will find him as invaluable as I have. Viscountess Reading, Jeffries. And now, have a tray brought to my wife in her rooms. She is tired from the journey and I will join her for dinner there."

He led Patricia into the hall, past the footmen and a curtsying maid, and up a wide, graceful stairway. Patricia concentrated on keeping her head high. She would make no ugly scenes, but she had every intention of telling Guy exactly what she thought of his high-handed ways and what the result of his trying to get the *ton* to accept her would be, as soon as they were private.

And tell him she did. Although Guy heard her out, his face set in an expression of polite interest, he had no comments until she was through.

"I understand you very well, Patricia, but I really could not let your fears and cowardice govern our lives forever," he said at last as he poured more wine into their glasses.

"I am not a coward! I only want to spare you the *ton*'s cruelty."

One dark eyebrow rose. "Thank you, but I fear you mistake the matter. We shall see which of us is right, shall we not? No, no more now. We will talk again tomorrow, for I can see you are fatigued. Sleep late, my heart, and I will join you here for breakfast."

Patricia watched him rise to pick up her hand and kiss it before he left her, and she felt bereft. They had never been apart for so long. How could Guy just walk away and leave her alone?

She wandered over to one of the long windows and stared down into the square. Most of the houses built around it had lights in them, and across the way a party was in progress, for carriages drew up and gaily dressed people entered the flambeau-lit doorway, talking and laughing together. Below her, two gentlemen strolled along, deep in conversation, and carriages and hackneys rumbled across the cobbles. It was crowded and sophisticated and brittle—it was London, just as she remembered it.

Shivering a little, she turned away to survey her rooms. They were large and well proportioned, and somehow she was surprised. Surely there was no need for such a massive, impressive house, not just for the two of them. She went to inspect the bedroom and dressing room, surprising a middle-aged servant who introduced herself as Findles, her new lady's maid. Patricia smiled and the maid helped her to undress and put on a new nightgown and robe that she had never seen, and then she brushed out her long chestnut hair, chatting all the while. Patricia thought her premonitions of disaster and the noise of town would keep her awake, but she fell asleep as soon as her head touched the pillow.

The next morning she became aware of a hum of activity

outside her rooms, but when Findles brought her her chocolate and asked if she wished a bath prepared, she did not
question her. Guy had said he would be with her for breakfast.
She would wait and ask him about it then.

As she was getting ready to rise and dress, Guy knocked
and entered, waving the maid away.

"Come, sleepyhead, breakfast awaits us in the sitting room,"
he said, throwing back the covers and holding out her robe.

"What is going on, Guy?" she asked when he had bent his
head and kissed her lips lightly. "What is all the bustle about
and why do we not eat downstairs?"

"I was sure you would not care for it, my love. You see,
the house is full of caterers and musicians and florists and
who knows what all, and there is such a crush of people
bringing champagne and chairs, and crystal and plates and
lobster patties and creams you would be sure to lose your
appetite."

Patricia stared at him as he seated her at the table, a terrible
premonition growing in her mind. "Whatever do you mean?"

"Why, tonight is the event that all London has been waiting for, love. The Viscount and Viscountess of Reading are
giving a gala ball, and all the *ton* has been invited."

Patricia dropped the napkin she had been unfolding. "You
are mad!"

Guy grinned at her and poured them both some coffee.
"No, not mad, simply impatient. Now eat your breakfast,
Patricia, for we have a lot to do. First you have a fitting at
Mme Pauline's on your new ball gown. I hope you approve
my choice, my heart. And then we must go to Rundell and
Bridge for the surprise I promised you, and after luncheon
and a long rest, Monsieur Henri, whom I have been told is all
the crack, is coming to give you a more fashionable crop and
to create a hairdo for you that will have all the other ladies
mad with jealousy. And then, before you know it, our guests
will be arriving. Do eat your breakfast, love."

He cut a slice of ham while Patricia stared at him aghast.
For a moment, she thought of running away, but then she
realized that there was no escape for her that way. If Guy had
indeed invited all society to meet her, she could not embar-
rass him by not appearing at her own ball. She opened
her mouth to speak, and then, thinking better of the idea,
shut it.

"Very wise, my dear. It would do no good at all." Her hitherto adoring husband grinned at her.

The day passed in a whirl. The gown Guy had chosen for her was the most beautiful one she had ever seen. It was made of a soft cloth of silver that shimmered with every step, and was cut so severely that only the draping of the material over her breasts and shoulders and the deep cowl back served as ornamentation. There were silver sandals to match, and long white kid gloves, and since Guy had brought one of her Paris gowns to town with him, very few last-minute alterations had to be made.

When they reached the jewelers and had been seated reverently by Mr. Bridge himself, he placed before her a tiara, necklace, and earrings of amethysts and diamonds, so delicate in design that they appeared to float in their settings of fine silver wire. Her eyes went to Guy's as Mr. Bridge turned away for a moment, and she was surprised to see the anxiety there, almost as if he were afraid she would not approve his choice.

"They are beautiful—the most beautiful jewels I have ever seen, Guy," she told him, her voice awed, and his face lit up in relief.

She was glad to rest that afternoon after luncheon and before her bath, and it seemed no time at all before Monsieur Henri proclaimed himself not only satisfied, but ecstatic, and Findles was hooking her into her gown and fastening the jewels around her neck and in her ears. The tiara sparkled above the chestnut waves and curls of her coiffure, and the maid clapped her hands and declared she had never seen anyone in such beauty.

Patricia went downstairs to join Guy for dinner, her heart jumping in an alarming way. She found him waiting for her in the hall, attired in black evening clothes, with only the pristine whiteness of his cravat and silk stockings and a single diamond stickpin to relieve the starkness. She thought he looked magnificent and told him so.

"But not to compare to you, beauty. You are always superb, but tonight you are breathtaking. But come, our guests await us!"

Patricia had not known they were to have company for dinner, but she swallowed her fear and allowed Guy to lead her to the drawing room. At once her face lit up in a welcoming smile, for there were James and Charlie, Grandmother Darrow and Lady Sylvia. By the time she had greeted them all warmly and exclaimed at the ladies' presence in town, dinner was announced.

Patricia tried not to think of the ball to come as she caught up on Bath news with Lady Sylvia, heard her grandmother tell Guy he was a very lucky man, and accepted James' and Charlie's fulsome compliments on her appearance.

At last Guy came to lead her from the table. "I would show you the ballroom, love," he told her, his gray eyes full of his adoration. "It is my biggest surprise. But first, these are for you."

He beckoned to a footman holding a white box and took out a large bouquet of violets in a silver holder covered with diamond and amethyst chips. "From River Court, my heart," he whispered as she inhaled their sweetness, "to give you courage."

Patricia smiled, but her throat was so tight she could not speak. Tucking her hand in his arm, Guy led her up the stairs to the ballroom. There were footmen on duty along the stairs, and when the butler opened the ballroom doors, more stood at attention around the walls of the huge room that ran the depth of the house. The crystal chandeliers glowed with hundreds of candles, an orchestra was playing softly at one end of the room, and Patricia gasped at the decorations. The walls had been covered with finely pleated violet silk and on every table were vases of white roses and purple iris. Below the raised dais where the musicians were seated was a miniature bank covered with mosses and ferns and thousands of violet plants, for all the world like a replica of the riverbank along the Arun. Even the chairs and sofas along the walls were covered in a matching brocade.

"How enchanting," Patricia exclaimed as the others crowded around to see.

"Only this perfect a setting would do for you, my heart," Guy assured her, and then the butler announced the arrival of the first guests and he drew her back to the hall to receive them.

When she thought of the ball in later years—and surely there was never another ball to match it—she remembered only Guy, always beside her, his voice and his face glowing with pride as he introduced her to his friends. Although she watched carefully, there was no drawing away, no stiffening of anyone's face, no disdainful sneers, and no cutting remarks to mar their evening. It seemed everyone smiled and welcomed her, from Lady Jersey and Mrs. Fitz-Smythe to Lord Alverney, as if they had been cast under a benevolent spell by a good fairy. She did not notice that Guy had placed James and Charlie close by to aid them, and had had Lady Darrow and his aunt seated where the guests must pass them as they went into the ballroom, showing their august approval by their smiles and comments, and she never did learn how much these four as well as Guy had done to promote her well-being, not only that night, but in the preceding weeks. Charlie had admired her quality and good taste wherever he went, and James had extolled her gentle goodness and beauty, claiming Guy was to be envied a wife who had two such disparate traits. The final seal on her acceptance was the arrival of the Prince Regent and some of his gentlemen. He pinched her cheek and gave her a ponderous compliment before he disappeared into the card room, and then at last they were able to leave the receiving line. Guy signaled the orchestra to play a waltz and took her in his arms.

"Well, my doubting Thomasina, well?" he asked, drawing her closer and smiling down at her glowing eyes and flushed face.

"You must be a magician, a veritable Merlin, sir," she admitted. "I do not know how you did it, for I would never have believed it possible for you to turn society up so sweet."

"Shall I tell you my secret, my heart?" he teased, never taking his eyes from her face. "It was easy. I had only to invite my own friends and those in the *ton* who had had dealings in the past with the late Alvin J. Biddles, as well as their relations. Not everyone, of course, for that would have been too sad a crush, and we are striving to be exclusive tonight. Everyone was delighted to have the chance to wish us joy while celebrating their release from his avaricious clutches."

Patricia smiled, her eyes sparkling, and Guy could not help dropping a light kiss on her hair as she said, "But surely you do not mean the Regent was also in his coils, Guy?"

Her husband admitted he had used another method to ensure Prinny's attendance, and his royal smiles were only his tribute to such a beautiful lady.

When the waltz was over, Patricia sank into a deep curtsy, and as Guy drew her up and raised her hand to kiss, she whispered, "I am delighted that society has approved of me and forgiven you for your waywardness in marrying me as well, and especially relieved, for now your son's acceptance in the *ton* is a foregone conclusion."

She laughed at her suddenly speechless husband, whose eyes flashed gray fire as she added, "Or perhaps it is your daughter, and in a few years you will be planning another ball like this for her? How unfortunate that you must wait so many months to find out, for some surprises cannot be hurried."

And then she stood on tiptoe to whisper, "And let that be a salutory lesson for you, my handsome, impatient kidnapper. You are not the only one with secrets!"

About the Author

Barbara Hazard was born, raised, and educated in New England, and although she has lived in New York for the past twenty years, she still considers herself a Yankee. She has studied music for many years, in addition to her formal training in art. Recently, she has had two one-man shows and exhibited in many group shows. She added the writing of Regencies to her many talents in 1978, but her other hobbies include listening to classical music, reading, quilting, cross-country skiing, and paddle tennis. Her previous Regencies, THE DISOBEDIENT DAUGHTER, A SURFEIT OF SUITORS, THE CALICO COUNTESS, and THE SINGULAR MISS CARRINGTON, are available in Signet editions.